For Maureen and Jennifer
Murdered, June 5, 1973
Rutland, MA

1

June, forty-five years ago

The old beat up truck edged to the side of the road and pulled to a stop in front of a sandy haired young man who tossed his things in the back bed of the pick-up, opened the passenger side door and climbed in.

"I called in sick," Dan said with a cheery smile.

"You don't look sick," Bobby replied. He turned the steering wheel to the left and pressed on the gas pedal.

"I don't feel sick either," Dan chuckled.

"You've only been out of school and working for four days," Bobby said. "Is it a good idea to call in sick already? And, on a day like this? Would seem pretty obvious you aren't sick."

"You only live once," Dan answered. The breeze from

the open window tousled his hair. "I don't know how I'm going to stand working every day. It's worse than being in school."

"You'll get used to it," Bobby said. "I'm glad to be making some money. I wouldn't want to be back in school."

"Well, the fish better bite in case I lose my job," Dan said.

"You better have a good day off, fish or no fish," Bobby said.

"The sun's shining. We got cold ones in the cooler. It's a good day already."

The truck traveled past farms and fields as they followed the back roads to the Howland State Park. The old, tinny speakers blared Three Dog Night's song *Shambala* and Bobby's fingers tapped the steering wheel in time to the beat. Dan sang along, his voice high, loud, and pitchy.

"Ugh." Bobby groaned at the singing and took one hand off the wheel to cover his right ear in mock disgust. Dan sang louder.

After another mile, Bobby slowed his vehicle and turned onto the dirt lane that led to the clearing in the woods. From there, they would walk the trail down to the lake. The truck bumped along as the wheels dipped and rose over the ruts. A branch swished against the side of the truck. After a few more yards, Bobby pulled over as far as he could to get the truck off the narrow back road. There would be barely enough room to turn the pick-up around when it was time to leave.

"Jeez, how am I going to get out? I'm rammed right up against the trees," Dan protested.

"Climb out my way," Bobby told him.

Bobby took the cooler and Dan pulled the fishing gear out of the back. They walked along the wooded dirt road towards the field and the trails to the lake. The air was still, and the early morning sun was blazing in the hazy June sky.

"I hope you brought some bug spray." Dan swatted at mosquitoes.

"Just gonna have to suffer."

The clearing was up ahead. The two young men saw a dark blue Ford parked in the tall grass. The sun glinting off the hot metal was blinding.

"Looks like we'll have company at the lake," Bobby said. "Why'd they park in the middle of the field?

The young men stepped through the long grass towards the car. The left rear door was open.

"They left the door open," Bobby noted. "Battery'll be dead."

"I'll shut it." Dan headed over to the car but when he got close he stopped short. He stood frozen, his eyes wide, staring at the ground next to the Ford.

"No." His voice quivered. He took a clumsy step back.

"No." Dan's strained voice was just above a whisper. "Bobby, get over here."

The sound of Dan's voice made the hair on Bobby's arms stand up. "What's the matter with you?" He came up on Dan's left side and saw what was lying beside the car. "What the...?" He dropped the cooler. His stomach felt like it was filled with ice water. He turned around and vomited into the grass.

A young woman was on the ground, lying face up, her head partially under the left side of the car. Her eyes were open but she didn't see anything. The blood that had soaked her yellow shirt and white shorts was dry now. The throat was slashed, the wound parted wide. Blood covered the pale skin and had run down both sides of her neck onto the grass.

"What the hell?" Bobby wiped his mouth with the back of his hand. Sweat was beading on his forehead. He shot a quick glance at Dan, averting his gaze from what was on the ground. His eyes were wild as they swept around the clearing. "Who'd do this? Who'd do this?" He choked on his words. His chest heaved up and down. He shuffled his feet two steps backwards. "We gotta get out of here. We gotta report this."

"Hold on. Wait." Dan stepped around the woman to peer into the car.

"What are you doing? Come on, Dan. Don't touch nothing." Bobby wouldn't look at the blue car. He took

4

two more steps away from the scene and wheeled around.

"There's a kid. A little girl. In the front seat."

Bobby kept his eyes focused in the direction of his truck. "A girl? She okay?"

Dan whispered a curse.

"What? What now?"

"Man," Dan muttered.

"What is it?" Bobby asked but he didn't want to know.

"She's dead. Throat's slit."

"Oh, no." Bobby lurched away. He was shaking. His head buzzed. "A kid? What the hell? We gotta get out of here. Dan, come on." Bobby took off through the field. He wasn't waiting to see if Dan was following.

Dan's legs wouldn't move. He was stuck in the spot, staring through watery eyes at the little girl sprawled in the front seat. She was half leaning against the passenger side door of the car, her skin white, so white, the ends of her long blonde hair crusted with blood. Her eyes were open. Flies buzzed around her.

Dan's lower lip trembled. "Damn bugs," he whispered. His blood had drained out of his head. He swallowed some air. His breath was coming in gasps. A tear escaped from his eye and rolled down his cheek.

"Come on!" Bobby yelled to him from across the field.

Dan shook himself, backed away, and ran after Bobby to the truck.

A kid, a kid.

2

June – Present day

OLIVIA SAT cross-legged on the living room floor of the two-hundred-year old Colonial house going through stacks of old newspapers. She had promised her cousin John that she would help clean out the attic while she was staying at his house. Now that she saw all the stuff crammed up there, she was sorry she said she would do it.

John groaned as he lugged his suitcase down the stairs and let it thud against the front door.

"You travel light, huh, John?" Olivia said, her eyes on the papers.

John waved his hand in the air. "I'm always afraid I don't have enough clothes with me," he said. He wiped the sweat off his forehead with his arm. "This humidity kills me. It seems like the weather gets hotter and more humid every year."

He plopped in the big, soft easy chair across from Olivia. A chocolate Lab roused itself from a nap and tried to climb into the chair with John. Her long, pink tongue rolled over John's face and he put his two hands against her chest to push her away.

"Lily. Jeez. No."

"You said you were hot. She's trying to cool you off," Olivia said without looking up. She pulled the elastic from her wrist and used it to put her hair up into a high ponytail. The fan on the coffee table wasn't doing much but blowing the hot air around.

"Liv, there are two portable air conditioning units in the basement. If this heat keeps up, you might want to bring them up. They're easy to install. I should have done it but I didn't know a heat wave was settling in."

"Okay. I might use them if the heat doesn't break soon." Olivia was reading the headline of the old newspaper from forty-five years ago reporting a double murder. On the front page was a picture of a dark haired young woman and beside it, a picture of a blonde girl about four years old.

"Why did your dad keep these?" Olivia asked.

"Oh, you know how my dad was. He loved old newspapers." John looked down to see what Olivia was reading.

"That's Mary and her daughter Kimmy. They were murdered here in town, about forty-five years ago."

Olivia grimaced.

"They were our cousins," John added.

Olivia looked up. "What?"

"Yeah, second cousins or something. The killer was never caught."

"I never heard about this," Olivia said.

"Everybody sort of forgot about it, I guess. It was long before we were born, Liv."

"Our cousins?" Olivia bent over to read the article more closely. She pushed a stray lock of her brown hair behind her ear. "What happened?"

"Distant cousins. They were stabbed. They both had their throats slit. Two young guys found the bodies. Over in the state park."

Olivia looked up, her blue eyes wide. "A little girl? Who could do that to a child?" she asked. "A little girl and her mother?" She tilted closer to the paper on the floor to read more details.

"It's gruesome," John said, still leaning back in the easy chair.

"What happened? Who did it? Why?" Olivia asked.

"Nothing happened. No arrest."

"Why, not? The case just got dropped?"

"I suppose. They probably couldn't figure it out."

"But," Olivia said. "How could it just get dropped? What about the family? Didn't townspeople push for answers? Couldn't the police find the killer?"

John shrugged. "I don't know. Not enough evidence maybe. People want to move on from painful things."

Olivia looked across the room. Her eyes didn't focus on anything; she just gazed off into space. *Painful things.* Olivia knew plenty about painful things. The aunt who raised her had been murdered just over a year ago. Olivia had spent the past year as a first year law student, throwing herself into the work to keep from thinking about painful things. She thought she had coped with the violence that ripped her aunt from her life, but recently she wasn't so sure. Nightmares had begun plaguing her, she felt fatigued for no reason, and sometimes headaches hammered her head so hard that all she could do was go to sleep.

"But," Olivia said, "the killer is just walking around? For all of these years? Just living his life?"

"There was an article in the paper a few years back about unsolved cases in Massachusetts," John said. "Mary and Kimmy were one of the cases discussed. The District Attorney talked about doing DNA testing on some evidence that had been collected back then from the crime scene. But I never heard what came of it. Never saw anything about it in the news."

Olivia stared at the pictures of her distant cousins looking back at her from the first page of the old newspaper. Her heart contracted.

"Who could do that to a little girl? Was the girl killed in front of her mother?"

"I don't remember." John checked his watch. "Liv, thanks for staying here while I'm gone. I appreciate it. The contractors are supposed to show up tomorrow to start on the sunroom. It's bad timing with the office asking me to go away at the last minute. But it couldn't be helped. I have to make this trip. And I just couldn't put Lily in a kennel for two or three weeks." John ran his hand through his hair. "I'm sorry I don't have a firm return date."

"It's no problem at all. I can stay for three full weeks if you need me to," Olivia said. "I'll keep an eye on the sunroom renovation. Joe has taught me a thing or two."

Joe lived in the house next door to Olivia and her aunt Aggie for over twenty years. He had been Aggie's best friend and was like a dad to Olivia. Joe owned a restoration and construction business specializing in antique homes.

"Lily and I are buddies," Olivia continued. "We'll keep each other company. It will be a nice relaxing few weeks."

Lily was stretched out on the rug next to Olivia and she lifted her head at hearing her name. Olivia reached over and scratched the dog behind her ears. Lily flopped over on her side and nudged her neck closer to Olivia's fingers.

In May, after completing her first year of law school, Olivia went to the Netherlands for a three week internship. She had just returned to Massachusetts and was feeling worn out. It would do her good to have some time off before she started a summer course at the beginning of July.

The doorbell rang and John rose to open the front door for his co-worker.

"Hey," Dave said. "I'm a few minutes late, but we have plenty of time to make it to the airport. How're you doing, Liv?"

Olivia stood up and shook Dave's hand. "I'm good, Dave. It's nice to see you again."

John turned to Olivia and hugged her. "Call me or email me if you need anything. I really do appreciate this."

"We'll be fine. Don't worry. Have a good trip."

John lifted his suitcase and the men walked across the front porch and out to the car. Olivia waved, closed the door, and looked at Lily.

"Want to go out, girl?" Lily jumped up and wagged her tail. "Come on. Let's go out back for a bit."

Olivia was thankful that John's huge back yard was fenced to keep Lily from wandering. There was also a small barn in the yard where John enjoyed his woodworking hobby. Lily could stay outside and use the barn for shelter or shade whenever John was going to be gone for more than a few hours. John told Olivia that if she had errands or such, she could keep the barn door open and leave Lily in the yard.

As Olivia led the dog to the back door off the kitchen, she glanced down at the newspaper on the floor. Her cousins stared back at her from the front page. She paused for a moment looking at the two smiling faces. Olivia breathed a heavy sigh and turned away.

A PUFF of the night breeze pushed the sheer curtain of Olivia's bedroom window over the windowsill and it fluttered in the dark before settling back into place. The light from the full moon streamed in through the open window and pooled on the wide pine floorboards. Olivia's sleep had been fitful with strange dreams tormenting her.

Her eyes flew open as though some loud sound in the house was the cause for waking her. Her tank top was wet with sweat. She lay still, listening. She turned her head slightly and shifted her gaze to the foot of the bed. A little girl with long blonde hair stood there watching her. Olivia bolted upright, her heart pounding.

The girl was gone.

Stupid dream.

Olivia shook her head and sucked in a long breath of the humid air. Lily was sitting in the corner of the room her tail swishing back and forth across the pine floor, her posture alert, friendly, and attentive. She was looking at the spot at the foot of Olivia's bed where the little girl had been standing in the dream. Lily whined. Olivia's brow furrowed as her gaze shifted from the dog to the end of the bed.

"Lily," Olivia whispered, even though she and the dog were the only ones in the house. Lily's tail thumped. The dog stood, crossed the room and rested her head on the mattress.

Olivia pushed the sheet back and swung her legs over the side of the bed. She rubbed her forehead, stood and walked barefoot to the bathroom where she splashed her face with cold water. She let the water run over her hands and then rubbed them up and down her arms trying to cool off. She padded along the hall to her room and climbed back into her bed. Lily sat on the floor and looked up at Olivia with wishful eyes.

"Oh, okay," Olivia told the dog. "But it will just make both of us hotter." She patted the mattress inviting Lily to jump up. The Lab accepted the invitation and snuggled along Olivia's legs. Olivia glanced once more at the foot of the bed before she scrunched down under the sheet and tried to fall sleep.

3

Olivia woke to the sounds of a truck's door slamming shut. Lily had her front paws on the sill of the second floor window and was looking outside. A low growl vibrated from her throat. Olivia shot a look at the clock as she pulled on her shorts. Eight, already. She peeked out over Lily's head and saw a cherry red pick-up truck in the driveway. The doorbell rang and Lily checked Olivia's reaction to decide if she should bark or not.

"It's okay, Lily. It's the contractor. Come on, girl." At the bottom of the staircase, Olivia unlocked the front door and swung it open while holding onto Lily's collar. A tall, tanned, young blonde in jeans and a t-shirt stood on the front porch. She smiled showing a perfect row of white teeth. She extended her hand.

"Hi. Olivia Miller? I'm Jackie Connors. The contractor."

"Oh. I was expecting a man," Olivia said. "Ugh. That was a pretty stupid comment, wasn't it? I'm sorry."

Jackie shook her head and smiled. "It's okay. It happens all the time. People tend to hover around me at first when I start a job thinking I probably don't know what I'm doing." She referred to her clipboard. "So we're expanding and improving the sunroom, right?"

Olivia nodded. "Yes. My cousin showed me the plans."

Lily sniffed Jackie and gave her a lick on the hand. Jackie petted Lily's head.

"I just like to review everything before we get started," Jackie said.

A blue truck pulled up the driveway and two guys got out carrying paper coffee cups. "Morning," one called to Jackie as he put his cup on the roof of the truck and swung his tool belt around his waist.

Jackie raised a hand to the men in greeting. "Here's some of my crew," she told Olivia. "Can we look at the sunroom together?"

Olivia, Jackie, and Lily walked along the brick walkway to the rear of the house. Jackie indicated from the plans what they were contracted to do and reviewed everything with Olivia.

"So that's it. We'll be done with the whole thing in two or three weeks. Some days the crew will only be here half days. We're running about four different projects at once so I'll be here off and on going between here and the other places we're working on. But all that is built into the estimate I gave your cousin and it won't interfere with the time frame we quoted. As long as the weather holds for the first week, we'll be good. The interior finishing won't be dependent on the weather conditions. You'll see other members of my team working here. It won't always be these two guys. They're all good experienced workers. My cell phone number is on the paperwork I gave your cousin. Call me with any questions or concerns you have. Anything at all. Every few days, I like to meet with the owner to review where we are on the project."

"Sounds good," Olivia said. Lily was following the men back and forth to the truck as they brought out the lumber and tools. "This is Lily by the way. Looks like she plans on helping." Olivia chuckled.

Jackie smiled at the dog. "Nice dog. We'll be glad for her company. Okay, we'll get to work then. I'll be here most of the day today. I like to stay when the project starts in case any surprises show up."

"Thanks. Let me know if you need anything. Hopefully nothing unexpected will rear its head," Olivia said. She started back to the front of the house.

"Hopefully not," Jackie agreed.

OLIVIA HELD up the old newspaper article in front of her laptop so Brad could see it as they Skyped.

"Here are their pictures on the front page," Olivia said to her boyfriend.

"That's horrible, Liv. Who could do something like that?" Brad asked. Brad was in Maine running his bookstore while Olivia was minding her cousin's house.

"That's exactly what I said," Olivia answered.

"Nobody ever mentioned the murders to you?" Brad asked.

"No. I guess it was so long ago that it just never came up. I didn't even know that I had these distant cousins." Olivia put the newspaper on the kitchen table next to her laptop. "It just seems so terrible that no one was caught and brought to justice. It seems so wrong." Olivia glanced down at Mary and Kimmy's pictures.

"There mustn't have been enough evidence," Brad offered.

"They must have collected and retained evidence from the crime scene. Why can't they run it through some DNA testing thing now?"

"Don't know. Maybe they lost it," Brad said.

Olivia got a far away look in her eyes.

"What are you thinking?" Brad asked.

"Well, I was thinking of going to the police station and asking about it. Or maybe go to the District Attorney's office and ask what became of re-looking at the case a few years back. You know how John told me there was a newspaper article about cold cases in Massachusetts and this was one that the DA's office was looking at again."

"It was almost forty-five years ago that the crime was committed," Brad said. "They must have given it their full attention back then. There must have been a lot of pressure to solve it, what with a young mom and her little girl killed. And, so violently. Maybe there just wasn't enough evidence to arrest and prosecute."

"I just want to know," Olivia said.

"You're not going to start looking into this are you?" Brad asked. "Not after last summer? Please don't."

Last summer Olivia was consumed by finding out the cause of her aunt's death and the events of that nearly got her killed.

Olivia didn't answer.

"Liv." Brad had an edge to his voice. "No. Let it be. None of us want a summer like last year. Don't stir anything up. Please. Just spend some time relaxing. Clean out John's attic like you said you would. Take your class in July and then come home to us for a few weeks before your fall classes start."

Olivia still didn't say anything.

Brad sighed. "Joe and I are still recovering from last

year. Joe has just started to sleep through the night without waking up in terror." Brad and Joe had helped Olivia uncover her aunt Aggie's killers. Brad continued, "I couldn't take another summer like last year. Don't do this, Liv. Let it alone."

"Brad, I'm not going to stir anything up. It was forty-five years ago. What could I possibly stir up? I just want to know why no one was arrested for this."

"Olivia." Brad never called her that unless he was being serious about something. "I know you. It won't stop there."

"I think I'll go down to the library and look up some old newspapers from to find out what was written about the murders."

Brad's face was stern.

"Come on, nothing's going to happen to me in a library, Brad."

"I wouldn't count on that," Brad muttered.

Olivia ignored his comment and changed the subject. "I'm looking forward to you and Joe coming down to visit. Lily will love you two. You'll like her. She's a perfect dog."

"I'll be glad to see you. And, the dog." Brad grinned. "Joe's already planning the meal for Friday night, but he won't tell me what he's making."

"I won't ask. I want to be surprised. Are you bringing the blueberry cake?"

"You bet." He smiled. "I need to get back to work, Liv. Talk tomorrow?"

"Yes," Olivia smiled back at him.

"Stay out of trouble," Brad warned.

Olivia shook her head. "You worry too much," she told him.

"I'm dealing with *you*, so no, I don't worry too much." Brad's face was serious. "And maybe you don't worry enough."

"Good night, Brad."

"Night, Liv. Love you," Brad said.

Olivia's heart still warmed whenever he said those words to her. "Love you, too." Olivia closed the Skype session just as Lily put her warm nose against Olivia's thigh and nuzzled her to go out.

4

The night never cooled off and the day dawned hot and muggy. Olivia tossed and turned all night in the bedroom's sauna-like conditions and when morning arrived, she felt as if she hadn't slept at all. She decided she would install John's air conditioning unit in her bedroom later in the day. She showered, made breakfast for herself and Lily, and let the dog out so that she could spend the day in the yard supervising the sunroom workers. Olivia checked with them to be sure Lily wouldn't get in their way while she spent a few hours at the library. The men reported that they were pleased to have the dog's company.

Olivia made the ten minute drive to the library and parked in the front parking area. She got out, walked across the lot, and climbed the granite steps to the old, oak door of the Howland Public Library. She stopped at the information desk to inquire about old newspapers and was directed to the third floor microfiche library. The librarian showed Olivia how to use the machine to scroll through the articles and how to print the ones she wanted. Olivia flipped through the newspaper films until she found what she was looking for.

The first article reported that on the day following the murders, two local men, eighteen and twenty years old, had discovered the car and the bodies around 10am in a clearing approximately seventy-five yards up a wooded dirt road in the Howland State Park, two miles west of the Howland town center and three miles west of the Monahan's home. The young men were on their way to fish at the lake when they made the discovery. They went immediately to the police to report the grisly murders.

Mary Monahan was found fully clothed on the ground with her head partially under the vehicle. The daughter was in the front seat of the car. Mrs. Monahan's throat was slashed twice and she suffered multiple stab wounds to the chest and abdomen. Olivia winced recalling being stabbed in the gut herself last summer. Her hand moved instinctively to her stomach as she continued reading.

The daughter was stabbed once in the chest and her throat had been slashed. The left rear car door was open. Sperm was found at the scene but neither the mother nor daughter had been sexually assaulted. The husband,

George Monahan, reported his wife and daughter missing around suppertime on the day of the murders.

Mrs. Monahan had dropped her son off at kindergarten, did an errand in the nearby town, stopped at a hardware store in the town next to Howland around 2:00pm, and then was not seen again that day. There were stories about Mary and Kimmy in the newspapers every day for ten days, and after that, the articles were more sporadic until they disappeared altogether. A nineteen-year-old local man was a suspect and the police felt that the case was solved but no arrest could be made due to lack of evidence.

Olivia wondered how there could be a lack of evidence. Mary must have fought back. She must have had the killer's blood and skin under her nails. There was sperm at the scene. If the police suspected the nineteen-year-old man and felt the crime was solved, how could they not make an arrest? How could they let him off?

Olivia rubbed her temples and shifted her gaze away from the microfiche reader. Her eyes burned. A headache was brewing from reading for so long on the tiny screen and she felt hot and miserable. The accounts of the murders of the young mother and her little daughter made Olivia's stomach roil from the horror of it as she imagined the mom's panic and desperation to protect her child and the utter despair that must have crushed her when she knew there was no escape.

Olivia's heart pounded and a cold sweat broke out all over her skin from thinking about the killings. She printed the articles that she wanted to keep, paid the librarian, and left the building taking the steps two at a time. She needed to get out of there, to get away from the horrible words on the screen.

Her orange Jeep was an inferno from having sat closed up in the parking lot. Olivia fiddled with the controls for the air conditioning as she pulled onto Main Street and headed back to the house. She took the turn to John's Colonial and parked next to the blue and red trucks in the driveway. Jackie was pulling a metal case out of the truck bed and she turned her head when she heard Olivia's car. She waved to her.

"You don't look so good," Jackie said eyeing Olivia's pale face.

"I don't feel so good," Olivia confirmed. "I'm going to lie down for a bit."

"Need anything?" Jackie asked.

"I'm okay, thanks," Olivia said even though she didn't feel okay. It was like knives were cutting into her head.

"It's probably this heat," Jackie said.

Olivia nodded and moved toward the house, her head pounding.

"Just yell if you need something," Jackie called after her. "I'll be here a couple of more hours."

Olivia checked on Lily and let her stay outside to

hang out with the contractors. She went to the kitchen and splashed her face with cold water while leaning over the sink, took two aspirins and drank a large glass of ice cold water. Her headache was in full force now and her eyes squinted against the too bright light streaming in through the windows. Olivia's legs shook as she shuffled down the hallway. Her stomach threatened to heave. She made it to the living room couch, stretched out, and immediately fell asleep.

~

OLIVIA WOBBLED around the kitchen still groggy from her nap. She had slept for two hours and woke up sweaty and weary but the headache had subsided. She let the dog in and Lily sat near the back door watching Olivia move about the room. Olivia ate a banana and then went upstairs for a shower. She could hear hammering coming from the sunroom and was surprised that the construction workers hadn't quit for the day.

After she cleaned up and changed clothes, Olivia walked barefoot through the house to the sunroom toweling off her hair. Jackie was putting some tools in a metal box.

"Hey," Olivia said. "I thought you'd be gone by now."

"Oh, hi. No, I'm still here. A guy decided to call in sick today so I'm doing a little extra. How are you feeling?"

"Better. I didn't sleep well last night and I was at the library reading small print for a couple of hours this afternoon and the combination just made for a whopper of a headache."

"Doing some sort of research?" Jackie asked as she cleaned up the wood scraps and stray nails.

"Just for my own interest. Not for any official project or anything."

"Did you find what you were looking for?" Jackie asked.

"Somewhat. I just started really," Olivia said. She sat on a saw horse that was in the sunroom. "Did you grow up around here?"

"Yeah," Jackie replied. "I left to go to college, but I came back to the area to do graduate work in Boston and married my high school sweetheart." She looked up at Olivia with a big grin on her face. "You don't hear that much anymore, do you?"

"No, you don't," Olivia smiled. "How long have you been married?"

"Well, next month it will be six years."

"Wow. A long time," Olivia noted. "What did you do your graduate work in?"

Jackie took a swig from her water bottle and stretched. "I got a Ph.D. in counseling psychology."

Olivia's eyes widened and she cocked her head to the side.

Jackie laughed. "I know, so what I am doing in construction?"

"That was my exact question." Olivia smiled.

"I got married while working on my Ph.D. When I finally finished it, I worked for a year and then decided that it just wasn't for me and that I preferred designing and creating structures. My dad had worked as an architect and had a small construction business. I worked for him all through high school, and off and on when I was doing graduate work. So I started small with contracting and built my business over time." Jackie snapped the metal case shut. "I love it."

"I'm impressed," Olivia told her. "Especially since you spent all that time in school and you weren't afraid to make a change."

"Oh, I had my detractors and naysayers. But this is my life and I only get one shot. I want to be happy in my work."

"What did your husband think?" Olivia asked.

"He's a musician. He's used to flexible schedules and doing his own thing," Jackie grinned. "So he was fine with it."

"I'm glad it worked out," Olivia said. "Lots of people would be afraid to make such a big career change."

Jackie picked up the case and Olivia and Lily walked her to her truck.

"My husband is traveling with his band for a couple of weeks. If you're free, would you be interested in grabbing a bite to eat later?" Jackie asked Olivia.

"I sure would," Olivia responded. "I'm not used to all this country quiet. I have an apartment in Cambridge while I'm at school and it's a lot busier than Howland. My home's in Maine and Ogunquit's busy in the nice weather. I'm not used to things being so spread out and having to use the car all the time."

"Yeah, a place like Howland is a definite change of pace. I'll run home and jump in the shower. Do you know the Sports Bar Restaurant in the center of town?" Jackie asked. "It has good food and good prices. Want to meet around 8pm?"

"Sounds great. See you there." Olivia waved as Jackie backed out of the driveway and turned onto the road.

OLIVIA ARRIVED first and took a booth by a window. Jackie arrived shortly after and hurried over to where Olivia was sitting.

"It took me a little longer than I thought," Jackie said. "I had to swing by and talk to a client."

"It's okay," Olivia said. "I haven't been here long at all." Olivia was sipping an iced tea and browsing the menu. The restaurant's clientele changed gradually around 8pm each night as the families finished up their meals and headed home and the couples and singles arrived and gathered around the bar for drinks and appetizers. A Red Sox game played on the television over the bar. The restaurant was in the midst of the customer shift as Jackie took her seat across from Olivia.

Jackie ordered a burger and cole slaw and Olivia decided on the veggie burger and salad. They shared an appetizer of hummus and pita bread. They were both grateful for the air conditioned temperature of the restaurant and for a chance to get out of the heat for a couple of hours.

"The heat doesn't usually bother me, but the humidity is killing me," Olivia said.

"Yeah, it's bad this year. It came on strong. I haven't had time to build up my tolerance for it," Jackie said.

They worked on polishing off the appetizer. "So your cousin John said you had finished your school year and would be staying at his house for a couple of weeks, but he didn't mention what you're studying."

"I just finished my first year of law school."

"That's great. How did it go? Are you enjoying it?"

Olivia laughed. "I'm not sure you could say it was

enjoyable. I survived though. I just came back from the Netherlands. I did a three week internship there."

"Nice. That was where we spent our honeymoon," Jackie said. "We spent two weeks on a bike trip traveling the country. It was wonderful. What did your internship entail?" Jackie asked.

"I was working at the International Court of Justice at The Hague. I think it probably sounds more exciting than it was. It involved mostly doing research and writing up findings. But I learned a lot."

"Sounds terrific." Jackie told her. "So what were you researching today at the library? Something law related?" Jackie asked.

"Not really, no." Olivia put ketchup on the veggie burger that the waitress placed in front of her. "I'm cleaning out my cousin John's attic and I came across some old newspapers up there. I found a story about a double murder that happened here in town about forty-five years ago."

Jackie bit into her burger. "Before I was born," she mumbled after swallowing. She wiped her chin with her napkin. "It rings a bell though. Was one of the victims a young mom?"

"A mom and her four year old daughter," Olivia said.

Jackie put her burger on her plate. "I remember hearing about that. My parents brought it up once." She looked thoughtful. "The killer was never arrested, right?"

Olivia nodded. "Right. The story caught my interest and I went to the library to look at old newspapers to find out more details about the killings."

"What did you find?"

Olivia filled Jackie in on the information that she had gathered from her research.

"Awful," Jackie said. "What kind of a monster could do that? In broad daylight, too. Doesn't seem smart to kidnap two people in the light of day. Could it have been a crime of emotion? Or was it just random?" Jackie took a swallow of her beer. "This was a small town in those days. Lots of open space and people who had lived in town for years. Most people knew each other. The killings seem out of place. Seems like something more likely to happen in a city. What do you think about the killer? Someone just passing through? Someone from town?"

"The newspaper article said the police suspected a local guy. A nineteen-year-old. But there wasn't enough evidence to make an arrest. As far as the police were concerned, the case was solved," Olivia said.

"Really? That seems awful that they knew who did it but then he got off without being arrested." Jackie shook her head.

"John said that the Monahans were relatives of ours," Olivia said.

Jackie's eyes widened. "Were they?"

Olivia nodded. "I'd never heard about the killings

before. I saw the old newspaper up in the attic and John told me about it. I wonder if Mrs. Monahan knew the killer. Like you said, it was broad daylight. Maybe someone stopped Mrs. Monahan for something, to talk or whatever, and then the person kidnapped them. Maybe Mrs. Monahan was unsuspecting because she knew him?"

"It doesn't seem like it would be premeditated though," Jackie offered. "If you were planning ahead, wouldn't you want it to be dark when you approached?"

"But the person must have had a knife with him since the Monahans were stabbed and their throats were cut," Olivia said. "So maybe it was planned." Olivia's stomach was churning and her throat felt dry. Talking about the Monahans having their throats cut caused violent images of last summer to flash through her mind. Her palms were clammy and she reached for her water glass to moisten her throat. She took a long drink and continued. "But like you said, it seems dumb to plan an abduction and murder for the middle of the day. And how would someone even know where the Monahans would be that day?"

"And 'why' is another question. What could have been the motive?" Jackie asked.

"It seems beyond brutal to kill a woman and her child," Olivia's voice was soft. "The mom must have been terrified. Her one thought must have been to protect her daughter. She must have fought like hell."

They sat thinking for a while.

"My dad grew up here in town," Jackie said. "Lived here all of his life. I'll ask him what he heard about it."

"I'd be interested in what he has to say," Olivia said.

"Dad would have been in his early twenties then. He must remember some of the details. I'll let you know."

They finished off their burgers.

"The town must be a lot bigger now than back in the day," Olivia said.

"Oh, yeah. The location of Howland is really great. About a half hour on the train to Boston. Good schools. Highway access is nearby. But it still has a very rural, country flavor even with the huge influx of people over the years. Actually all the building and expanding started about forty-five years ago, a couple of years before those murders," Jackie said. "That mom and her daughter must have been in the first wave of newcomers to move in. It was the beginning of the changes in Howland."

"I imagine those murders certainly changed the atmosphere here," Olivia said.

"Yeah." Jackie's face was serious. "I bet that's for sure."

5

Olivia had spent the morning working on the attic. John had designated the things that should be thrown out, those he wanted to keep, and things he wanted to sell in a yard sale. She carried the things that would be thrown out into the garage. A trash removal company would be coming in the morning to haul the unwanted articles away. Olivia brushed a strand of hair out of her eyes and wiped her dirty hands on her old shorts.

She spotted Mr. Andrews, the landscaper, parking his truck in the driveway alongside one of the construction worker's vans. Olivia's cousin had hired Mr. Andrews to cut and trim the lawn at the house. Olivia waved to him and then went into the kitchen through the door from the garage.

Mr. Andrews rang the bell when he had finished his

work. He was a spry silver-haired man in his late sixties. His skin was dark and leathery from years of working outside.

"Hey, Mr. Andrews, come on in. John left an envelope for you. Come to the kitchen. How about a cold drink?" Olivia said.

"A cold drink sounds good. Damn heat," Mr. Andrews said wiping his forehead with a handkerchief that he retrieved from his back pocket. He followed Olivia to the kitchen at the rear of the house.

Olivia put ice cubes into a tall glass and poured lemonade into it. She put a slice of orange on the rim before handing it to Mr. Andrews.

"That looks great. Thanks."

"Have a seat. John left the envelope on the desk in the den. I'll be right back with it," Olivia told him.

When she returned with the envelope, Mr. Andrews was scanning the account of the murders in the old newspaper that she left on the kitchen table.

"This was a damned thing," he said still looking at the front page. "I remember it well. Forty-five years ago? Hard to believe it was so long ago."

"You lived in Howland back then?"

"Oh, sure. We've been here since 1968. The Monahans lived on the next street over from us. We had kids close in age." He shook his head. "Bah. Hadn't thought about it for a long time."

"Were you friends?"

"Can't say we were friends, exactly. Friendly. My wife knew her. We'd see them at church. The women taught Sunday School. They'd help out at the church when there was a funeral. Things like that."

"I read in the old papers that the police thought the killer was a local guy, a young man from town," Olivia said.

"Yeah, I heard that. Nothing came of it, far as I know."

"No one was ever arrested," Olivia said.

"Damn shame. Something like that and no arrest."

"What was the talk? Did people think it was the local guy?"

"Some did. There was lots of gossip. Some thought one of the priests at St. Catherine's was involved. Don't know if there was any truth to any of it."

"Why would someone suspect the priest?" Olivia asked.

"Never knew the details. Women were attracted to him. Ask me, he probably encouraged the attention. I never liked the guy. He seemed like a ladies' man."

"The victims were John's and my distant cousins," Olivia said.

"Were they? Gosh."

"I've been reading about the murders. I'd like to know why no one was arrested."

Mr. Andrews read a bit more of the old article. "Look,

Olivia, why don't you give my wife a call. She might remember more than I do about what happened and what people were thinking. Our number is on the invoice for the lawn." He pointed to the bill he had left on the table.

"I'd hate to bother her. She wouldn't mind?"

Andrews scoffed. "She never minds talking, that one. She'd be glad to talk to you." He checked his watch. "I gotta get a move on. Still have a number of lawns to do. Thank you for the cold drink."

Olivia walked Mr. Andrews to the front door.

When she returned to the kitchen, Olivia glanced at the old newspaper on the table. She played Brad's words in her head. *It was so long ago. Leave it alone. Don't stir anything up. None of us want a summer like last year.* She turned the paper over so that the Monahans' photos weren't visible and she headed for the garage to finish preparing the attic junk for the trash company. When Olivia reached the door to the garage, she stopped in front of it. Holding the door knob, she turned her head and looked back at the overturned newspaper. After several seconds of mental debate, Olivia pulled her phone from her shorts pocket, walked back to the table, and leaned over the landscaping invoice to find the number to phone Mr. Andrew's wife.

6

Olivia followed the directions that Mrs. Andrews gave her and she turned her Jeep onto Magnolia Hill Drive. She drove along the winding road past woods of pines, maples, and oaks until it widened slightly and opened to several miles of what Olivia could only describe as mansions. The homes lined both sides of the road, each one set back on expansive acreage. Olivia considered her cousin John's 2800 square foot antique Colonial to be a huge house, but four to six houses the size of John's would easily fit inside the palaces she passed. The mansions had an air of understated elegance, as if they were owned by a doctor or lawyer or successful businessperson, but some also exuded an opulence associated with a celebrity or professional sports star.

It was just before noon when Olivia spotted the

granite mailbox post with number twenty-eight engraved onto it. She turned the Jeep into the long driveway that led to a stately brick mansion. There were shade trees and mature plantings neatly meandering around the ground's of the home.

Olivia wondered how a lawn business owner could afford such a place and she suspected that she had the wrong address. She glanced at the paper on the console to confirm the address she had written down to be sure this was the house she was looking for. She slowed the Jeep and parked near the three car garage.

A woman came around the side of the house. She was slender and petite, her silver hair cut short and stylishly with wisps framing her face. She was dressed in a short sleeved striped shirt and tan chinos and carried a basket of flowers in one hand and some garden clippers in the other. She seemed energetic and efficient and she greeted Olivia with a bright smile.

"I was in the back yard and heard the car so I came out to see if it was you. Olivia, right?" She extended her hand.

"Yes, hello Mrs. Andrews," Olivia said. "Thank you for seeing me."

"No need for thanks. I'm happy to speak with you. And please, call me Lydia."

She led Olivia along the stone path to the back of the house. There was a large glass room off the rear of the home. All of the floor to ceiling windows were open, allowing what little breeze there was to enter the room.

"This is a beautiful home," Olivia said.

"Thank you, hon. People are sometimes surprised that a lawn service man owns a house like this." She laughed. "Bob owned a construction business all his life. He did quite well, made good investments, and that's what paid for this place. He retired a few years back, gave the business to our son. But Bob is a man who must keep busy or he goes crazy which means he then drives me crazy." She winked. "So he decided to start the lawn business. It works out nicely as we live here in spring, summer, and fall and then head out to Arizona in the winter."

"Lucky," Olivia said. "I wouldn't mind escaping some of the New England winters myself. Your husband seems like a real nice man."

"Oh, he's a peach. But don't tell him I said that," she smiled. "Come on in, Olivia. I want to get these flowers in water. Then we can have some tea and sit and talk." They entered an enormous kitchen that had a center island, granite counters, high end appliances, and a gleaming wood floor. Mrs. Andrews removed a cut glass vase from a cabinet, filled it with water, and arranged the flowers. She made tea and she and Olivia took their mugs out to the sunroom.

"Please, sit," Lydia said. They each took a seat in plush

chairs. The room provided a view of green lawn, tall maple trees, and flower beds edging the property line.

"What a peaceful, relaxing spot," Olivia observed. "Even in the heat of the day this room is so cool."

"It really is a lovely place to sit and enjoy the yard. Somehow it catches the breeze." They sipped their tea. "So, Olivia, Bob tells me that you are related to Mary Monahan and her daughter."

"Yes, distantly, though. I didn't know about them at all until a few days ago when my cousin John told me what happened. No one had ever talked about them to me. Or, of the murders."

"Not surprising. It was so long ago," Lydia said. "Time passes and people move on. Sad things are forgotten." She sipped her tea with a faraway look on her face. "Not forgotten, just left unspoken." She gave Olivia a sad smile. "How can I help? What can I tell you?"

"I guess I'm trying to piece things together and understand what happened. Why no one was arrested. Your husband said that you and Mary were acquaintances."

"I would say more than acquaintances, but not full-fledged friends. We both taught at Sunday School and attended the same town events because of our kids, so I got to know her. She was a nice woman, a good conversationalist, kind, helpful. She doted on those kids." She shook her head slowly and sighed. "Those murders took a toll on me. It hit close to home. I used to imagine being torn from my family like that. My daughter murdered. My husband and two sons left behind. Lives destroyed. Why? For what? The tenuous nature of life...I thought a good deal about that. I believe it made me more grateful for each day. It's a cliché, I know, but I do believe that I became more mindful of the things that were most important." She squeezed her hands together in her lap. "I haven't thought about the murders for a long time."

"It must have been a terrible shock to everyone in town."

"Oh, my, yes. It was unbelievable that something like that could happen here in Howland."

"What did people think? Did the townspeople talk about suspects?"

"Oh, sure. There was plenty of gossip. There was talk of an escaped prisoner, a young man from town. Rumors were swirling."

"What did you think? Did you have any feelings one way or the other?" Olivia asked.

"I wasn't sure what to think. I wanted the police to figure it out and make an arrest. Keep us all safe. But you know that didn't work out."

"What's the story on the young man from Howland? Did you think he was a valid suspect?"

"There was never much in the papers regarding him, but we all knew he was taken in for questioning," Lydia said. "His name was Kenny Overman. I think he was

about nineteen when it happened. Kenny was a high
school dropout, had a tough family life. We saw Kenny as
a young man ruined by his upbringing. He did odd jobs
for a while, landscaping, delivery man, snowplowing. He
was a big drinker. Kind of a lost soul. My best friend,
Angela... her younger sister, Emily, dated Kenny for some
time. They weren't a match at all, but she was drawn to
his bad boy tendencies. Emily was a rebel. Her parents
were strict Catholics, very wealthy, old money. They have
a huge mansion here in the Magnolia Hill section of
Howland. Emily chafed at their control. She knew dating
Kenny would make them furious. Emily told Angela that
Kenny had quite a temper, but Emily could match him on
that one. She was always fighting with her parents."

"Was Angela on Emily's side in her arguments with
the parents?"

"There were five years between Angela and Emily.
They were never really close. Angela was married already
when Emily was in high school. Angela tried to stay
neutral in the battles between Emily and the parents. I
think Angela felt badly that her parents had so much
turmoil going on in their house. After the murders, the
parents told Emily that if she didn't break off with Kenny
then they would cut her off financially, so Emily stopped
seeing him. They were always on again, off again anyway.
My friends and I were on the fence about Kenny and the
murders. On one hand, we just couldn't believe he could

commit a crime like that, but on the other hand, what Emily told Angela about his temper and his drinking, well, we wondered if it may have been possible under certain circumstances."

"What happened to him? Is he still in town?" Olivia asked.

"Oh, no. He's long gone. Who knows where? Imagine living in a town where everyone thinks you're a murderer? As soon as he was cleared of suspicion, he took off. I don't think Emily was sad to see him go. He was too much trouble. She knew it would never work."

"Is Emily living in town now?"

"She lives about twenty minutes from here. She never married. She was engaged for a while to a man she knew since elementary school, but she broke it off. Never had kids. Emily works as an accountant...has her own business now in multiple locations... owns real estate...is very successful. Would you be interested in speaking with her, Olivia?"

"I would. Do you think she'd be willing?" Olivia wondered what the girl who had been dating the suspect would have to say about him.

"I don't see why not. I'll make a call to my friend, Angela, and ask her to talk to Emily. I'll give Angela your cell number and if Emily is amenable, my friend can pass the number to her and ask her to give you a call."

"Yes, please. I'd appreciate it," Olivia said.

"In fact, if you want another opinion on Kenny, maybe you should also speak to Angela and Emily's mom, Isabel Bradford. She must be in her early nineties now, but she still lives in the family home. Her version of Kenny would certainly be a different viewpoint than Emily's will be."

"That would be great if she would talk with me," Olivia said.

"I'll bring it up with Angela and see what she thinks."

"There was a newspaper story a few years back about unsolved cases in Massachusetts," Olivia said. "They profiled the case on Mary and Kimmy. The article indicated that the police knew who killed them but there wasn't enough evidence for a conviction."

"Hmm...not enough evidence or botched evidence?"

"What do you mean?" Olivia asked.

"There was semen at the scene. Mary had skin under her fingernails. She fought back. Her hands and wrists had cuts on them. She must have had blood from the killer on her. With DNA testing now, how can they not figure it out? Especially, if they have a suspect in mind?"

"So you think the evidence was lost or mishandled?"

"It sounds like it to me. But what do I know?" Lydia said. "Things get lost. Evidence gets contaminated." She paused. "Sometimes, intentionally."

Olivia raised her eyebrows. "Intentionally? Why?"

"Well...there was some talk back then. Some talk about the priest at the church. It was probably idle gossip.

That he was interested in Mary. That perhaps he made advances and she rebuffed him."

"Your husband mentioned the priest. So what? People think he might have killed her?"

"It was scuttlebutt. Father Anthony was a handsome man, young, friendly, energetic. The women in the parish were gaga over him. They loved to talk. There was gossip."

"You think there was some substance to it?"

"I don't know." She put her mug down and sighed. "Maybe."

"Why?" Olivia asked.

"Mary and I, as I said, we both taught Sunday School. Sometimes I would catch Father Anthony looking at Mary. She would be arranging her materials in the classroom and he would always come by and chat with her. Another time I arrived to the church hall to help set up for a funeral meal. I heard loud noises coming from the kitchen. An argument. Angry voices. I couldn't hear what they were saying. Of course, I didn't want to go in there with that going on, so I started setting up chairs and tables at the far end of the hall, banging things around...making as much noise as I could so whoever was arguing in the kitchen would know that I was out there. All of a sudden, Father Anthony stormed out of the kitchen and left the building. He didn't acknowledge me at all. I was thinking whether I should go into the kitchen to see who was still in there but then two other women came into the hall from outside to help out. They went right into the kitchen and started bustling about. I walked in to help get the meal started, and it was Mary who was in there. We made eye contact. She looked flustered, upset. I think she knew that I had heard the argument going on but she said nothing. She turned to the sink and started washing out serving platters. I never mentioned anything to her. We acted like nothing had happened."

"Do you think they were having an affair?"

"No, I don't. What I knew of Mary, that wasn't something she would have done. But, Anthony? Maybe it was something he was interested in. Maybe he didn't like being refused."

"Is Father Anthony still at the church?"

"No, he isn't. He was transferred to another church." She paused for effect. "About a month after the murders."

Olivia leaned forward. "Transferred? Was that in the works prior to the killings?"

"Not to my knowledge. Nor to any of my friends' knowledge either."

"That seems very suspicious. Where did he get transferred to?"

"Somewhere in California," Lydia said.

"California? That's about as far away from here as you can go without leaving the country."

"Uh-huh."

"Do you think Father Anthony did it, Lydia? Do you think he killed them?"

Lydia moved her hand in the air. "Oh I don't know. It must have been coincidence that he left our church. Wouldn't it be incredibly obvious to the police if he transferred without reason? He must have been called to a church that needed him. Or it was planned ahead of the murders but wasn't discussed with the congregation. The police must have looked into it." They sat in silence for several seconds. "Don't you think?"

"It would be absurd if they didn't look into it," Olivia said. "Of course...times were different back then."

Lydia nodded her head. "That crossed my mind as well. Don't make waves. Don't make people lose faith. Keep it quiet. Transfer him."

They exchanged a long look.

"I'm not saying he did it, Olivia. I'm just telling you what happened."

"I understand."

"It could have been Kenny for all we know," Lydia said. "Not enough evidence, so what are they going to do? The person gets off. Leaves the area. That's the end of that."

"Doesn't seem right does it?" Olivia said.

"Not at all," Lydia said firmly.

7

Olivia was returning from running errands and saw Jackie's red truck parked in the driveway of John's Colonial. Olivia walked around to the back of the house to the sunroom. Jackie was hammering alongside one of her workers when she saw Olivia approaching. She grabbed her water bottle and stepped outside to meet her. They sat down on the deck.

"I talked to my parents last night about that murder case," Jackie told Olivia. "My sister and I had dinner with them."

"What did they have to say?" Olivia asked. "Did your dad remember it?"

"He sure did. He said it was a shocking event that had the whole town talking. People who never locked their doors, started locking up. People didn't want their kids walking around alone. It just changed the whole tone of things. He said people seemed more distrustful of each other. He said he never felt like things went back to the way they were before the murders."

"I can imagine," Olivia said.

"Dad said there were lots of rumors flying around about who may have done it. There was talk of a local kid involved and a guy who was living in the woods was suspected."

"So what was the consensus? Did townspeople have any strong opinions one way or the other?"

"Not really. It all depended on who you talked to."

Olivia nodded.

"Dad said that a guy who had been living in the woods was suspected because he had kidnapped a couple of local women at knifepoint about a month before the murders. Dad was sure he read about it in the papers back then. He suggested you go back to the library to look it up if you're interested."

"I'll probably go back to the library a couple of more times. I'll look it up."

"My sister brought up something that I never knew."

Olivia looked at Jackie with interest.

"My sister Lynn has a friend who is a psychic or a medium or an intuit, whatever you want to call her."

Olivia's face took on a look of disbelief.

"I know, I know. It sounds crazy. But this woman has worked on unsolved cases all over the country. The police actually call her in. She lives here in town. The Howland police called on her a few years back to look into these two murders."

Olivia sat up straight eager to hear more. "Really? She works with the police? She worked on this case?"

"Lynn said you should go talk to her. The woman's name is Hannah. She might be able to tell you some things. Lynn gave me her name and email address." Jackie handed Olivia a piece of paper with the information written on it.

"I've read about psychics assisting the police, but I never really believed it could help," Olivia said. "Sort of seems like nonsense."

"Yeah," Jackie said. "I'm not sure what I think about it. I went to this woman a couple of years ago for a reading after my sister convinced me. It was impressive what she said about me. But I'm skeptical. I never knew she worked with the police."

"Guess it couldn't hurt to talk to her," Olivia considered.

"Sure, send her an email. My sister said to mention her name as this psychic is booked months in advance."

"Thanks, Jackie. I'll let you know what comes of it."

Lily sat down next to Olivia and pushed her nose at Olivia's hand trying to encourage some patting. "In my research the other day, I found out that Mary's son, Michael, is living about sixty miles from here."

"Is he?" Jackie asked.

"I'd like to talk to him."

"He was just a little boy when his mom and sister were murdered. I doubt he'd be able to tell you much."

"I know. But maybe the police have kept in touch with him. He must know some details about why no one was arrested."

"Are you going to try to contact him?" Jackie asked.

"I can't find a phone number or email address for him. But I did find his physical address." Olivia stopped patting Lily but the dog nudged her hand and Olivia returned to scratching. "What if I just drive up there? Ring the bell and introduce myself?"

"Hmmm. I don't know. That might be too much of a surprise," Jackie said.

"I'd just really like to talk to him."

"It might not be a good idea."

"There's no other way to get in touch." Olivia sighed. "I might just take the chance."

Jackie looked at her. "Can you brace yourself for disappointment? Because that might be all you get out of it."

"I guess I'll have to."

LATER THAT NIGHT, Olivia sent an email to the psychic introducing herself, explaining what she was researching, and asking if she might be able to arrange a meeting sometime soon.

Olivia stayed up until well past one in the morning debating with herself about whether or not to make the drive to call on Michael Monahan in person. She sat curled on the sofa with just one lamp on the side table turned on. A scented jar candle was in the center of the coffee table and the flame flickered and caused long shadows to dance on the walls. Olivia poked at the edge of the notebook where she had jotted notes and facts about the murders. The notebook opened to the page listing the information about Mary Monahan's husband and son. Olivia imagined driving to Michael Monahan's house, introducing herself, and being invited in to hear how he had coped with the loss of his mother and sister. She rested back on the sofa and stared at the ceiling. No matter how many ways she tried to convince herself that arriving unannounced at Monahan's front door would work out well, she couldn't shake the reality that he would find her visit intrusive. Olivia decided to talk it over with Brad the next day. She pushed herself up from the sofa and leaned forward to blow out the candle. She turned off the lamp, called to Lily, and the two climbed the stairs and went to bed.

8

Emily Bradford, the girl who had dated the nineteen-year-old murder suspect, contacted Olivia and they arranged to meet at a coffee shop in Brookline center. From her seat near the window, Olivia watched a sleek silver Mercedes pull into the lot and park. An attractive, slender woman with honey blonde hair cut into a long bob emerged from the driver side. She was wearing a tight, bright blue skirt, heels, and a fitted navy blazer. She looked trim and strong. Olivia calculated she must be in her early sixties.

The woman strode to the door of the coffee shop with confidence and purpose, entered, and spotted Olivia right away. She crossed the space to Olivia's table and extended her hand as she took a seat on the opposite side of the booth.

"Emily Bradford."

"Thanks for getting in touch with me," Olivia said as she shook hands with the woman.

"I was surprised as hell when my sister called to tell me someone wanted to speak with me about the murders," Emily said. Her voice carried a tone of authority. "No one has asked me anything about it since the year it all happened."

"I just wanted to get some of your impressions from the time. I understand you were dating one of the original suspects?" Olivia asked.

"Yes. Kenny. Kenny Overman. We dated off and on through high school and during my first year of college. I thought he was so cool, smoking, drinking...even in the ninth grade." She leaned forward, a slight smile on her face. "He seemed so dangerous and outlandish. Just did whatever he wanted. So different from my straight-laced, rule-based, Catholic parents." She chuckled. "That was part of the appeal. That and how good-looking he was." She sipped her coffee. "He was sweet at heart...when he wasn't drinking."

"What about the priest at St. Catherine's? Father Anthony?" Olivia asked.

Emily's eyebrows went up. "What about him?"

"Your family attended the church. Did you know him at all?'

"Sure. He led the youth group. Why do you ask about him?"

"People mentioned his name...suggested I look him up...said he might have some information. I was hoping to get his take on what happened since he lived here in Howland at the time of the murders," Olivia said. "Do you know where he might be located now? Which parish he's assigned to?"

"I don't. No," Emily said. Her face was blank. "I haven't seen him for years. I don't know what people think he could offer about the murders."

"What did you think of him?" Olivia asked.

"He was good at organizing. Friendly. It was an active youth group. It was more of a young adult group, I guess. We were all between seventeen and twenty. We had a lot of fun."

"Did he seem overly friendly with the women?" Olivia asked.

Emily shifted in her seat. "How do you mean?"

"Some people have said that he enjoyed being around women."

"I hadn't heard that." Emily's face took on a hard look. "I never noticed."

Olivia worried that she might have offended Emily and decided she better change her line of questioning. "Why do you think the police suspected Kenny? Was there evidence that tied him to the crime? Was he connected to the victims in some way?"

"Kenny knew the husband more than the wife and

daughter. He had done some work around their house. Some painting, raking, things like that. They suspected him because Kenny's car was parked alongside a road about three miles from the crime scene. Mary and her daughter stopped at a hardware store to pick up some things on the day of the murders. The store wasn't far from where Kenny's car was parked. Kenny said the car broke down and he left it there. He said the police tried to get him to say that Mary picked him up to give him a lift."

"Did anyone see Kenny with Mary that day?"

"Not that I know of. But the police didn't give out information like that to the public."

"Why suspect Kenny just because his car was on the road?"

"Kenny had an argument with Mary's husband a month prior to the murders. Kenny was accused of taking a couple of expensive tools from the garage of Mary and Tom's house. There was no way to prove who owned the things. There was animosity between the guys. Kenny told me he bought those tools himself, but who knows? Maybe he did steal them."

"Where did Kenny say he was at the time of the murders? Did he have an alibi?"

"He went into Boston the day of the killings. He was planning to talk to an Army recruiter, but he told me he changed his mind when he got to the door of the recruiting office. He said he went over to Fenway Park and just hung around outside. He couldn't afford a ticket to the game."

"Did you see Kenny that day? The day Mary and her daughter were killed?"

"Yeah. He always called or dropped by every day, unless we were having a fight, which we ended up having that night. He came by...I don't know, could have been like 10pm or so. He asked if I wanted to go for a ride on his motorcycle. You can imagine how my parents loved that. I didn't want to go because I was feeling sick. I had gone to New York City for the day. I took the bus there so I had to get up really early. Kenny and I had bus tickets to go together but he backed out two days before. He said he didn't want to waste the day hanging around in some overpopulated city. He said he wanted to go talk to the Army recruiter, and that maybe he should join the military. I was furious at him for changing the plans especially since I already had the bus tickets. I decided to go myself...wanted a day alone...walk around, do some shopping. I was exhausted when I got home. I had a terrible headache. Kenny got so annoyed with me because I wouldn't go out with him that night...he thought I was making it all up that I didn't feel well because he hadn't gone to New York with me. We had a fight about it of course. He seemed more annoyed with me than usual which pissed me off."

She sighed and passed her hand over her forehead.

"I think back on it sometimes. I thought a lot about it at the time, after the police brought him in for questioning. If he had gone with me to New York, I would have been able to vouch for his whereabouts." She looked out of the coffee shop window for a minute, and then turned back to Olivia. "So anyway, he left right away when I told him I didn't want to go out that night. Which, of course, annoyed me because I was sick and I wanted him to stay with me but, no, he just took off when I refused to go ride around with him. That's what our relationship was like...a series of petty annoyances and arguments." She shook her head. "After being with Kenny, all I wanted was a nice, quiet, even-keeled life. No drama."

"I bet. Did Kenny seem different that night, different than usual?"

"I don't really remember. I can't say anything was different from normal."

"So the police brought him in for questioning?"

"They did. That was frightening to me, to think maybe I was dating a murderer. Kenny was a wreck. My parents freaked out. They told me to stop seeing him or they would stop supporting me. I had just finished my freshman year in college. I commuted in to Boston for my classes. My parents wouldn't allow me to live on campus." She rolled her eyes. "I couldn't afford to continue college without their support. And I sure as heck didn't intend to stay in Howland for the rest of my life. I wanted a career. I didn't want to be dependent on anyone else."

"So you stopped seeing him?"

"I stopped our romantic connection, but not because my parents told me to. I was tired of our relationship, his millions of problems, his moods, our fights. The murders gave me an excuse to end it. It shut my parents up too and kept the tuition money coming. But Kenny and I stayed in touch during the time right after the murders. My parents didn't know that detail. I felt bad for Kenny. He was so alone. He lived with his father...a mean, abusive, hateful drunk. Sometimes I would sneak out at night to see Kenny just so he could talk. He always professed his innocence. The police told him to stick around and not to leave the area, but after a while they had nothing to pin on him and they said he was free to do as he pleased."

"Then he moved away?"

Emily nodded her head. "I met him one night, late. I snuck out and met him in the field behind my house. He said he needed to take off...that everybody in town thought he was a killer. He needed a new start. He had sold his old truck to get some money. I asked where he was going but he said he didn't know. He said that he would contact me later to let me know where he was. He never did though. That was it. I never saw him after that. I don't know where he ended up or what happened to him."

"You think he could have done something like that? Killed Mary and Kimmy? Was he capable of doing that?" Olivia asked.

Emily was quiet for a moment. "His temper...especially when he drank...I hate to say it, but now that I'm older and I think back...maybe... maybe he could have."

9

Olivia had spent hours reading about the murders and the father and son who were left behind. She knew how it was to have someone you loved violently wrenched from your life leaving a gaping hole in your world.

Olivia's research had revealed that Mary's husband, George Monahan, had passed away a few years ago. Mary's son, Michael, was a dentist, had never married, no children. Olivia found another old article online discussing the cold case of Mary and Kimmy's murders. The reporter had interviewed Michael Monahan as part of the story. In the news article, Monahan described himself as someone who had a good life, who had no interest in the details of the murders. He believed that dwelling on tragedy was not helpful for anyone and that it was important to move on.

Olivia stared at her laptop screen as she and Brad Skyped while he ate his lunch at his bookstore.

"Did you read the article I sent you?" she asked.

"Yeah," Brad said between swallows of his sandwich. "It's pretty clear from the article that Monahan doesn't need to have the crime solved. He just wants to live his life. He doesn't want to know the details."

"I know." Olivia's hand held her chin. "Do you think he'd talk to me?"

"I don't think he would want to."

Olivia didn't say anything.

"I don't think you should contact him," Brad said. "He wouldn't be able to tell you much anyway. He was in kindergarten when it happened and he's never wanted to know any specifics. He couldn't tell you anything of worth."

"I guess you're right."

"I know you're disappointed. I know you'd like to connect with him. But I think you should respect how he needs to handle what happened."

"I understand." Olivia said. "Sort of."

Brad gave her a look. "How would it help with the case? From the article, it doesn't seem like he knows much or wants to know much. You probably know more than he does."

Olivia could see that Monahan just wanted to move forward and leave the past behind. He didn't need to know what happened. He was a little boy when the murders took place. Olivia wondered if maybe kids were better at adapting to changes and loss than grownups were.

"You're right, Brad. There's no reason to contact him."

10

Hannah the psychic responded to Olivia's email telling her that she was booked solid with client readings for the next few months but invited Olivia to come to her farm to talk. She wrote that she had a good deal of chores to do, and if Olivia didn't mind, she could chat with her as she worked in the barn.

Olivia maneuvered the Jeep along the skinny country road looking for Hannah's farm. She turned into the long winding driveway that snaked along stone walls, open fields, and mature trees. Olivia parked between a big antique Colonial house and a red barn. There were flower beds surrounding the house spilling with blossoms and a crushed stone walkway led to the front door. A wide door on the barn was open, so Olivia decided to see if the psychic was working inside.

A tall black horse stood on the cement floor cross tied between two rows of stalls and a petite woman was working on the animal's coat with a hand brush.

"Hey," Olivia said. "Hannah?"

The woman straightened and turned. She had her light brown hair pulled back in a ponytail. She wore jeans, boots, and a tank top which showed off the muscles in her lightly tanned shoulders and arms. She projected an air of competence and good health. She gave Olivia a big smile, put the brush in a box, and wiped her hands on her jeans as she walked over to shake hands.

"Hi. Nice to meet you. Come on in." Hannah welcomed Olivia into the barn. "I'm just finishing up with the General here," she motioned to the stately horse.

"He's a beauty," Olivia said.

"He is, isn't he? He's a wonderful horse. Despite his size, he's as gentle as a lamb. I use him to teach new riders because he's so smart and steady. Do you ride?" Hannah asked as she reached for another brush.

"Oh, no. I've never been on a horse unless you count pony rides at a fair when I was little."

"You should try it. I bet you'd enjoy riding." Hannah pointed to some hay bales along the wall. "Have a seat here if you like while I finish up."

Olivia sat and made herself at home. The barn smelled of horse, hay, and fresh air. Hannah kept the place spotless.

"So I understand that you have some questions for me?" Hannah said as she bent to brush the horse's legs.

"Yeah." Olivia wasn't sure where to start. "Well, you know I'm staying at my cousin's house while he's away and I found some old newspapers in the attic." Olivia proceeded to explain her interest in and connection to the decades-old murder case.

"So it just seems so horrible that no one was prosecuted for the crime and I wonder what happened with the investigation," Olivia said.

Hannah unhooked the horse from the ties and turned him toward the other end of the barn where the far door was also open. "I'm going to put General in the pasture." Olivia rose from her hay bale perch and walked with them. They stepped into the sunlight and headed down the path to the far field.

"At the time of the murders, a young man from the area was considered a suspect but there wasn't enough evidence to arrest and go to trial," Hannah began. "The police asked me to assist in the case several years ago. A detective contacted me and asked for my input. They were hoping that working together we might come up with a lead that could tie the murders to the suspect." Hannah paused. "I'm reluctant to get involved in these cases because they're exhausting for me."

She sighed and continued. "I connect with people on the other side. Sometimes I see and hear them or sometimes there's no visual but they speak to me. In cases involving murder, the police don't tell me much. They often bring me to the place where the crime occurred and I open myself to sensations. In most cases, I transfer into the body of the victim. Sometimes I can see and feel what the victim saw and felt. In essence, I am sensorially aware of the murder."

Olivia stared at her. "You mean it's like you're the victim?"

Hannah nodded.

"You can feel what the victim felt?"

Hannah nodded again. "Sometimes."

Hannah opened the gate to the field and unhooked the lead from General's halter. The horse trotted off to the tree line along the edge of the field where three other horses were standing in the shade. The two women leaned on the rail fence and watched the horses.

After a few minutes, Hannah continued. "So in this case, I entered the body of Mary. Some things I saw, some I heard, and some I felt. I was able to confirm aspects of the case that were known to the police and some things that the police had suspected. I was able to provide some details that they didn't know at all." Hannah turned to Olivia and held her eyes for several seconds. "Your cousin is grateful for your concern."

Olivia's eyes went wide. "She...what?"

"She appreciates your concern. She appreciates that

you care, even though you never met them. But she isn't bothered that the killer hasn't been punished. She believes that the killer will have to account for what was done...in time...but maybe not in this lifetime."

Olivia shook her head. Her eyes were wide. Thoughts swirled through her brain. "I don't even know what to ask."

Hannah gave a slight nod and waited for Olivia to process what she had just heard.

"Mary talks to you?" Olivia asked. "You didn't just experience the crime and that was it?"

"Let's walk back to the house," Hannah said and they started up the path. "Right after the police called me about getting involved, I was in my kitchen and I turned around and Mary...her spirit...was standing there watching me. She didn't speak to me, so I just let her follow me around. I acknowledged her but didn't ask anything or say anything to her. She stayed almost all day just watching me. It went on for days before she finally spoke. I guess she was sizing me up." Hannah chuckled.

"She was in your kitchen? She spoke to you?" Olivia asked. She was finding all of this extremely hard to believe.

Hannah nodded. "We've become friends."

"You're...friends?" Olivia stopped walking and stared. "But. She's dead."

Hannah smiled. "I know how it sounds, Olivia. It

sounds crazy. But it is what it is. I used to be afraid of my abilities. The whole thing really annoyed me. I didn't want to be seeing and hearing people from the other side. In high school, I just shut it down and wouldn't acknowledge it at all."

Hannah headed to the patio behind the house. It was surrounded by flower gardens and bird feeders were placed in different spots.

"Please sit, Olivia. I have some lemonade and iced tea in the fridge. I'll get us some glasses."

"Can I help?"

"I'll just be a minute. Have a seat."

Hannah returned with a tray carrying two glass pitchers, glasses, and a plate with fruit and veggies on it. She placed the tray on the patio table, adjusted the umbrella for maximum shade, and poured the drinks. She sat down and picked up her story right where she had left off.

"So as I got older, I became intrigued by what I could do. My grandfather has the same skills, so he worked with me on accepting my abilities. It took a while to come to terms with it all. My grandfather was a tremendous help to me, very supportive and encouraging. He helped me develop my skills. I decided to use them in service to others."

Olivia sipped her iced tea. "My mind is racing," she confessed. "I don't know what to make of all this. It's a lot to take in. I've never heard anything like this before."

"I understand. I always suggest that people keep an open mind," Hannah said.

"Do you know who killed them?" Olivia asked.

"I have an idea, but there's something confusing about it. It's unclear."

"Can you tell me?"

"I can't, no. Since it's part of an ongoing police investigation. I'm not at liberty to divulge information."

Olivia nodded. "The police are still looking into this case?"

"From time to time."

"Do you think they'll ever make an arrest?"

"I don't know. The police don't tell me things like that."

Olivia took a long sip from her glass and thought about everything she heard. "So Mary appears to you?"

"Yes."

"Why doesn't Mary just tell you who the killer is?'

"It doesn't work that way. It's hard to explain," Hannah said.

Olivia took a deep breath. "I can't believe I'm asking these things. Mary's okay?"

"She's okay now. It took a long time to work through her anger, but she is in a good place now."

"What about Kimmy?"

"They're together. They weren't initially. When it happened, Kimmy was enveloped in a sort of blinding, white light, a caring benevolent presence took her away, wrapped in love and safety. After time passed, Mary and Kimmy were reunited."

"You still see them?"

"At least once a week," Hannah said.

Olivia shook her head. Her mind was racing. "People accept this? The things you're saying?"

"Some people do. Yes." Hannah held Olivia's eyes. "And some people don't."

"You're not making this up?"

"If I say it's true, will it help you accept it?"

"I don't know. Maybe, not."

"It's true, Olivia. Every word of it."

"Is there anything I can do?" Olivia asked. "Can I do something to bring the killer to justice?"

"I'm not sure. I can't predict the future. I can only see the ones who have passed. And they don't know the future either. Why don't you speak to the police? Go see the detective who is handling the case. Or the District Attorney. Maybe one of them can tell you something."

Hannah scrutinized Olivia for several seconds. "Have you lost someone recently...over the past year? Someone you love?"

Olivia's eyebrows went up. Her heart started to race. "What?" she whispered.

"Someone close to you." Hannah nodded her head slightly. "Your mother?"

Olivia blinked back tears. She cleared her throat. "My aunt," she said softly.

Hannah looked puzzled for a moment, but her face cleared. "She took care of you. Like a mother."

Olivia nodded. "Yes."

"She looks out for you." Hannah smiled. "She calls you 'Livvy'."

Olivia's hands started to shake. Her face turned pale. Tears spilled from her eyes. How could Hannah know this?

"She's all right, Olivia. She has peace in her heart." Hannah took Olivia's hand. "She's proud of you." Olivia pressed against the back of the patio chair trying to steady herself. Her heart pounded against her chest.

A little girl with dark hair opened the back door. "Mom, your appointment is here."

"I have a client now," Hannah said.

Olivia nodded.

"I'm glad we met. Come back again, if you like."

11

O livia drove back to the house with more questions than she had when she left. She held tight to the steering wheel. Her head was a buzzing mess of confusion. She wanted to talk to Brad and was glad that they had arranged to Skype that afternoon.

"That's what she told me, Brad," Olivia said to her boyfriend over the computer connection. "How could she do that? How could she see people who have passed? How could she know about Aggie?"

"I don't know, Liv," Brad said. "Maybe she looked you up on the internet. Maybe she read the stories online about you last summer. Maybe she saw Aggie's obituary."

Olivia pondered that. "I didn't think of that. That's possible. Maybe she did."

"It's weird, though," Brad said. "How'd she know what Aggie called you? That was never in the news stories."

"Yeah...right. How would she know that?" Olivia felt dizzy.

"Could she have read your mind?"

Olivia looked stunned. "Read my mind? But I wasn't even thinking of what Aggie called me." Olivia shook her head. "It would be pretty impressive if she could read my mind. But that wasn't even in my mind. My mind was blank. I was so shocked at what she said about Aggie."

Brad stared at Olivia through the screen. "I have no idea. I really don't know."

"It scares me. Could it be possible? Could she be in touch with people who have passed?"

Brad shrugged. "I don't know. How could it be possible?"

"Could people who have passed...could they leave something behind when they go? Like energy or something? Could she tap into that and know things?" Olivia asked.

"That's too wild for me. I don't know what's going on. And she claims to have assisted police across the country?" He paused, thinking. "Maybe she *can* sense those who have passed?"

Olivia ran her hands through her hair. "I wish you were here, Brad. I wish you could get away."

"I..." Brad started.

Olivia waved her hand. "I know...I know you can't. I understand. I just mean I wish you were here so you could hear things first hand."

"Yeah. I'm sorry, I can't."

"It's okay." Olivia smiled. "You can't leave the store. I know that. I'm not trying to make you feel bad. I like having you around, that's all."

Brad grinned at her. "Thanks. You're not so bad yourself."

"I suppose I'm not going to be able to understand this stuff. Maybe it's unknowable and unexplainable for most people. It raises a lot of questions and there aren't any answers. The more I think about it the more my brain gets muddled. I'm going to have to focus on the murders and forget about whether or not that psychic can really do what she says she can do."

"Why don't you just forget about it? What difference does it make anymore? Why get wrapped up in it?" Brad asked. "Mary's own son doesn't want to know about the killer or what happened. He doesn't need the murders resolved."

Olivia thought for a minute. "That doesn't make it okay. Just because he wants to leave it in the past. That's his personal choice. But, it isn't right that the killer has been living his life for the past forty-five years. Kimmy was four, Brad. She never got a chance to live her life."

"I know," Brad said softly. "But what if you could solve

it? What good would it do? It was so long ago. What does it matter anymore?"

Olivia leaned closer to her laptop screen and sighed. "It doesn't matter if it was four years ago, or forty years, or four hundred years. It matters that their lives were taken from them. It matters that someone went unpunished. *They* matter."

12

Emily Bradford's mother, Isabel, phoned Olivia and told her she would be willing to meet and discuss the "unfortunate events of the past" which is how she put it. Her older daughter Angela would be coming for afternoon tea and Olivia was invited to join them.

Olivia found the house easily. It was a huge red brick mansion at the end of a long driveway hidden from view from the main street of the Magnolia Hill neighborhood. Olivia rang the bell and the door was answered by a trim older woman with blonde chin length hair. She was well-dressed in cream colored linen slacks and a crisp white shirt.

"Hello. Olivia? I'm Angela Kildare. Emily's older sister." They shook hands. "My friend, Lydia Andrews, said you would be interested in speaking with my mother.

I'm glad you could join us. Please come in. Mother is in the family room."

"It's nice to meet you, Angela. Lydia spoke highly of you. I appreciate that your mom is willing to talk with me."

Angela led Olivia through the foyer and down a long central hallway to the back of the house. They entered an enormous family room that had a cathedral ceiling and a full wall of glass looking out over a stone terrace and a beautifully landscaped in-ground pool. Several panels of the glass wall slid back to open the room to the outside.

A petite woman with snow white hair was sitting in an ivory straight-backed chair sipping tea from a china cup. She was dressed in a linen skirt and pale blue blouse. She turned to Olivia and Angela as they entered the room.

"Hello, Olivia. I'm Isabel Bradford. Please excuse me for not rising to greet you. My arthritis is kicking up." She indicated a white sofa positioned directly across from her, a glass coffee table in between. "Please sit. Angela, would you pour our guest some tea?" There was a heavy, blue and white vase in the center of the table and on either side of it was a three-tiered plate holder laden with various squares and miniature cookies. "Help yourself to some treats, Olivia."

Angela and Olivia sat side by side on the white sofa.

"Thank you for seeing me, Mrs. Bradford."

"I'm glad to help if I can. What can I tell you?"

"Well, I'm interested in finding out about the murders of my cousins. I'm talking with people who lived in town at the time."

"Your cousin was a lovely woman. An active member of our church." She closed her eyes for a moment and took a deep breath. "It is still unimaginable, even after all these years. The brutality of it. Killing a mother and child. It shook our community to its core." She spoke of it as if the very words were foul-tasting.

"Are you sure it's not too troubling for you to recall?" Olivia asked.

"It's terribly troubling. However, I do wish to assist you if I can. I'm an old woman, Olivia. There are exceedingly limited ways for me to be useful. What can I tell you that might be helpful?"

"I appreciate it," Olivia told her. "I wonder about the suspects. And, of course, why no one was brought to justice. I understand that you knew Kenny Overman."

"I knew him." Her words dripped with disgust. "I cringed every time he set foot in this house. Which my late husband and I tried to keep to a minimum. I gather you've spoken to Emily?"

Olivia nodded. "I met with her at a coffee shop in Brookline."

"How nice. She probably said more to you in your short visit than she has to me in the past few years."

"Mother..." Angela started.

"Never mind." Isabel raised her hand. "I'm sure Emily informed you that we are estranged."

"You're not estranged," Angela said.

"Angela," Isabel said sharply. "I do not need to be corrected. Call it what you will. Emily and I have very little to do with one another. We don't get along. It's been like this since my husband and I asked her to leave the house a few months after the murders. We withdrew financial support shortly after that."

"Was that because of her relationship with Kenny?"

"It was due to her behavior and attitude towards us. But our family issues aren't what you're interested in. It's Kenny you want to know about. Yes?"

Olivia nodded.

"There isn't much to say about him. If I may be blunt, he was not of our social status. Emily should not have been dating him. He was uneducated. No prospects. He had a drinking problem, inherited from that louse of a father. He was ill-mannered, rough. Emily defied our wishes. It was constant fighting. It was like living in hell with the tension and stress that girl caused us. Thankfully, Angela was married and living in her own place and didn't have to suffer what we went through."

"It sounds very difficult," Olivia said. "Mrs. Bradford, do you remember if Kenny came to your house on the evening of the murders?"

She took a deep breath. "Yes he did. I would not let him in the house. Emily had to speak to him at the front portico."

"Did you usually let him in?"

"Unfortunately, yes."

"What was the difference this time?"

Mrs. Bradford fiddled with the napkin on her lap.

"Mother..." Angela said.

Mrs. Bradford flashed Angela a warning look.

"Tell Olivia what happened that night," Angela said. "It's long in the past. It doesn't matter now."

Mrs. Bradford sighed and adjusted herself in her chair. "Emily and I had an altercation earlier that evening."

"About Kenny?"

"Amazingly, no. I had gone to Boston to meet a friend for shopping and dinner. The friend took ill and we had to cancel our dinner plans and I returned home earlier than expected. When I came into the house, I could smell smoke coming from the living room. I ran in and Emily was standing at the fireplace. A fire was blazing and smoke was filling the room. I yelled at her, 'What are you doing? Did you open the damper?' I rushed over to her. She wheeled on me...she had such a look of hate on her face. She had the fireplace poker in her hands and as I approached her, she lifted the poker with both her hands, horizontally to the floor, and she smashed it into my chest. She yelled,

'Don't come over here, leave me alone.' I was completely caught off guard. The force she hit me with sent me reeling backwards and I hit the floor. I smashed my head into the coffee table. I knew there was animosity between us, but that day I clearly understood her hatred of us."

"Why did she have a fire going?" Olivia asked. "It was June."

"That's what I asked her. I pulled myself up off the floor. I wouldn't give her the satisfaction of thinking she injured me. I stood there seething. I asked, 'Why the hell do you have a fire going in June?' She glared at me and told me she just felt like it. I stormed over to the fireplace to put the screen across it...Emily had it wide open with the roaring fire going full blast...sparks could have ignited the rug. I told her if she touched me again, I would call the police and have her arrested. She threw the poker on the floor and told me to go ahead and call them. She stormed out of the room. It was a terrible, terrible day. My own daughter striking me like that. Can you imagine?"

"I'm sorry to hear how difficult it was," Olivia said. "Did you send her away immediately?"

"No. My husband and I thought it best if we stayed quiet until the end of the summer. We thought if we kicked Emily out right away it would just drive her into Kenny's arms. Once Overman was suspected, we were hoping that he would be taken into custody before the end of the summer. That didn't happen. When September came, we told Emily that we would pay for that year's college expenses and that would be it. She would have to take loans for the final two years of school or find a job and pay for it that way. We told her it was time she got her own place and started her life as an adult."

"Did you notice if she was burning something in the fireplace?" Olivia asked.

"I assumed it was wood," Mrs. Bradford said with an edge to her voice.

Angela asked Olivia, "What do you mean?"

Olivia turned to Angela. "Is it possible that she might have been trying to destroy something? Burn it to get rid of it."

"You didn't notice anything mixed in with the wood? Or in the ashes later on?" Olivia asked Mrs. Bradford.

Mrs. Bradford sipped her tea. "I don't recall looking into the fireplace. What could she have been burning? Since you asked, you must have something in mind."

"I wondered if she might have been helping Kenny by burning something related to the case. His shirt. Something he took from the victims. To get rid of evidence," Olivia said.

Mrs. Bradford looked over her porcelain cup at Olivia with a steely gaze. "My daughter went to New York City that day. I don't believe she would have had time to be an accomplice to that ne'er-do-well."

"Oh. No," Olivia said. "I didn't mean to imply that Emily was an accomplice. I just wondered if Kenny may have asked her to get rid of something for him without telling her what was going on. Maybe she burned something for him because he asked her to."

"I doubt it. She was fooling around with the fireplace before Overman showed up here." Mrs. Bradford placed her cup on the table. "To be honest, I can't tell you much about Kenny. I didn't care to know the young man. I tried to avoid him whenever he dropped by. I admit he had a difficult life, but that wasn't something we wanted seeping into our lives. That's really all I can help you with, Olivia. I'm sorry I can't provide more information."

"You've been very helpful. Thank you for seeing me," Olivia said. "I appreciate it."

"Angela will see you out," Mrs. Bradford said looking off into the yard.

At the front door, Angela said, "Mother can come off as a very stern person. She is kind, but she sees things in black and white. There are no shades of gray with her. She's a product of a strict upbringing from a wealthy family. She expected certain standards of behavior from us and she could be cold and harsh if we didn't toe the line."

"Emily sounds to have had a tough time with it,"

Olivia said. "Two clashing personalities. Are you and your sister close?"

"We keep in touch, but we aren't close. There was the five-year age difference separating us...we were always at different stages in life. Emily thought I was the favored one, but I just knew how to keep my mouth closed and go along with things. She and I are opposites in just about every way. She was at the top of her class, a great athlete. She thinks I wasted my life taking care of my husband and children and not having a career. Our father did very well with investments that he made over the course of his working life. When he died, he left my mother, Emily, and me very wealthy women. Emily didn't have to work a day in her life but career has been her focus. She's very driven. Her business is everything to her. She owns some strip malls and office buildings. We don't have much in common. She works out every day. Runs marathons, goes rock climbing, does triathlons. I enjoy cooking and gardening and quilting. Emily turns her nose up at those things. She thinks I've squandered my life. And let's me know it. "

"Different choices," Olivia said. "Emily never wanted to marry?"

"I suppose she did early on, but things happened that turned her away from relationships."

"Kenny?" Olivia asked.

"Well, Kenny, yes. That must have been frightening to

be dating someone who is suspected of murder." Angela paused. "There was something else though. Emily was in a serious relationship with a young man from town. It started shortly after Overman left Howland. The young man had been in her high school class. He came from a good family. The Martins attended our church. Mother was pleased. James was in youth group with Emily. He had a crush on her. After Overman took off, Emily started dating James. They went out for about a year."

"They broke up?" Olivia asked.

Angela sighed. "James died." She cleared her throat. "He drowned in his family's backyard pool."

"How awful," Olivia said. "The poor family. Poor Emily."

Angela nodded. "Emily was there when it happened."

Olivia's eyes widened.

"James' parents were out. Emily and James had spent the evening barbecuing and swimming. They were drinking. It got late. Emily went inside to use the restroom and when she came back out, James was at the bottom of the pool. Emily was frantic. She tried to pull him out of the water. She called the police but he was dead by the time they arrived."

"That's terrible."

"I think Emily really loved him," Angela said. "She never seemed the same towards relationships after that.

She became very driven and focused on becoming successful."

Olivia had a faraway look in her eyes. "So sad," she whispered.

"A couple of years later, Emily was engaged briefly to a man from town but she broke it off. He was in Emily's classes all through school. They knew each other from the time they were little."

"Do you know why she broke off the engagement?"

"She just said he wasn't for her," Angela reported.

"Her former fiancé went to high school with her?"

Angela nodded.

"Is he still around? I wonder if he would talk to me about Kenny. It might be helpful to talk to a classmate. He might have some insight."

"His office is in Chestnut Hill. Name's Don Chandler. He's an attorney. It must be easy to find his number."

"I might look him up," Olivia said.

"It couldn't hurt. Let me give you my cell number in case there's anything more we can answer for you."

Olivia added Angela to her contacts.

"Thank you for your time, Angela. I appreciate your help."

13

During their chat earlier in the week, Olivia learned from Lydia Andrews that Pastor Mike Sullivan had been at St. Catherine's Church since before the murders and that maybe he could shed some light on the crime.

Olivia knocked on St. Catherine's parish house door. She hoped to have a talk with the priest. After a few minutes, an older woman opened the door and peered out at Olivia. The woman was small and stooped with silver gray hair. She was wiping her hands on her apron.

"Yes?" she asked politely but seemed slightly put out that she had been interrupted from her work.

"I'm Olivia Miller. Is the pastor available?"

"Father Mike is in back tending the garden. You can go around to see him if you like." She indicted the back of the house with a wave of her hand.

"I'll do that, thanks. Sorry to bother."

"No bother, hon."

Olivia found Father Mike bent over a row of soil. He was placing seedlings in small holes that had been neatly dug down the row. He was sitting on an overturned bucket.

"Father Mike?"

He stood just as Olivia spoke and he turned to her voice, his floppy straw hat shading his face. "Hello." His voice was deep and kind. His face was lined and craggy and beads of sweat covered his brow. He took an unsteady step towards Olivia, his legs stiff from sitting on the bucket.

"I'm Olivia Miller. Sorry to bother you. I was wondering if you had a minute to talk."

"Of course. Why don't we sit on the bench." He indicated a wooden bench placed in the shade of an apple tree. "I'd be glad for a break," he smiled. He tottered a bit towards the seat, and Olivia reached over and took his arm.

"Not as spry as I once was but I keep active. It just takes time to get these old legs going once I've been sitting."

When they were settled side by side on the bench, Father Mike wiped his face with a handkerchief and commented, "We haven't met."

"No," Olivia confirmed. "I'm staying at my cousin

John's house for a couple of weeks. John Miller. He isn't a church member so maybe you don't know him."

"I know who John is. We've served together on the town Recreation Committee for several years. Good man," Father Mike said.

"He's away right now," Olivia said. "He's having some work done on his house which happened to coincide with an unexpected business trip. So I'm keeping an eye on things for him and taking care of his dog."

"I see." His kind eyes met Olivia's. "What brings you to see me, dear? What's on your mind?" Father Mike asked.

"When we were cleaning out the attic at John's house, we came across some old newspapers. Some of them have articles about the murders that happened here in town a number of years ago. A young mother and her daughter. They were our cousins."

Father Mike winced. His shoulders seemed to slump and he looked down at the ground. "A terrible thing. That was a terrible day. I was the priest who said their funeral mass."

"I didn't know that. How long have you been a priest, Father?"

He straightened a bit. "Just over sixty years. The last fifty years right here in Howland. Things have changed a good deal. Not so many men entering the priesthood today."

"You're the only priest here at the parish?"

"Yes. Time was, back in the day, there might be three priests at one parish. Not anymore. Some priests are even traveling between churches now. That's hard. That makes it very difficult to get to know the people."

"I imagine it does."

"I'm lucky though. We have a strong group here, many active participants which makes for a nice community of people."

"There was another priest here when my cousin Mary went to church here?"

"Yes. There were two of us, and then just before the murders, a third priest arrived to join us."

"What were their names?"

"Father Paul Carlson was new. Father Anthony Foley had been with me here for maybe three years. Both were young men just starting out. The murders were trying for all of us."

"Mary taught Sunday school here."

"Yes she did. She had worked as a teacher in elementary schools before she had her own children. She was a natural with the kids, very sweet and kind. Mary did a lot for the church, helped out with funeral meals when she could, served on some committees. A hard worker. Cheerful, pleasant. Someone that people enjoyed being around."

"I'm curious about my cousins...the case," Olivia said. "I want to talk to people in town who lived here when it happened. I guess I'm trying to get a sense of them. Was Mary friendly with the other priests?"

"Father Paul was only here for a couple of weeks before the crime. Father Anthony was friendly with most of the young families. They would organize softball games, hikes, canoe excursions. Lots of activities that appealed to the younger crowd." He chuckled. "Even back then, I preferred the spaghetti suppers and things of that nature."

"Would you say Mary and Father Anthony got along well?"

The priest looked directly at Olivia. "Olivia, I know the talk that went around. I heard the gossip."

"I'm sorry, but I have to ask. I'm just trying to understand what happened to my cousins."

The priest said, "To my knowledge, there was nothing unseemly between them."

"It would be quite an accusation. It would have hurt the congregation if something like that was true," Olivia said.

"It would have been a blow, yes. But it wasn't true. Mary was an upstanding woman. She wouldn't have engaged in such behavior."

"What about Father Anthony? I apologize for being blunt...but, what if he had had a willing partner?"

The priest's face clouded. "Speculation is unfair, especially when a person is not available to defend himself."

Olivia nodded. "He was transferred I understand," she said.

"He was."

"Very soon after the murders."

"Yes."

"Where did he transfer to?" Olivia asked.

"California. I can't recall the specifics."

"You aren't in touch then?"

"At first we kept in touch. But then busy schedules got in the way and we no longer kept up contact."

"You don't remember what parish he was in?"

Father Mike sighed. "My memory isn't what it was, I'm afraid."

Olivia held his eyes.

"You could try the diocese office. I'm sure they have records."

"I'm not accusing, Father, really I'm not," Olivia said.

"And I'm not trying to protect him. Or conceal anything," Father Mike said.

"I'm just trying to figure out what happened to my cousins," Olivia told him.

"Anthony had a magnetic personality," Father Mike said. "He was fun, witty, engaging. Everyone was drawn to him. He was a handsome man." Father Mike paused, and then said, "I cautioned him to be wary of people's perceptions. To be careful not to give the wrong impression to people...to the women, especially. Sometimes friendliness and caring can be misconstrued to be something other than it is. It's a fine line and a delicate balance to maintain, especially for an attractive, young priest."

Olivia said, "I can see that could be hard...to maintain boundaries."

Father Mike looked down at his hands. "In some ways it seems very long ago and in other ways, it feels like yesterday. I remember the horror I felt when I found out. The terrible anger." He looked at Olivia. "Mary and her daughter stopped in at the church hall sometime around 2:30pm that day. She dropped off some paint for the recreation hall."

Olivia sat up. "Did you see them?"

"No. I didn't."

"How do you know they were there?"

"The new gallons of paint were in the rec hall."

"But how do you know what time they brought the paint to the hall?"

"The police know that they stopped at the hardware store to buy the paint around 2pm that day. And they were killed between 3 and 4pm." The priest sighed. "I often thought what might have been if I had seen Mary that day when she stopped by. Just a short conversation may have eliminated her encounter with the killer. A few minutes here and there may have made all the difference." He paused. "It would be easy to lose faith when such a terrible thing like that happens."

Olivia understood those feelings. "How do you cope with such a thing? How do you support your parishioners through that? I would feel so ...so..." Olivia's voice trailed off.

"Betrayed? Abandoned? Hopeless?" Father Mike said.

Olivia adjusted her position on the seat to face the old priest. "Yes, all of those things." Her voice was soft. "Where was God then, Father? When they were having their throats slit?" Olivia looked out across the green lawn. "Where is God's loving hand when someone decides to kill? Why doesn't His hand stop it...keep it from happening...keep good people safe?"

"Do you believe, Olivia?"

She shook her head slightly. "No. I'm sorry, I don't. I suppose I'm an atheist...or maybe an agnostic...or a humanist." She smiled weakly, and Father Mike nodded.

"I understand," Father Mike said. "Belief is...complicated. And, sometimes, infuriating. And there are times when I question...oh my, there are times."

"But you still have your faith?"

He nodded. "I do. Through all I have seen, I come back to it. My belief remains."

"In a way, I envy that," Olivia said.

They sat in silence for a minute.

"I believe in everlasting life, Olivia. I believe that your cousins are at peace. I also believe that punishment may not be meted out in this lifetime, but that what needs to be accounted for...will be...in time."

Olivia sighed and nodded. "Thank you for talking with me."

Father Mike patted Olivia's hand and said, "I hope you find what you're looking for."

14

Olivia sat hunched over one of the microfiche readers at the Howland Public Library. She had spent an hour looking through reels of old newspaper stories and found the information that Jackie's father had shared about the guy who pulled a knife on two women from the next town.

The story reported that a month before the murders, two women were in Howland taking a walk on a wooded trail when they were approached by a man and a woman who asked for a ride to the next town over. They said their car had broken down. The women agreed.

Once they had traveled several miles, the man sitting in the back seat of the car pulled a knife on the women and ordered them to drive to the town north of Howland. The man and the woman got out near a bus stop and disappeared. The next day, that woman was captured and identified the man as an escaped convict who had been living for several weeks in the Howland state park near the old abandoned prison camp. The man remained at large but was picked up in another state on June 5 on a misdemeanor charge.

So the convict couldn't have been the murderer, Olivia concluded, as he was arrested in another state on the day of the killings.

Olivia checked the library wall clock and decided it was time to head back to the house. She wanted to go for a walk and thought Lily would like an outing. She packed her notes and printouts in her bag, took the stairs down to the lobby, and stepped outside into bright sunshine. Olivia squinted as she walked to her car.

When Olivia reached for the Jeep's door, she noticed something white fluttering on the windshield. She reached around and pulled a piece of paper from under the windshield wiper.

LEAVE IT ALONE was printed in the middle of the paper.

Olivia's heart thudded. She glanced around the parking lot but there were only a few cars parked here and there. No people were around. She looked at the paper again. The words sent a chill down her back. Not many people knew she was researching the murders. *Who would write this? Why?*

Whoever it was knew what kind of car Olivia drove

and that she was at the library. Olivia's eyes narrowed and she could feel anger pricking her skin. She crumpled up the paper and stuffed it into her bag. She got into the Jeep, started it up and pulled away from the library going much faster than she should.

Olivia turned into the driveway of the house just as Jackie's red truck was starting to back out. Olivia parked her car and got out slamming the driver side door. Jackie stopped her truck.

"Hey, how's it going? How was the library?" she called out of her truck window.

Olivia stared at her. "How did you know I was at the library?" she said evenly.

"You told me."

"Oh. Right," Olivia said.

Jackie studied Olivia for a few seconds. "What's wrong?"

"Nothing," Olivia answered. "Sorry, I'm distracted. I need to go for a long walk."

"Okay." Jackie moved the truck backward again preparing to leave. "I'll see you tomorrow."

Olivia stormed into the house and into the kitchen. She filled a glass with cold water and downed it in three gulps placing the empty glass on the counter. *Who left that note? Why should I leave it alone? Who has something to hide?*

Olivia jumped as Lily's wet tongue lapped a path across the bare skin of her leg.

"Lily," she laughed. "I didn't hear you come up." Olivia scratched her behind the ears and Lily did a little jumping thing with her two front paws. The dog's eyes were bright and happy. Olivia's distress and anger started to fade.

"You're a good one," Olivia told her. "How about we go for a walk? Let's go to the rail trail." The Howland area had an extensive system of rail trails, former rail lines that had been converted to passive use trails which threaded throughout Massachusetts beside roadways or through woods and forests. Now these pathways were used for walking, biking, and jogging.

Lily woofed and she followed Olivia upstairs. The dog sat patiently tapping her tail while Olivia changed into her exercise shorts and shoes.

15

Before the events of last summer, Olivia had been a jogger. She never called herself a runner because she felt she was too slow for that description. She always said that she didn't go very fast, but she could go pretty far. In college, she had no trouble "running" six or seven miles every other day with a shorter jog of two to four miles on her off days. Because of the stabbing injury to her gut last year, Olivia had been taking long brisk walks but hadn't tried to do any jogging. Jackie had recently taken up running and had worked up to doing two to three miles a day, five days a week.

There was a club of runners in the Howland area that got together each week to run and Jackie was at the point where she felt she could keep up with some of the slower members. Jackie's friend had been nagging her to take part in the running club but Jackie always refused. The next running event was going to be held on the rail trails in Howland and Jackie couldn't think of a good excuse not to go, so she asked Olivia if she wanted to try it out with her. Olivia was reluctant.

"But you're in good shape from all the walking you've been doing," Jackie said. "And there are different groups. There are people from elite runners to the slow pokes and everyone in between. You pick which group you're going to run with. They have different routes and distances mapped out for each group. It might be a fun way to get back into jogging."

"I don't know, Jackie," Olivia said. "I'm not going to be able to keep up with anyone."

"I bet you'll surprise yourself. It could be fun. It's no pressure and my friend says it's a great group of people. And they all go out for beers afterwards."

"Well, in that case," Olivia laughed, then hesitated. "Maybe. Let me think about it."

"Come on," Jackie said. "Don't make me go alone. I can't tell my friend I'm not doing this event."

"You can run with your friend."

"She's in the advanced group." Jackie made a sad face.

"Oh, okay. I'll go," Olivia conceded. "Can I bring Lily?"

"Great, thank you," Jackie said. "Dogs are welcome but they have to be leashed. I'm glad you're not making me do this on my own."

THE WEATHER on the evening of the running club event was perfect for exercising. The air was dry and comfortable. Jackie picked up Olivia and Lily and they headed for the state park.

"Perfect day," Jackie noted.

"I was hoping it would rain," Olivia deadpanned.

Jackie chuckled. "You'll do fine."

"I don't know why I'm nervous," Olivia said.

"It's just because you haven't run for a while," Jackie told her. "You can alternate jogging and walking. It's a good way to start again."

People were parking in one of the big fields next to the rail trails. Jackie pulled the truck in beside a line of cars and they got out and headed in the direction that other runners were walking. Every body type and shape was represented in the gathering, from long lean marathoner looking bodies to short and stout men and women. There were teenagers in athletic clothes standing around chatting, adults stretching and signing in at a table, and a number of dogs greeting one another.

Lily looked eagerly at the other dogs and wagged her tail. Jackie and Olivia followed behind Lily and headed for the check in table. As they passed a Mercedes wagon, a blonde woman in a tank top and shorts was pulling a big box out of the back of the vehicle and it slipped from her hands and crashed to the ground causing the contents to spill over. A round of cursing followed the impact. The woman bent to gather the materials and Olivia walked over to help.

"Let me help you," she said.

The woman looked up. "Olivia."

"Emily," Olivia said.

They both stood.

Olivia introduced Emily and Jackie. "And this is Lily."

Emily shook hands with Jackie but ignored the dog.

"I'm running late. I'm supposed to be checking people in," Emily said. "I've got all this stuff to carry."

"We can help," Olivia offered. She bent to gather the things that had fallen from the box. Olivia picked up cords of rope, some sort of pick type things, metal loops, a harness, shoes with rubber soles, and gloves.

"That's my climbing equipment. Just throw it all back in the box," Emily said. "I was trying to move it to the side of the hatch to get the folding table out."

"Let me give you a hand," Jackie offered. There was a mountain bike on top of the table and the two women pulled the bike out and then removed the metal table.

"This is the car I use for all my athletic equipment," Emily said. "I should replace it with a van. I really need to get this stuff in order."

Olivia put the box of equipment back in the hatch.

"Could you carry this box of t-shirts over to the check-in table?" Emily asked. "And there's a container of forms and pencils in the hatch somewhere."

The women picked up the boxes and headed for the first registration table.

"I don't know why I offered to help with this. I have a triathlon to train for next month," Emily said.

"Wow," Jackie said. "Ambitious."

"Training for that must take up all your time," Olivia said.

"I swim or bike in the mornings and run here on the trails on the weekends. After work, I run on the roads. This is going to be my last one, though. Too time consuming with my other commitments. Only marathons from now on."

There was a long line of runners waiting to check-in and only one young guy trying to handle all of them. "I thought you'd never get here," he grumped at Emily.

"I run a business," she snapped. "You're lucky I made it here at all."

Jackie and Olivia exchanged glances as they set up the table and placed the container of forms and the box of t-shirts on top of it.

"Can we do anything else?" Olivia asked.

"Thanks. I'll handle it from here," Emily said.

"Somebody's stressed out," Jackie said as they walked to the back of the line.

"When I met with Emily's sister, she told me that Emily pushes herself in every area of her life," Olivia said. "She's sure hard-driving."

"Not one of my characteristics," Jackie smiled.

"She's got a ton of money. Obviously she's smart, good-looking, fit. But she doesn't seem happy, does she?" Olivia said.

"Some people are just sour."

"Born that way or made that way by life?" Olivia asked, thinking of Emily's past troubles...her controlling parents, Kenny Overman suspected of murder, her boyfriend James drowning in his pool.

"Maybe some of both," Jackie said.

16

Olivia sat at the bar of Howland's Sports Bar Restaurant. She was meeting Jackie for dinner and decided to arrive early and get a drink at the bar. The edges of a headache had been threatening all day and she wanted to get in out of the unseasonable heat that had returned to the area. She took a sip of her iced tea just as her cell phone vibrated in her pocket. The text message indicated that Jackie was running late. Olivia didn't mind, she was enjoying the air-conditioned coolness and listening to the comments of the other patrons who were watching the Red Sox game on the big flat screen television over the bar. A group of middle aged guys were cursing and praising different players.

Look at the pitcher. He's improved.

That young outfielder could become a major force. Just needs more experience.

Whoa, whoa, whoa. A fast ball was hit to center field causing the group to moan.

Yeah! Nice play! The guy next to Olivia hit the bar with his hand to emphasize his appreciation of the talents of the Red Sox centerfielder. He turned to Olivia.

"So, what do you think? Are they gonna make the playoffs this year?" he asked.

Olivia took another sip of her iced tea. "They have the talent. They're doing well. I hope they don't end up breaking our hearts," she told the guy.

The man shook his head. "Spoken like a long time member of Red Sox Nation."

Olivia smiled. She had been raised by a die hard fan. She and Aggie had always gone to Fenway Park for plenty of games each season. Aggie almost never missed a game on television. Now watching the Red Sox made Olivia happy and sad, happy because she loved the team and the times she shared that love with Aggie, and sad because Aggie was gone and now she was watching alone.

"You from Howland?" the guy asked.

"No," Olivia said. "I live in Cambridge. My cousin lives here. I'm visiting."

"So how do you like our town?"

"It's nice. It's a lot different than the city."

"The peace and quiet can be pretty good...or can drive you nuts," the guy chuckled. He extended his hand. "Glenn Masterson."

"Olivia Miller." She shook with him.

The guy was meaty and thick. His hand was the size of a bear's paw. He was graying at the temples and his complexion was bright red like he had been spending too much time in the sun without sunscreen.

"Have you lived here long?" Olivia asked.

"Oh, sure, my whole life. My folks lived here before I was born. Didn't get very far from home, did I?" Glenn smiled.

The guy next to Glenn leaned forward and said, "Don't let this guy bother you," he kidded with Olivia. "He'll talk your ear off if you give him a chance."

Glenn gave him a poke with his elbow and said, "Maybe you should learn how to hold a conversation." He turned back to Olivia. "This is Tom."

Olivia liked the easy banter between the men. They seemed to be good friends, comfortable in each other's company. A woman with a few extra pounds came up behind Glenn, and gave him a peck on the side of his face.

"The traffic was terrible coming home. There must have been an accident," she told him.

He put his arm around her and gave her a hug. "This

is my wife, Robin," Glenn told Olivia. "Hon, this is Olivia. She's in Howland visiting her cousin."

"Nice to meet you, Olivia." The woman's smile was warm and welcoming. The bartender greeted Robin and placed a glass of red wine in front of her.

"How are you enjoying your visit?" she asked Olivia.

"It's been nice. I'm minding my cousin's house and dog while he's away on business," Olivia said.

A plate of appetizers arrived and they dug in. "Help yourself," Glenn indicated to Olivia, as he bit into a mozzarella stick.

"Who's your cousin, hon, if you don't mind my asking?" Robin nibbled a chicken tender dripping with buffalo sauce.

"John Miller, he owns the yellow Colonial out on Streeter Road," Olivia answered.

"Oh, I know who John is. He has the nice chocolate Lab...Lily, isn't it? I run into them walking in the state park. We have a Jack Russell terrier, crazy as a hoot. That dog can't run enough. I take him to the park almost every day or he'll tear up the house with all of his excess energy." She shook her head, smiling.

"I don't know if I could keep up with a Jack Russell," Olivia said.

"You'd think that dog would help me lose weight, but nope. Guess it doesn't help meeting this gang here twice a week for a few drinks and appetizers."

"You get together every week?"

"Just about," Glenn answered. "We watch the game, shoot the breeze. We've all been friends since high school."

"Yeah? You all went to high school together?" Olivia asked.

"We did," Robin said. "Seems like a hundred years ago." She lifted the wine glass to her lips.

The group of friends seemed to be in their early sixties, Olivia guessed. Close in age to Kenny Overman and Emily Bradford. Olivia didn't want to put a damper on the conversation, but she had to ask.

"Did you know Kenny Overman in high school?"

Glenn, Robin, and Tom turned as one toward Olivia, their eyes wide.

Robin spoke, "Where'd you hear that name?"

Glenn snorted. "Everyone knew Kenny Overman."

"One bad apple," said Tom.

"When I first got here, John and I were going through some old newspapers that were up in his attic. Kenny Overman's name came up in connection to a crime that happened here in Howland," Olivia told them.

"Oh, boy," Robin said. "Did it ever."

"Police questioned Overman about a double murder that happened here in town decades ago," Glenn said. "Did you read the accounts in the newspapers you found?"

Olivia nodded. "John told me the victims were distant cousins of ours."

"The woman and her daughter went to the same church as my family. It was devastating. People in town were shocked, terrified for a while," Robin said. "Our parents didn't want us out late, had to know where we were going and who we were with."

"When you're a teenager," Glenn said, "you never think anything bad is going to happen to you, but I have to admit those killings had us in a knot for a while."

"So what did you think about Overman?" Olivia asked. "You knew him?"

"We never hung around with him," Tom said. "He was in my gym class one year. He was always in trouble."

"We all steered clear of him," Glenn said.

"Do you think he committed the crime?" Olivia asked.

"Could have," Glenn said. "There are some people you'd say 'oh, no, he couldn't have done such a thing.' But with Kenny, I wouldn't be able to say that."

"I never believed he did it," Robin said. "He was in my homeroom junior year. Yeah, he was always in trouble, had attitude, never did homework, smoked, drank, probably did drugs. But there was something about him. I couldn't see him as a killer."

"Why, not?" Olivia questioned.

Robin looked thoughtful. "I don't know if I can explain it. He seemed kind of like a lost lamb. Like he needed to put on that tough guy veneer to keep people away."

"You just felt sorry for him, Robin," Tom said. "That old man of his was always beating on him."

"He'd come to school with bruises, black eyes," Robin said. "He'd just say he fell or got in a fight with kids from the next town over. I didn't believe that. He never claimed his father did it. But we all knew. Our parents talked."

"Kenny was a mean one," Tom said. "He could've murdered the mom and child. I wouldn't be a bit surprised."

"Yeah," Glenn added. "I think he did it. But the cops didn't have any evidence. So what can you do?"

"I don't think he was mean," Robin said thoughtfully. "Angry, yes. But not mean."

"Did you ever notice a violent streak? He got into fights?" Olivia questioned.

The group thought for a moment. "Never heard of any fights with kids from our school. Not sure," Glenn said. The other two shrugged.

"Is he living anywhere around here?" Olivia asked, even though she knew he wasn't.

"No, long gone," Glenn told her. "And, good riddance."

"People in town all thought he did it," Robin said. "A person can't stay in a place where everyone thinks you're guilty."

"I'd high-tail it out of town if everybody thought I was a killer," Tom said. "Start over somewhere else."

"Where'd he go?" Olivia asked.

"Never heard," Glenn said.

"Are any of his relatives in town?" Olivia asked.

"Not that I know of," Glenn said. "It was just him and the nasty father."

"Is his father dead?"

"I don't know," Tom said. "He and Kenny lived in a beat up ranch house they rented. After Kenny took off, the old man lived in an old shack in the woods for a long time until the town tore it down. I don't know what happened to the rotten old goat."

"What was the father like?" Olivia questioned.

"He was a mean piece of work," Glenn said. "Abusive, a drunk, a drug addict. Never worked. Was on welfare. The place was like a crap hole, if you'll excuse my language."

"What about friends? Did Kenny hang out with anybody? Did he have any friends?"

"No. He dated a girl in town for a while. But he was a loner," Tom said. "Had a chip on his shoulder. Didn't want any friends. Or maybe couldn't keep a friend. He hung out sometimes with the kids who congregated at the smoking area in the school parking lot."

"Sounds pretty sad," Olivia sighed

"He did have a friend," Robin said. "Well, maybe not a real friend. But he and James Martin were friendly."

The name rang a bell for Olivia. She thought for moment and then it came to her. "James Martin. I heard that name. He passed away?"

"Yeah, that's right," Robin said. "He was in a swimming accident."

"I understand James came from a wealthy family. How'd he and Kenny match up?" Olivia asked.

"Not sure. I think they made friends in kindergarten. James was a sweetie. I think he was good to Kenny because they were friends as little kids," Robin said. "Too bad James isn't around. He'd probably be able to tell you about Kenny better than most can. Give another side of him." Robin sipped her wine. "You know, Olivia, my friend...her brother, Dan Waters, was one of the guys who found the bodies in the state park."

Olivia's eyes went wide. "Really? Did your friend ever tell you much about what her brother had to say?"

"No. He never talked about it much. He's coming to Howland to visit his sister soon. Would you like me to see if he'd talk to you?"

"Yes, please," Olivia said. "You think he would?"

"He might," Robin said. "He's been interviewed now and then when reporters bring the case up. Let's exchange cell phone numbers and I'll let you know."

Olivia's temples were pulsing and she rubbed at them, hoping a full blown headache wasn't in the works.

"How about another?" Glenn pointed at Olivia's glass.

"Oh, no, thanks," Olivia told him. "My friend should be here any minute."

Right on cue, Jackie walked into the restaurant and glanced around trying to spot Olivia. Olivia waved.

"Here she is now. Nice talking with you all," Olivia told the group.

"Take care. See you again sometime," Glenn told her.

"Have a nice visit here, Olivia," Robin said. "Maybe I'll see you in the park with the dog. And I'll let you know if Dan Waters will meet you."

Tom tipped his glass to her as she slipped off the stool and headed to greet Jackie. The hostess seated them at a booth near the window.

"Make some new friends?" Jackie asked, opening the menu.

"Yeah," Olivia smiled. "They're real nice." Olivia rubbed her temples.

"You getting another headache?" Jackie eyed Olivia over the top of her menu.

"Maybe," Olivia said.

Jackie put the menu down and gave Olivia a serious look.

"What?" Olivia asked.

"You've been getting a lot of them?"

Olivia shrugged. "I guess so."

Jackie said. "Have you always had trouble with headaches?"

"Not always. The past few months though."

"Why do you think?"

Olivia drank a gulp of water from her glass then held the glass next to her temple. "I don't know."

"Have you been under a lot of stress?"

Olivia laughed out loud but it had no mirth in it.

"Boyfriend trouble?" Jackie asked.

"No. Not that," Olivia's voice was small.

"You want to talk about it?"

Olivia sighed. "I guess you don't watch the news?"

Jackie looked puzzled.

"Last year my aunt Aggie was murdered. She was more than my aunt. She raised me since I was one. Everyone said she had a heart attack but I didn't believe it. In the course of trying to figure out who murdered her, I killed a man. And, almost got killed myself. Twice."

"Wow." Jackie stared at Olivia.

"Yeah," Olivia said.

"So...did you figure it out? Did you find out who killed your aunt?" Jackie asked.

"I was on the right track, but I didn't really figure it out," Olivia said. "It was more like I got in the killers' way. They got careless and greedy and that's what did them in. It was a group of criminals. A father and son.

Some guys that worked for them. A State Police detective."

Jackie's eyebrows went up. "A cop?"

Olivia nodded. "They were moving drugs, smuggling valuables. My aunt crossed their paths and ended up as collateral damage."

"Are they all in custody?"

"The smaller players are. The cop is dead. The father shot his son and he died later in the hospital."

"And, the father?" Jackie asked.

Olivia was sweating. She used her napkin to mop her upper lip. "I killed him," she whispered.

Jackie reached across the table and held Olivia's hand. Olivia dabbed at the tears that were escaping from her eyes.

"I killed him," Olivia said. "He attacked me. It was self-defense. He's the one who killed my aunt. I feel awful about the whole thing but I'm not sorry I did it." She let out a long slow sigh. "Does that make any sense?"

"Of course, it does," Jackie said.

"The son. He asked me out. I only went once. He was messed up. I know he only asked me out to get information from me. But when I think back on it, he seemed kind of desperate for someone to help him. He kept asking me to meet him. He said he needed to tell me something. I blew him off. I think about it, Jackie. If I had met him, would he be alive today? I should have tried to help him."

"You said he was messed up," Jackie said. "It would be natural to want to avoid him."

"They were all terrible, evil people," Olivia said. "But he needed someone to be kind to him."

"Things look different in retrospect. You did what felt right at the time."

"I still think I should have listened to what he had to tell me."

"You can't second guess. It probably wouldn't have changed anything. Was he involved in your aunt's death?"

Olivia nodded. "I can't forgive him for that." She took a long sip of water. "But he tried to help me in the end. He tried to help me escape from his father."

"Is that how you survived?"

"No. The father shot him and then attacked me." She paused and swallowed hard. "And then I slit his throat." Olivia shifted her gaze out the window. "I'm glad they're dead and they can't ever hurt anyone else. But it won't bring Aggie back to me."

"I'm sorry," Jackie said.

Olivia nodded. "It's all a long story. I'll tell you more of the details some time."

"When did you say this happened?"

"My aunt was killed a year ago May. The whole mess was resolved by August."

"The facts and details were resolved maybe, but not your feelings about it," Jackie said.

Olivia let out a long breath. "I was doing really well. I started law school last fall, worked really hard. But over the past few months I've been having trouble sleeping. Getting headaches. Feeling moments of terror. Flashes of what happened pop into my mind."

"When those things *aren't* happening, do you feel yourself?" Jackie asked.

"Mostly."

"Sometime feel down? Get short-tempered?"

"Sometimes."

"Tired?"

"I'm exhausted."

Jackie leaned forward. "Did you get counseling, Olivia?"

"I went for a while, but stopped going."

"Why?" Jackie asked.

"It didn't seem like I needed it. I didn't like yapping about it with a stranger. I didn't want to go over it and over it...I wanted to be done with it all. But I guess I'm not." Olivia sipped her water. "You have your PhD in counseling, Jackie. What's wrong with me?"

"It's like post-traumatic stress," Jackie said.

Olivia made a face.

"It's anxiety. It affects your ability to cope. At times you might feel numb, distracted. You might have distressing flashes of memories of the event, avoiding people or places that evoke the memories, problems with concentration, problems with anger, trouble sleeping."

"Yes, that's me." Olivia's eyes filled with tears again. "I haven't been home in a year. Brad and Joe, they... Brad's my boyfriend and Joe is like my dad...they come down to Cambridge to visit me. At Christmas, we went to California. When I think of going back to my house in Ogunquit, I feel sick. I've been renting the house out for the past year. I haven't told Brad or Joe the truth about why I never make it home. I just say I'm drowning in work." Olivia lifted her eyes to Jackie. "Am I crazy?"

Jackie shook her head vigorously. "No, not at all. It's a normal reaction to what you experienced. You should talk to someone."

"I'm talking to you," Olivia said.

"You should talk to someone who's practicing."

Olivia took a deep breath. "What good would it do?"

"Well, for one thing, you can work on identifying the thoughts and sensations that upset you or make you afraid. Then practice replacing those thoughts with something less distressing." Jackie paused. "And talk about your grief."

"I don't know."

Grief. Wrapping itself around her heart when she least expected it. Choking her. Hot tears behind her eyes.

"Olivia, do you think it's a good idea looking into your cousins' murders right now?"

"Why, not?" Olivia asked.

"Come on. You know why. It's too close to what you've recently been through."

Olivia looked away from Jackie. The bartender caught her eye and waved his hand to call her over. "The bartender is waving to me."

Jackie turned her head. "What's he want?"

"I'll go find out. Be right back."

"Say 'no' if he asks you out," Jackie said.

Olivia chuckled. "I think I'm a bit young for him."

Glenn, Robin, and Tom had moved away from the bar and were sitting at a table near the far wall with some other friends. Olivia approached the bar.

"What's up?" Olivia asked.

"I heard you talking about Kenny Overman. You seemed interested in knowing what happened to his father. I know he's in a nursing home over in Worcester."

"How do you know?"

"My father-in-law's in the same place. I saw Overman there. He doesn't look too good. I thought I'd let you know."

"Thanks," Olivia told him. "What's the name of the place?"

The bartender wrote the name of the nursing home

on a bar coaster. Olivia took it, put it in her pocket, returned to her table, and reported to Jackie.

"I'm going to go to the nursing home and talk to him. Maybe I can find out where Kenny is."

"Why bother driving out there?" Jackie asked. "Overman wasn't right in the head back forty-five years ago. He must be in great shape now. Probably can't even string a few words together. He probably doesn't even know who Kenny is anymore."

"I guess I'll find out."

Jackie narrowed her eyes. "Olivia, why don't you give up on this? Now isn't the right time for you to go investigating. Take some time for yourself. Forget about the murders."

Olivia had a faraway look on her face as she traced the condensation on the outside of her glass with her finger. She thought of her cousins' smiling faces on the front page of the old newspaper and a heaviness settled around her heart.

"I don't think I can do that," she responded.

17

Olivia dragged herself out of bed when Lily's wet nose gave her a poke. Even though she had installed the air conditioner in the bedroom, she had tossed and turned during the night and did not feel rested at all. If not for the dog, she would have stayed in bed until noon.

Olivia and Lily took a long walk around the neighborhood before returning for breakfast. Olivia showered and put on a light-weight floral summer dress. She pulled her hair into a high ponytail, grabbed her keys and the bar coaster with the address written on it.

She steered her Jeep to the highway and even though the early morning was hazy and hot, she kept the windows down and didn't turn on the air conditioning, preferring the breeze rushing through the car windows.

Olivia had no idea what she was going to find at the nursing home. Probably, nothing.

After forty-five minutes of highway driving, she pulled off the exit and turned right onto Salisbury Street. She traveled several miles along tree-lined streets through suburban neighborhoods and then turned onto West Street. She took a left into a driveway marked by a small sign indicating the Manor Senior Living Community. The place was well-landscaped with flower beds and brick walkways winding throughout the property. There were several two story buildings spread over the campus. Olivia followed the signs to the nursing portion of the community. She parked and walked along a stone pathway that led to the front door. The place filled Olivia with a sense of despair and for a moment she was sorry she had made the trip.

Olivia opened the door and stepped into the foyer. A plump middle-aged receptionist smiled at her. "Hello. Can I help you?"

The place was furnished with cherry furniture and sofas and chairs of muted shades of green and peach. Matching swags framed the windows. The wood floors were shiny and clean. Huge windows looked over the lawns and gardens. There was a small vase of fresh flowers on the desk. Olivia understood how costly a full time nursing facility could be and from the looks of this place, she was sure that only the wealthy could afford to have a loved one in residence here. She wondered how Kenny's father managed to pay the bill. It didn't seem possible that he could live here and Olivia began to worry that she was in the wrong place.

An elderly gentleman scuffled up to the desk.

"Morning, John," the receptionist greeted him.

He mumbled something that Olivia couldn't understand, but the receptionist answered, "Here are some envelopes you can stamp for me. Come around and sit here at the end of the table." He shuffled around and took a seat.

She winked at Olivia. "He likes to keep busy, so I have a job for him each morning."

Olivia smiled. "I'm here to visit one of the residents. Lee Overman."

The receptionist's eyebrows went up. "Are you a relative?"

"Oh, no," Olivia answered. "I didn't know I had to be a relative to visit."

"I didn't mean that, hon. You can visit, relative or not. Lee doesn't usually have visitors. Let me ring one of the nurses." She picked up the phone and said a few words. "She'll be right along."

"Does Mr. Overman's son ever visit?"

"Not since I've been here. To tell you the truth, no one ever visits Mr. Overman."

"Have you worked here long?"

"Almost six years."

A nurse came around the corner after a minute. Her face was questioning. "You're here to visit Lee?"

"Yes. I'm Olivia Miller. I just thought I'd stop in. I'm living in the town where Lee used to live." It wasn't much of an explanation, but Olivia waited to see if she needed to add anything.

The nurse nodded. "This way."

They walked along an immaculate corridor. A woman sat in a wheelchair holding a baby doll. She was rocking it and cooing to it like it was real.

"Lee isn't what you're probably expecting," the nurse said. "He doesn't speak much. He's confused. Stays in his wheelchair and looks out the window. He needs help with his meals." They walked past a few more rooms. "Here we are."

A man sat in a wheelchair by a window in the room. He was hunched over and had a blanket over his knees.

"Lee? Someone's here to see you," the nurse spoke gently.

No response.

The nurse pulled a chair over next to the man. He just kept staring out the window. The nurse checked the cup that was sitting on a table. "I'm going to go get you some more juice," she said. "Are you warm enough?"

No response.

"You can sit here," she said to Olivia indicating the chair next to Lee. "I'll be right back."

Olivia edged over and sat down. The man's eyes were cloudy and distant. He was skinny and his face was blotched with liver spots. The hair was white and thin on top. The blue black veins on the hands were visible through the almost translucent skin.

"Mr. Overman?" Olivia's voice was soft.

Nothing.

"Mr. Overman? Lee? I'm Olivia Miller. I came from Howland."

The man blinked but that was it.

"I came to ask about Kenny," Olivia tried again.

It was like the man was deaf. Olivia was afraid she might upset the old man if she mentioned the murders, but if things kept going as they were, she had wasted her time coming to the nursing home.

"Lee, I know Kenny was in trouble in Howland years ago." Olivia watched the man's face. "Because of a woman who was murdered. A woman and her child."

The man's face betrayed no emotion.

"I know the police questioned Kenny. They suspected him of killing the woman and the child." Olivia paused. "But the police let him go."

The man remained still and quiet.

Olivia waited. "Do you know where Kenny is?"

The nurse came back with some juice in the cup. "Want a drink, Lee?"

No response.

She held the cup to Overman's mouth so that he could sip through the straw. She looked at Olivia and shrugged. "He's not much for talking." She returned the cup to the side table. "I'll come back in a few minutes to put him in bed for a rest."

Olivia nodded.

"Is Kenny still alive?" Olivia tried again.

The old man's eyes stared out the window.

"I'd really like to talk to Kenny." She watched the birds at a feeder that was placed just outside the window. "He's not in any trouble."

No response.

"The woman and the child were my cousins."

Silence. The man sat like a statue.

Olivia didn't know what else to say.

The nurse returned. "I need to get him into bed. To change his position."

Olivia nodded and stood up. She tried one more time. She bent down closer to the man's face. "Can you tell me where Kenny is?"

Lee didn't even look at Olivia, just past her, out the window.

The nurse moved the wheelchair closer to the bed.

"Thanks for letting me visit," Olivia said.

"It was nice of you to come by. Lee doesn't get any visitors," the nurse said.

"No one?" Olivia asked.

The nurse shook her head.

"Do you mind if I ask? This seems like it must be a very expensive facility. I understand Mr. Overman wasn't a wealthy man. I wonder how he manages the cost."

"I don't know. You're right though. This place costs an arm and leg. The residents here have hefty bank accounts. Or their relatives do. It is a sought after senior community because of the quality of the care."

Olivia nodded. "Well, thanks. I was just wondering."

"Nice of you to stop by," the nurse said.

"Bye, Mr. Overman," Olivia said.

She headed for the hall and returned to her Jeep in the parking lot. Olivia stood next to her car rummaging through her bag for the key. In the short time she had been inside the nursing home, the temperature had risen several degrees and the light was white hot reflecting off the metal of the Jeep. She wished she was still in the air conditioned comfort of the nursing facility. *How does Overman afford this place? He didn't have any money. Who would be paying the bill?*

18

Robin from the Sports Bar Restaurant phoned Olivia with the news that Dan Waters, one of the young men who had found the Monahans' bodies in the field so many years ago, would meet with her at the coffee shop in the center of Howland. Olivia was nervous. She felt intrusive talking to Mr. Waters about that awful day. She hoped he didn't feel obligated to talk to her because Robin told him she was related to the victims.

Olivia parked her Jeep in the coffee shop lot and started for the door. A man in his sixties with salt and pepper hair approached the coffee shop from the right, and reached the door just as Olivia was climbing the steps. He held the door open for her and said, "Olivia?"

Olivia smiled. "Mr. Waters." She extended her hand to shake his.

"I recognized you from Robin's description." His eyes were kind. He had an easy, gentle manner.

They found an open booth near the big glass windows and ordered drinks.

"Robin tells me you're related to the Monahans."

Olivia explained that she only heard of her distant cousins and the murders when she arrived to house-sit for John.

"It's just so disturbing that such a crime could be committed and no one was ever arrested," Olivia said. She held Mr. Waters' eyes. "It really bothers me."

"Me, too." His voice was soft.

"I've been talking to people who lived in town back then." Olivia shifted her gaze to her tea cup. "I'm not trying to play detective. I just...I don't know." She looked up and sighed. "I can't stop thinking 'why'. Why did it happen? Why would someone murder a child? Why did someone get away with killing them?"

"I understand," Waters said. "The same thoughts go through my mind."

Olivia clasped her hands together and raised her eyes. "My aunt was murdered last year."

Waters' face muscles shifted from surprise to sadness in a split second. "I'm so sorry."

"I know that my concern over this is magnified by what happened to us last summer. I'm hypersensitive to the injustice of it." Olivia paused. "I'm telling you this because I want you to know that I'm not being morbid or ghoulish trying to find out details about my cousins. I just...I just wonder if there's some tiny detail that the police overlooked that might reveal something new. That's the reason I'm talking to people."

Waters nodded.

"So if you're uncomfortable telling me anything," Olivia said, "please just say so. I know it must be hard to talk about it." She swallowed hard. "I have a hard time talking about last year. I still..." She shook her head.

"It's okay," Waters said. "Time passes. It gets easier. I couldn't talk about what I saw in that field for years. Sure, I had to tell the police and answer their questions, but for a very long time, I didn't want to talk about it with anyone."

The waitress came to their table and re-filled Waters' mug with coffee.

"Can you tell me about that day?" Olivia asked.

"I was eighteen years old," Waters said. "I had just graduated high school and started a job. My friend Bobby and I were going fishing. Bobby picked me up and we drove to the state park. We had to walk through a field to get to the trails. We saw the car parked there. The back door was open. I went over to shut it so the battery wouldn't die." He cleared his throat. "That's when I saw Mrs. Monahan on the ground. She was covered in blood. I knew she was dead." He took a gulp of his coffee. "In those days, Howland had a chief of police and a part time officer. Officer Cooper owned the variety store here in Howland. If anybody needed him, they would call or go to the store to get him. There was no police station back then." Waters adjusted himself on his seat. "We took off after we saw the bodies. We ran to the truck and drove like wild men to the store to get Officer Cooper. We were babbling at him to come quick. We brought him to the field. When we were ranting at him about what we saw he didn't realize the woman and child were dead. Somehow we didn't get that across in our frenzy. He just thought someone was hurt in the park. He had a shock when we got back to the field." Dan took another long swallow of his coffee. He stared out the window. "Police swarmed the crime scene. Bobby and I stayed there and watched. That would never be allowed today. Police took photographs of the scene...of the mom and the little girl with one of those Polaroid instant picture cameras. The police spread the photos out on the back of the police car. I looked at them. It was horrible. I wish I had never seen them. Even though I was right there...even though Bobby and I found the victims...there was just something about those photos. The photos seemed to make the whole thing real." He shook his head. "Those awful images are stuck in my brain." He let out a long, slow breath. "I knew the family from church but I didn't recognize them in the field. We found out later in the day who they were. I was sick for days after that. I had no appetite, couldn't eat at all. Couldn't sleep. The images still haunt me. The horror of it." Dan looked at Olivia. "Who could do that to a little child? I still can't drive by the state park without thinking about it," he said. "I'm glad I moved away so I don't have to drive by that place. I always hoped that they'd figure out who did it. Arrest someone. Send him to prison. It's been so long now. I've given up hope that it will ever be solved."

"Is it okay if I ask you some questions?"

"Of course," Waters said.

"You found the mom first? Near the car?"

Waters nodded. "Her head was partially under the car...near the open door. She was on her back."

"And then you found the little girl?"

"That's right. She was in the front seat. Leaning against the door."

"Were there any signs that they might have been molested?"

"They were both fully clothed, so, I would say they weren't." He hesitated. "Well, you know there was semen there?"

Olivia nodded.

"My assumption has always been that the semen happened after they were dead but I don't know what the police would say."

"Do you know where the semen was found? In the

grass? Near the bodies?

"It was on the front of Mrs. Monahan's shorts."

Disgust rose in Olivia's throat.

"Could you get a sense of what happened from the crime scene?" Olivia asked. "Do you think Mrs. Monahan was driving? Do you think the killer was in the back seat directing where she should go? Or do you think the killer was driving and Mrs. Monahan was in the back? She wouldn't have tried to escape because her daughter was in the front."

Waters didn't answer for a few seconds. His brow furrowed as he thought. "I couldn't say for sure but if I had to guess, I would think the guy was in the back seat. When they got to the field, he probably jumped out, left the back door open, pulled Mrs. Monahan from the front. There was probably a struggle. He killed her. The little girl was probably screaming. Was probably too afraid to run. He must have killed her then. I picture him going back to the mother's dead body and, you know...that's how the semen got there."

"It makes sense." Olivia said.

"I'm just guessing, of course. I don't have any information from the police about the order of events."

Olivia nodded in agreement. "Did you and your friend Bobby talk about it? What might have happened to the Monahans? Who killed them? How the crime was committed?"

"No. We didn't. You might think that strange, but the whole thing freaked us out so bad that we avoided the topic. We even stopped hanging out together. Seeing each other just brought the whole thing back and neither one of us wanted that. Right after it happened, people would stare at us and whisper. I figured they must think that me and Bobby were suspects. I hated being associated with the whole mess. I wanted to move away from it. I assume Bobby felt the same. Anyway, the friendship faded. He passed away a couple of years ago. My sister told me it was a heart attack."

"Did you know Kenny Overman?" Olivia asked. "He must have been a year ahead of you in school?"

"Yeah, he was. I knew who he was but never hung around with him."

"I know he was a suspect," Olivia asked. "What did you think? Did you think he might have done it?"

"Overman seemed too convenient to me. The State Police took over the case from the local cops. Seemed like they would have loved to pin it on Overman. Get a conviction. Tie it up nice and neat."

"But that didn't happen," Olivia said.

"Probably not for lack of trying. Overman was the perfect person to charge with the crime. A loser. No family that would fight the arrest. Somehow the cops couldn't pin it on him though. Lucky, for him."

"So you don't think it was Overman?"

"Could have been him. But it wasn't my feeling."

"Did you have any thoughts on who might have done it?"

Waters hesitated. "Have you heard anything about the priest at St. Catherine's?"

"Father Anthony? There was some gossip," Olivia said.

Waters waved to the waitress indicating he wanted more coffee. He looked at Olivia and let out a long breath. "My family went to St. Catherine's."

Olivia waited for him to continue.

"I was in the youth group. For a while. I thought it would be a great way to hang out with the girls."

"It wasn't?" Olivia asked.

"The girls were all into Anthony. He wasn't that much older than most of us. I think he must have been around twenty-five or twenty-six? Anyway, most of us guys couldn't get any attention from the girls. They were always flirting with Anthony. Thing was...he didn't seem to discourage it. I didn't think it was right. Part of it was jealousy on my side of it, but it just didn't seem right for a priest. To me, he seemed to encourage the attention."

"Do you think he had something to do with the murders?"

"I don't know. I suppose not. But I've always had a feeling. I imagine the police checked him out."

"Is your feeling based on his flirtations?"

Waters leaned back in the booth. "One time, the youth group went on a camping trip. We got to the place late. Some of us guys were putting up the tents. One guy had no experience, made a mess of one of them. Anthony came by. He yelled at the kid. Lost his temper. Knocked the poles down. Made a scene. Told him to figure it out and do it right. It was an odd over-reaction. I didn't like it. The guy seemed off to me. I quit the group after that. I thought the priest was volatile. I didn't want any part of him." He shrugged. "I wondered. In a certain situation, with that temper of his?" Waters leaned forward and lowered his voice. "They wouldn't let him off would they? Just because he was a priest?"

Olivia had no answer for that.

19

On Friday, Olivia took Lily to the state park for a long walk and a swim in the lake. After drying themselves in the sun on the bank of the water, they headed home, stopping first at the florist so Olivia could buy a bunch of mixed flowers for the dining table.

Joe and Brad were coming for the weekend and Olivia couldn't wait to see them. They were bringing a kayak and a canoe so that they could spend Saturday on the lake and the river that fed into it. The canoe was so Lily could go along too. Joe had prepared something special for dinner for Friday night, but wouldn't tell Olivia what it was. Olivia decided she would put together a green salad with strawberries to go with whatever Joe was bringing.

The oppressive heat of the past few days had been

chased away by a late night thunderstorm and now the air was warm and pleasant. Olivia had cleaned the house, made the beds with fresh sheets, and put out fluffy towels in the bathrooms.

She was feeling tired suddenly and decided to sit on the front porch in one of the big wooden rockers and take a break for a little while. She called Lily as she opened the screened door and the dog came bounding from the kitchen. There was a cushion in the corner of the porch for the dog but Lily lay down in front of the gate that John had placed across the steps to contain her safely on the porch. She surveyed the occasional cars driving past, the two squirrels playing in the big oak, and she snapped at a fly that buzzed too close to her head. Olivia sank into the cushioned rocker thankful for the quiet at the house today. The work crew had taken the day off from renovating the sunroom. Olivia moved gently back and forth in the rocker, the movement lulling her to drift into sleep.

Olivia dreamed of a sunny field of wildflowers and long grasses. She wandered through the field happily picking some daisies for a small bouquet. Black-grey clouds appeared on the horizon and rushed overhead turning the day into evening. Olivia looked up at the darkened sky and huddled in the field, trembling. The wind whipped around her. Lightening flashed. Olivia heard a low rumbling, an engine, the sound getting louder and louder, closer and closer. Over the ridge to her right, a blue sedan flew over the hill, went airborne and hurtled toward her. She knew she didn't have time to run so she knelt on the ground and crouched into a ball. She clamped her eyes shut. The sound of shattering glass and crunching metal deafened her. Tiny shards of glass rained over her. She opened her eyes. All was black.

She was inside now but the place was unknown to her. She stood and took a few steps in the darkness trying to get her bearings. Her foot bumped into metal. She tripped over something and fell to the concrete floor. Her foot was caught in the wheel spokes of Aggie's bicycle. She struggled to free herself. A light was coming toward her. It was blinding. Olivia shaded her eyes. It was a man, an eerie blue-red light glowing from him. It was Aggie's killer. He had a knife. The silver blade reflected the light emanating from the man. Olivia tried to scramble away but her foot was still tangled in the wheel. She smashed at the metal spokes with her free foot while she jerked the trapped leg from side to side. The knife flew from the man's hand like a missile and plunged into Olivia's stomach. She screamed.

Olivia startled awake from Lily's nose nudging at her. Sweat beaded on Olivia's brow, her clammy hands pulled at the sweaty t-shirt stuck to her chest and back. Her breath came in short, fast gasps. Adrenaline was surging through her veins.

Lily put her head on Olivia's knees and Olivia stroked

the soft smooth fur of the dog's head. After several minutes of patting, Olivia's breathing evened out and her heart beat returned to its regular pace. Anxiety is no match for the tenderness of a gentle dog.

"These stupid dreams, Lily. When are they going to stop?" Olivia sighed. Lily tapped her tail on the floorboards of the porch. The big pink tongue shot out and licked Olivia's arm. Lily stood up and put her paws on the rocker on the outside of Olivia's knees and tried to push up onto her lap. Olivia laughed.

"Lily, we both can't fit in this chair." Lily's tongue slurped a big kiss over Olivia's face. Olivia turned her head away. "Ugh," she laughed again and gently pressed Lily back down. She scratched behind the dog's ears.

"Good dog. Come on, let's go get ourselves a cool drink." Olivia and the dog headed for the kitchen. Olivia splashed her face with water and went to the bedroom to change her sweaty t-shirt. When she returned to the kitchen, Lily was sitting next to her food dish thumping the floor with her tail.

"I get the message," Olivia told her. She opened a can of dog food and scooped it into Lily's bowl along with a container of dry dog pellets. Lily gobbled her meal while Olivia freshened the water in her bowl. Olivia sipped cold water from a glass, her hip leaning against the counter, and watched the dog enjoying its meal.

Lily and Olivia turned their heads at the sound of two

car doors slamming. Olivia smiled at Lily. "They're here, girl. Let's go see Joe and Brad." Lily looked eagerly at Olivia, and then cocked her head at the sounds in the driveway. They both trotted to the front porch to greet the visitors.

Brad was removing an overnight bag from the back seat and straightened when he heard the slap of the screen door closing. He grinned at Olivia. Lily let out a friendly woof. Joe was hidden by the open trunk of Brad's car, but leaned left to reveal his tanned, craggy face, his light blue eyes beaming at Olivia. She hadn't seen them for over a month and the sight of them filled her with warmth and calm and light.

Olivia slid the porch gate back and Lily bounded down the stairs and danced around the men. Brad dropped his bag and enveloped Olivia in his arms. He leaned back a bit, brushed a strand of hair from her face, and tenderly cupped her chin in his hand. He kissed her.

"Okay, it's my turn," Joe kidded. Brad and Olivia laughed and stepped apart. Joe gave Olivia a bear hug.

"You look good, Liv," Joe told her, his voice was soft.

She hugged him tight.

"So do you," she smiled.

Lily bounced around them. Brad greeted the dog and patted her head. Joe scratched her ears. They carried in bags of food and the two small suitcases.

Joe produced a huge pan of pasta and eggplant

parmesan and a plate of garlic bread. He instructed Olivia to preheat the oven to 350 degrees. Brad pulled whipped cream from the cooler and put it in the fridge. He placed the blueberry cake on the counter and pushed it back to the wall in case the dog got exuberant and decided to help itself.

Olivia had set the table earlier, so the men had glasses of beer and Olivia poured herself a glass of iced tea. They sat around the dining table, the candles flickering, waiting for the meal to heat through. Olivia filled them in on what she had discovered so far about the murders.

"So it sounds like that Kenny Overman kid is the one that did it," Joe said.

"But the police didn't arrest him, so maybe not," Brad said.

"Whoever it was, he was pretty darn bold," Joe said. "Taking the woman and child in the daylight. Killing them outside...someone might have heard screams." He was quiet for a minute. "Were they..." he paused.

"Molested?" Olivia finished it for him. "No, they weren't, but there was semen found at the scene."

"Ugh," Joe muttered.

"So the guy kills them and then stands there and ..." Brad shook his head.

"I know," Olivia said. "It's sickening."

"If the police think Overman did it and they found some guy's bodily fluids at the scene, why don't they run a

DNA test on it now?" Brad asked. "Wouldn't that prove he did it?"

"I guess it would," Olivia said.

They were silent thinking it over.

"Would the police need something to go on besides speculation in order to ask someone for a DNA sample? In order to match it to the DNA from the crime scene," Joe said. "I wouldn't think they could just ask to take a sample without cause. Without something concrete. Would they need something like a search warrant?"

"That's a good point," Brad said.

The oven timer went off and Joe took the eggplant out of the oven. It was getting dark outside and a light breeze floated in through the windows. Olivia put some music on and they enjoyed the delicious meal.

After the dishes were cleaned up, the three of them took Lily for a walk around the neighborhood and then they sat on the front porch rocking. Brad and Joe caught Olivia up on the news and gossip from Ogunquit.

"It's nice having you here," Olivia told them. "I miss you two."

Brad reached over and held her hand. "The feeling's mutual," he said.

"I sure miss you, Liv. It's strange not having you next door," Joe said.

"How is the renter doing, Joe?" Olivia asked. Olivia decided that since she would be away in Cambridge for law school it would be best to rent out the Ogunquit beach house that Aggie had left to her. Joe was keeping an eye on the house for her.

"The woman is very nice. She takes good care of the place," Joe said. "She's quiet. A good neighbor. We sit around the fire pit together some nights now that the weather is good."

"That's great," Olivia said. "I'm glad it's working out."

"I'm looking forward to having you stay with me for the month of August," Joe told her. Olivia was going to stay at Joe's house during August after she returned from her summer class.

"Me too," she grinned. "You can make me tasty meals."

"Bah," Joe responded. "We'll take turns."

They chatted and rocked for another hour.

Joe stood up and stretched. "Time for me to hit the sack. I need a good night's sleep if I'm going to keep up with you two on the river tomorrow."

"Don't worry, Joe," Brad said. "We'll take it easy for you."

The three of them knew that it would be Joe who would be way ahead of Brad and Olivia when they hit the water with the kayak and canoe.

"Goodnight, children." Joe kissed the top of Olivia's head.

"Goodnight, Joe," they said in unison.

Brad and Olivia stayed outside on the porch for another half hour. Olivia sat in the rocker next to Brad with her legs pulled up under her and a blanket over her lap. She adjusted herself a bit in the chair so that she was slightly facing Brad. She watched him as he rocked, engrossed in a novel. His brown hair flopped over his forehead. Olivia admired the line of his chin, the curve of his bicep, his strong hands cradling the book. Lily lay at their feet, fireflies danced by the tree line, and crickets and peeper frogs chirped and called in the darkness. Olivia wondered if anything could be more perfect.

Brad shifted his position and caught Olivia looking at him.

"What?" he asked. He reached his arm across the space between the rockers, held his hand out to Olivia and she placed hers in his.

She gave him a soft, sweet smile. "Nothing."

He leaned closer to her and raised her hand to his lips and kissed it. "Time to go in?" he asked.

Olivia nodded. They stood and gathered their things. Brad put his arm around her waist and they went inside. The two climbed the stairs with the dog tagging along behind them.

20

Olivia, Joe, Brad, and Lily had a wonderful day on the water. Despite applying sunscreen, each one had a bit of sunburn on their faces. Except the dog. Lily was like the captain of the canoe or like a carved figurehead on the bow of a ship. All day she stood at the front of the canoe surveying everything around her as Brad and Joe took turns paddling from the back. Now she was sound asleep next to Olivia on the rear seat of Brad's car.

"I think that dog enjoyed the day more than anyone else," Joe laughed. "I don't think I've ever seen a creature who loved the water like Lily does."

"Yeah," Brad agreed. "She sure seemed disappointed when it was time to leave."

Olivia patted Lily's head as she watched the scenery passing the car window.

"I didn't realize this state park was so huge," Brad said.

"Yeah, miles of walking trails, the lake, river, a good size pond, fields," Olivia commented. *Fields.* "Brad, would you turn left up here and take the longer way back to the house?"

"Sure thing. What's up?"

"Would either of you mind if we stop at the field where the murders took place? I've been wanting to go take a look, but I just didn't want to go there by myself."

"I don't mind, Liv," Brad told her.

"Gives me the creeps," Joe admitted. "I'll stay in the car."

"Afraid of ghosts, Joe?" Brad asked.

"Nope," Joe said. "I'm afraid of the living. And the things they do."

"I won't be long, if you don't want to get out," Olivia told Joe.

Olivia gave Brad directions to the dirt road that would lead to the field where Mary and Kimmy were killed.

"Here. Here it is on the left." Olivia was craning her neck from the back seat to see the road. Lily sensed the car slowing and sat up to see where they were. Brad turned onto the dirt road and the Jeep bumped up and down as if traveling over a washboard.

"Pull over here," Olivia told him.

Brad pulled the car over as far to the side as he could.

They opened the doors and stepped out. Lily jumped out and sniffed the brush along the dirt way.

"I'm going to stay here," Joe said. "I think I'll just close my eyes while you two investigate." He hunkered down on the seat to get more comfortable.

"Okay, Joe, we'll be back in a bit," Olivia said.

"Take your time. I'm happy right here," Joe replied. His eyes were already shut.

Brad and Olivia made their way down the dirt road. Lily ran ahead. When the road opened to the field, Olivia said, "This is it, Brad. This is where they were killed."

They followed a small path that cut through the long grass.

"From the newspaper descriptions I read, the car must have been parked right around here," Olivia said.

"Strange to think what happened so many years ago," Brad said. "It's so peaceful." He shook his head as they stood quietly observing the place.

"It's hard to believe that two people were murdered here," Olivia said, her voice soft.

Lily bounced towards them from across the field.

"There's supposed to be a lake over that way," Olivia told Brad. "The guys who found the bodies were on their way to fish."

"Let's take a look," Brad said.

When Lily saw them coming towards her, she bolted back in the direction she had just come. Brad and Olivia followed the narrow path until it widened and edged along a clear blue lake that appeared to cover many acres.

"It's beautiful," Brad said. "Is swimming allowed?"

"I don't know," Olivia answered. "There's swimming at a lake over off of River Street. There's a town beach there. I take Lily to swim in the evenings. Dogs aren't allowed when the lifeguards are on duty. I'm not sure if this is the other side of that lake. I need a map of town. I can't get my bearings about where things are located in relation to each other."

"Want to follow along the trail for a while?" Brad asked.

"Yeah, let's," Olivia said. "Maybe something will look familiar. I've walked Lily at the state park. Maybe this trail leads to the other side of the park."

After walking for about fifteen minutes, the trail split.

"Which way?" Brad asked.

Olivia considered and pointed to the left. "This way."

They walked on for another ten minutes and came to a small clearing. They could see the trail picked up again between the trees on the other side of the field. They crossed to the far side and headed along the path which inclined up the side of a hill.

Brad said, "Maybe we should head back, Liv. Joe might be wondering where we are."

"Okay," Olivia replied and then smiled. "But he's probably still sound asleep."

Just before Olivia turned around, something in the distance caught her eye.

"What's that near the top of the hill?"

Brad leaned forward to get a better look between the trees. "It's a building."

"Let's go see."

The trail leading to where they were headed was overgrown, so they ducked and pushed aside branches as they trudged up the slight incline. They emerged from the woods into a large expanse of manicured lawn. An in-ground swimming pool could be seen near a large brick mansion situated at the top of the crest.

Olivia eyed the place. "This is the Bradford mansion. I talked with Isabel Bradford and her daughter, Angela here. I recognize the room with the wall of glass looking over the terrace and pool. This is Magnolia Hill."

"The area of Howland with all the mansions? This is quite a place," Brad said. "Do they have armed guards patrolling the grounds?" he joked.

"Emily Bradford told me that she used to meet Kenny Overman in a field behind her house. She would sneak out sometimes. That clearing we just came through at the bottom of the hill. That must be where she used to meet him," Olivia said. "I didn't realize that their property backed up to the state park land."

A dog barked somewhere in the distance and Lily's

ears perked up. She started to advance towards the sound but Olivia took hold of her collar.

"No, Lily. Come on." Olivia turned her around. "I guess we should get back to Joe," she told Brad. The three stumbled through the brush to return to the trail.

When they reached the car, Joe was snoring in the front seat. Brad and Olivia exchanged impish grins. Careful not to make any noise, they took small, slow steps until they were right next to the open car window. Brad looked at Olivia and mouthed, 'one, two, three,' and then he and Olivia let out blood-curdling shrieks.

Joe startled from his nap and jerked straight up in the seat, blinking, trying to orient himself to his surroundings.

"Idiots!" he shouted at Olivia and Brad who were doubled over, laughing. "Are you damn fools trying to give me a heart attack?" Joe grumped at them and shook his head.

21

On Sunday, Brad followed the line of cars past St. Catherine's Church and pulled into the field which was being used as an overflow parking area for those attending the annual church yard sale and festival. Joe, Olivia and Brad left the car in its spot and headed back to the sidewalk that led up to St. Catherine's.

"I had no idea this was such a popular town event," Olivia said.

"Quite a turnout," Joe remarked.

"You should have set up a table to sell all of the stuff you're removing from John's attic," Brad said.

"Yeah." Olivia grinned. "And then keep all the profits for myself," she joked.

The church parking lot, the rec hall, and the field behind the church held food vendors, games for kids, craft tables, and tables and booths filled with all kinds of items for sale from yard sale trinkets to professionally crafted specialties. A band was set up near the food tent and the musicians were playing a mix of country, blues, and pop songs.

Joe was fascinated by a booth that sold wooden decoys, bird houses and furniture and he struck up a conversation with the man who handcrafted all of the items. Olivia admired a table of handmade jewelry and purchased a pair of dangly sterling silver earrings. Brad lingered over a table of out of print books.

The sky was bright blue and the day was warm and clear. It seemed everyone in Howland was at the event.

"I wish I hadn't eaten lunch," Brad said, eyeing the food concessions.

"I bet that won't stop you," Olivia teased as they approached the food tent where sausages sizzled on grills, individual pizzas were made with every topping possible, and soft serve ice cream was dipped into chocolate, caramel, or strawberry icings.

"Oh, look, fried dough." Olivia trotted over to a food truck.

"Well, if she's going to indulge, I'm right behind her," Joe admitted.

"Sausage truck?" Brad asked.

"Yup," Joe said.

Olivia met the guys at one of the picnic tables set up

under a huge beech tree. She took the bench opposite them and bit into her fried dough. Powdered sugar dusted her nose and lips.

"Looks good on you, Liv," Brad told her between bites of his sub sandwich of sausage, peppers and onions. Joe had one too and they had a plate of onion rings set on the table between them. They each had a frosty mug of beer next to their plates.

Olivia took a sip from Brad's mug. "What should I get after this?" she asked.

"At this rate we'll have to roll back to the house," Joe noted.

"Or explode before we get there," Brad said.

As the guys made short work of the food, a man's voice spoke over the PA system announcing a tractor pull event at the far end of the back field. Joe and Brad grinned at each other.

"Go," Olivia said, rolling her eyes. "I'm happy sitting here in the shade. Come get me when it's over."

The guys jumped up and hurried off like little kids. Olivia shook her head and chuckled as she finished off her fried dough.

"Hey." A woman's voice called. Olivia turned to see Jackie heading towards her with a gigantic banana split. "My dad and brother took off on me when they heard that tractor pull announcement. We were going to share this," Jackie said. "Looks like you're going to have to help me now." She sat on the bench beside Olivia and placed the dessert between them.

"Oh, Jackie, no," Olivia groaned.

"Here's a napkin." Jackie put a napkin and spoon in front of Olivia. "Eat."

They dug in.

"Is it this crowded every year?" Olivia asked scooping a spoonful of ice cream into her mouth, hot fudge dripping off the spoon.

"Depends on the weather," Jackie said. She pointed at Olivia's chin where a blob of fudge had landed. Olivia swept her tongue over her chin and giggled.

"Nice manners," Jackie said.

In between bites, they ate and chatted, enjoyed the music and watched the people. Jackie and Olivia made plans to go for a jog the next day on the rail trails after Jackie finished up work. They polished off the banana split and Jackie left to go look for her relatives. She asked Olivia to join her.

"I'm not leaving this bench," Olivia said. "I'm too full to move. I need to digest a bit before I go off walking around," she kidded.

Just as Jackie left, Olivia saw Father Mike strolling towards the table, an older woman holding on to his arm. Olivia waved.

"Olivia," Father Mike puffed. "May we join you?"

"Please." Olivia indicated the opposite bench.

The priest put his cane against the picnic table, helped the woman balance as she arranged herself on the bench and then maneuvered his own legs over the seat and plopped down.

"The golden years," he chuckled. "Not sure what's so golden about them."

The woman nodded her head. She was petite and slightly stooped. She had straight, silver gray hair, cut short with bangs brushed to the side. She wore slacks, sensible shoes, and a cardigan.

"Martha, this is Olivia Miller," Father Mike said. "She is the young woman who is researching the Monahan's murders. Remember I mentioned her to you?"

The woman reached across the table to shake Olivia's hand.

"Olivia, this is Martha Martin. She was born in town and has lived all her life here."

"It's nice to meet you," Olivia said shaking Mrs. Martin's hand.

A young man delivered two plates of pasta, salad, and a French roll to the woman and the priest. They thanked the young man profusely.

"Olivia, can we share our meal with you?" Father Mike asked.

"Oh, thank you, but I've eaten way too much today already," Olivia told him.

Mrs. Martin picked at her meal. "Father Mike tells me you were cousin to Mary Monahan and her daughter."

Olivia nodded and told her that she never knew of them until she found the newspaper reporting the murders.

"A sad event in the history of our town," said Mrs. Martin.

"Did you know Mary and her daughter?" Olivia asked.

"Not well. But she and her family attended church here and I knew who the family was." She took a small bite of her roll and shook her head. "Long, ago. But the feelings seem fresh."

"True," Father Mike said. "I hadn't thought about the crime for so long...and then when Olivia asked me about it, I was surprised how emotions flooded back."

"Things changed here because of the murders," Mrs. Martin said. "Before the killings we were so easy-going. But after that we all locked our doors. We worried who the murderer could be. It made us suspicious of others." She sighed. "I made my son tell me where he was going and who he was with."

Father Mike nodded.

"I would feel the same way," Olivia said. "I'd want to know where my child was every minute."

"But it ends up that the natural events of the day are the real dangers," Mrs. Martin said.

Olivia wondered what she meant.

"Unfortunately," Father Mike said. He touched her shoulder.

"It's been almost forty-five years that James passed," Mrs. Martin continued.

When she heard Mrs. Martin's comment, Olivia's brain made the connection. James. James Martin. Angela Bradford told her that Emily dated James Martin after Kenny Overman left town.

"James was your son?" Olivia asked.

"Yes." She paused. "He suffered an accident."

"I'm sorry."

Mrs. Martin pushed the pasta around her plate. "He drowned in our backyard pool."

"How terrible," Olivia said.

A middle aged woman came over to Father Mike and whispered something into his ear.

"Would you ladies excuse me for a moment? Martha, are you all right sitting here for a bit?"

"Yes, Mike. Go ahead. I'm fine."

"I'll be here," Olivia said.

The middle aged woman helped Father Mike remove himself from the picnic table, handed him his cane and took hold of Mike's arm as they moved toward the recreation hall.

Mrs. Martin went on talking about the accident. "It was just over a year after the Monahans were killed that

James drowned. I wondered if there was some curse put on our little town. How could two such terrible events happen in Howland? That's what I wondered."

Olivia nodded.

"And, poor Emily." Mrs. Martin looked up from her plate. "That poor girl. Emily Bradford. Have you heard her name as you talk to people in town? She dated the young man who was considered a suspect in the Monahan murders."

"Yes," Olivia said. "In fact, Emily met with me to give her impressions."

"A lovely woman. After the murder suspect left Howland, Emily and James started to date. I hoped it would lead to something eventually. Emily was there the night James drowned. She had gone into the house to use the bathroom and when she went back outside he was at the bottom of the pool. She tried to get him out." Mrs. Martin put her fork down. "I don't think poor Emily ever recovered. I know I haven't."

"It must have been a terrible shock," Olivia told her.

"Oh, yes." Mrs. Martin looked off into the distance. "It's odd. I had an odd feeling that evening. Maybe it was a premonition of what was to come."

"A premonition?"

"My husband and I were to attend a function in Boston that night. James and Emily were sitting by the pool. They had used the grill to cook burgers for dinner. I was going to let them know we were leaving and say goodbye to them. When I entered the screen room off our kitchen...it overlooked the pool area...I could hear Emily crying. I stopped, wondering if I should go out to them or just leave them be. They seemed to be arguing over something. I didn't want to intrude on them so I went back in the house. We left for Boston without saying goodbye." Mrs. Martin's eyes were filled with sadness. "I should have said goodbye."

Olivia wanted to say something comforting but was unsure of what might help. "You didn't know what would happen."

Mrs. Martin gave Olivia a sheepish smile. "I don't know why I'm telling you this, dear. But when Father Mike brought up the Monahans, and it being this time of year, all those thoughts rushed into my head."

"It's okay," Olivia said. "I understand." Olivia didn't want Mrs. Martin to feel badly that she had talked about her son's accident, so Olivia asked, "Have you kept in touch with Emily?"

"Oh, my, she has been very helpful to me. My husband and I divorced about a year after James' passing. We both had to deal with our grief. We handled it in different ways. We weren't there for each other and we grew apart."

"I'm sorry." Olivia didn't really know what to say and felt inadequate murmuring such useless phrases.

"Emily visits me now and then. Calls me." Mrs. Martin leaned closer. "She has been very helpful to me financially."

Olivia was surprised. "That's very kind of her."

"I told her that it was unnecessary. That I could manage. But the truth is I would struggle without her help. I'm very grateful to her." Mrs. Martin's voice was wistful. "She would have made a lovely daughter-in-law."

"Do you know what Emily and James were arguing about that night?"

"When I was in the screen room that evening I thought I heard them talking about the Monahans. That's what I meant by a premonition...thinking they were discussing the Monahans made me feel that something bad was going to happen. Whatever it was, Emily sounded angry and upset. Almost, hysterical. That's why I stayed inside and didn't go out to them." Mrs. Martin sipped her water. "I asked Emily about it once. She brushed it aside. She said they had been drinking and that a minor thing got overblown. She said the argument was nonsense."

Olivia nodded. "Most arguments are." Olivia wondered why Emily and James would be discussing the Monahans and if they *were* talking about them, what could have caused Emily to be so upset?

Olivia noticed Father Mike tottering over to them.

"Everything okay?" he asked as he sat down.

"We had a chat." Olivia smiled.

"She is very pleasant company," Mrs. Martin told Father Bill.

"I guess I'll go find my friends now," Olivia said. "It was nice to see you Father Mike. Nice to meet you, Mrs. Martin." They shook hands.

As Olivia made her way to the back field, she wondered how on earth a tractor pull could keep two grown men's attention for so long.

22

Olivia, Brad and Joe took bikes to the rail trail after the church festival and completed a fifteen mile ride partly because they were guilty for all the eating they did at the church. When they returned to the house, Joe and Brad took Lily for a walk while Olivia made beef and veggie tacos for dinner. She made Spanish rice and a green salad to go with them. The guys and the dog returned from their walk just as Olivia was finishing setting the weathered wooden table on the deck with flowers, dishes, silverware and linen napkins. Joe and Brad carried the food to the table and Olivia fed Lily. They lit candles, opened a bottle of wine, and settled down to munch just as the sun was setting over the trees.

"I'm looking forward to you being home in August,"

Brad said to Olivia as he added homemade salsa to his tacos.

"It seems like you haven't been home in ages," Joe added.

"I know. It feels like that to me too," Olivia said. Thinking about being back home in Ogunquit caused the anxiety of last summer's violence to flash through her veins and coil hard in her stomach. She wanted to tell Brad and Joe about her fears and how those fears had prevented her from returning to Maine but she didn't know how to start. Her fingers shook as she reached for her wine glass.

"Well now that you've had a successful first year of law school, maybe you can come home some weekends this coming year," Brad said. "Now that you're used to the workload and the routine." He looked across the table at Olivia. "I miss you."

"Things aren't the same without you," Joe said.

Olivia's eyes misted and she swallowed hard. "I hope so. I want to."

They cleared the table when they were finished and Olivia brought out tea, coffee, apple pie and vanilla ice cream. It was nearly dark and the soft light from the candles flickered over their faces as they enjoyed the dessert.

When the pie was eaten and the coffee finished, Joe and Brad helped Olivia clean up, loaded their bags into the trunk, and fastened the canoe and kayak to the top of the car for the trip home.

"We'll see you soon, sweet pea." Joe hugged her. "Stay out of trouble."

"I'll try," Olivia said. "I can't promise though." She smiled at him.

Brad bear-hugged her and kissed her as he stroked her chestnut brown hair. Olivia couldn't help a tear escaping from her eye. Brad brushed it away. "I feel the same way," he whispered. "I'm counting the minutes until August 1."

She nodded and wrapped her arms around him for one last hug.

Olivia waved to them from the front porch with Lily beside her wagging her tail as the car backed up, turned, and headed down the driveway to the street. Olivia watched until the red tail lights disappeared. She sighed, patted Lily's head, and the two of them went into the house.

Olivia sat in her pajamas curled up on the sofa reading. Lily sprawled out on the floor at Olivia's feet. Olivia was sorry to see Brad and Joe leave. The weekend visit made her homesick for the coast of Maine, her house there, and the daily interaction with the men. Her thoughts of them made it difficult to focus on her book.

Lily lifted her head and turned to the front door. She woofed, low in her throat.

Olivia ran her toes over Lily's back. "It was just a dream, Lily. Go back to sleep, girl." Lily put her head back down on the rug.

A quiet thump from the direction of the front door caused Olivia to turn and Lily to bounce to her feet. A growl rumbled from the dog. Lily flicked her eyes at Olivia and turned her gaze to the front entrance. Olivia closed the book and rose from the sofa. She and Lily stood motionless, listening.

Olivia went to the window, turned the lamp off, moved the muslin curtain a bit to the side, and looked into the dark, front yard. The driveway was empty and she saw no movement on the lawn. She crept to the window on the far side of the front door which afforded a better view of the porch. Lily barked and Olivia jumped, her heart leaping into her throat.

"Sshhh, Lily," she said. Olivia put her ear next to the door. She heard nothing. Lily was beside her. Olivia unlocked the deadbolt and put her hand on Lily's collar.

"Lily, wait," she whispered.

Olivia pulled on the heavy wooden door and opened it a crack. Lily was eager to get out, but she stood still obeying Olivia's command. Olivia put one eye in the open crack, and seeing nothing she fully opened the door. Lily pushed against Olivia's leg but stayed beside her.

Olivia grimaced and gasped and pulled on Lily's collar preventing her from pushing open the screen door. On the floor of the porch just beyond the front door, were two dead squirrels, one larger than the other. Both of their throats had been slit and they were positioned with their heads yanked back, fully exposing the gashes. The bigger animal had stab wounds along the abdomen.

Olivia's stomach churned. Her eyes flashed about the yard and down to the street. She pulled Lily back into the house, slammed the door and turned the deadbolt. Her hands were shaking and her breath was coming in gasps. Anger flared in her chest. She closed her eyes for a second to blot out the gruesome sight, but shutting her lids made the image of the bloody creatures flash in her mind.

Bastard. Who did it?

Olivia darted up the stairs to the second floor of the house with Lily running behind. She dashed from bedroom to bedroom peering out of the windows trying to see anyone who might be lurking or running through the yard to the tree line.

Returning to the living room, Olivia played the past few minutes back in her head. She hadn't heard a car engine or feet creaking on the floorboards of the porch. She hadn't seen a gleam from headlights or a flashlight.

Lily had perked up right before Olivia heard a thump from the front of the house. Whoever was responsible must have been watching and waiting since the delivery of the deceased squirrels happened after Brad and Joe ended their visit. Olivia suspected the person must have checked around the house on other occasions in order to find the easiest and most hidden way to approach and retreat with the least chance of detection.

Olivia clenched her jaw. Her hands were balled into fists. As she moved to the coffee table for her cell phone to place a call to the police, Oliva was almost thankful that she hadn't discovered the perpetrator in the yard because she didn't want to be responsible for what she might have done to him.

THE POLICE ARRIVED and Olivia recounted how she found the animals on the porch. Olivia was grateful that one of the officers removed them so that she wouldn't have to see the mutilated bodies again. Olivia told the police that she had met with some residents of Howland to inquire about the decades-old murders of her cousins and the officers suggested that the dead animals on the porch were probably a prank by local teenagers who had heard that Olivia was asking questions about the forty-five-year old crime.

"So they grab some squirrels and slit their throats? For a prank?" Olivia asked.

"Kids do stupid stuff," the officer said. "They don't think beyond the moment. That's how they end up in trouble."

The second officer came inside from disposing of the squirrels. "They'd been shot."

"Kids must have been hunting and thought it would be funny to stage the old crime scene on the porch," the first officer said.

"Funny? That's terrible," Olivia said. Her stomach was still roiling. She shook her head at the cruelty that people were capable of. She wrapped her arms around herself.

The police concluded the visit by reassuring Olivia that it was most likely a harmless act committed by bored adolescents looking for some excitement.

"Not harmless for the squirrels," Olivia told them. There was a big, fat knot in her throat. After the officers left, she walked around the first floor pulling the window shades shut. She decided to read upstairs in bed.

"Come on, Lily. Let's go relax upstairs. Or try to, anyway." Olivia led the way up the staircase. She looked at Lily next to her and was glad she wasn't alone in the house.

23

Early the next morning, Olivia drove to meet Emily Bradford's former fiancé at his law offices in Chestnut Hill. She was still shaken over finding the dead squirrels on the front porch the night before and her emotions alternated between worry and fury. Worry that someone might return for another "prank" and fury at whoever did the cruel deed.

Olivia pulled the Jeep into the parking lot of the law offices of Chandler, Mitchell, and Kaplan. When Don Chandler's secretary buzzed him, he came out to greet Olivia and usher her into his office. Chandler was tall and slim and had the body of a long distance runner. He had sandy blonde hair and bright blue eyes. His charcoal suit was well tailored and he exuded a warm energy.

"Would you like something to drink, Olivia? Tea,

coffee, ice water?" Chandler asked. He indicated one of the dark grey matching club chairs and they sat opposite each other.

"Nothing, thank you," Olivia said. "I don't want to take much of your time. I appreciate you seeing me."

"Not at all. I don't know how much I can help, but I'm glad to answer your questions."

"I recently learned about the murders of my cousins forty-five years ago and I wondered why no one was ever arrested and prosecuted. I'm just asking people who lived in Howland for their impressions. I understand you were in Kenny Overman's high school class."

"I was. I was never friends with the guy. We were in some classes together now and then up until high school, then after that I really just saw him in passing."

"What did you think of him?"

"He was always in trouble for something it seemed. Minor things like not having his homework, misbehaving in class, teasing kids. He was absent a lot." Chandler looked thoughtful. "Tell you the truth, I didn't like being around him. He seemed like, I don't know, like something was simmering under the surface...anger...unhappiness. It's hard to describe. He seemed unhappy with himself. I found out when I got older that his home life was troubled. He seemed bright enough. If he'd been raised in a different family..." Chandler's voice trailed off and he shrugged.

Olivia nodded. "His father was an alcoholic, I guess. His mother took off and left them when Kenny was a little kid."

"Life sure isn't fair," Chandler said.

"Did you know Kenny to get into fights, was he ever violent?"

"Never saw that. Never saw or heard of any fights, but that doesn't mean they didn't happen. Once we got to high school, I didn't see much of him."

"What was the talk in Howland back then? Who was suspected for the murders?"

"Well, Overman for one. Some guy wandering through town was another suspect. There was gossip about the priest at St. Catherine's but that was probably idle chatter. No one was arrested, as you know."

"No evidence I suppose. Who did you think did it?"

"I hoped it wasn't Overman. A guy, my age. Who I knew? That scared the heck out of me. I just wanted the police to figure it out. Get the killer off the streets."

Olivia nodded. "I understand that you were engaged to Emily Bradford. Her sister spoke with me recently. Emily dated Kenny in high school."

"Yes."

"What do you think attracted her to Kenny?"

"Emily was headstrong. She had her own ways of doing things. She was involved in all the clubs at school, star student, a fantastic athlete. Her parents drove her nuts. They were very controlling. It was Emily's way of rebelling against them, I suppose. Overman was a good looking guy back then. That didn't hurt the attraction either, I'm sure."

"What's your feeling? Do you think Kenny could have killed my cousins? Was it in him to do something so vicious and violent?"

Chandler inhaled a deep breath. "That is something I just can't answer." He shook his head slowly. "I don't know, Olivia. I just don't know."

They sat in silence for a few moments. Olivia noticed the collection of photographs on Chandler's credenza.

"Your family?"

Chandler followed Olivia's gaze and smiled.

"Yeah. Quite a group."

"They're beautiful. How many kids do you have?"

"Five. Three boys and two girls. Most in their twenties now. Youngest is eighteen. Going off to college in the fall. It will be an adjustment for my wife and I, empty nest and all."

Olivia nodded. "Do you mind if I ask you about Emily?"

Chandler turned back to Olivia. "I don't mind."

"Any guesses why she never married? Do you think Kenny's troubles and then James Martin's death turned her off to relationships?"

"Could be. We started dating during our last year of

college. I went to law school in Boston and she went to grad school in the city as well. We always had separate apartments. I proposed to her right before we graduated. She accepted. We never got around to setting a date. Emily was very career-minded. Worked long hours, was determined to make something of herself. I worked hard too, but family was important to me." He chuckled. "As you can see from the pictures."

"Is that why she broke off the engagement? Because she was a workaholic?"

Chandler looked surprised. "*I* was the one who broke it off. She was furious. She didn't want kids and I wanted a lot of them. I hoped she would soften to the idea. She didn't and was adamant about never having a child." He paused. "She could be...well, sort of cold."

"How do you mean?"

"She was a great person, but could be very controlling and critical." Chandler looked down at his hands. "She was...she wasn't as warm as I wanted my partner to be. She was determined she would never become pregnant. Intimacy was not high on her list. A close, loving relationship was important to me. I couldn't see my life, my future, with someone like that."

Olivia turned her head and smiled at the pictures of Chandler's children. "It seems you have a very happy life."

"That I do. And I'm grateful for it. I guess Emily's

business was her baby, her child. She's thrown everything she has into it. She's very successful. I've always wished her nothing but the best."

24

Olivia needed a hair trim and Jackie gave her the name of the person who cut and colored her hair. The stylist squeezed Olivia in around several of her customers which meant Olivia spent a good deal of time sitting and waiting while the stylist worked on other people. After the appointment at the hair salon, Olivia stopped on her way home to pick up some groceries. It was after 9pm when she pulled into the driveway.

There was heavy cloud cover and the moon was obscured. The yard was pitch black and it made Olivia feel like she was driving into an empty void. She forgot to put the porch light on before she left and the front of the house was draped in shadow. The wind was starting to pick up signaling the possibility of rain approaching.

Olivia pressed the button on the garage door opener

attached to the car visor but the door stayed closed. She pressed again. Nothing. *Ugh. The battery must need to be changed.* She pulled the Jeep close to one of the garage bays, turned the key in the ignition and shut down the engine. Olivia gathered her purse and the three grocery bags from the passenger seat, and walked along the brick walkway to the front door of John's house.

As she was taking the steps, a bag slipped from her hand and hit the floorboards of the porch. Some cans of soup tumbled out. Olivia bent and blocked them with the other bags to keep them from rolling off the porch. In her peripheral vision, she saw a man's work boots by the front door. Her eyes traveled up from the boots. Her breath caught in her throat. A man stood in the shadows of the porch blocking the entrance to the house. Olivia stumbled back and froze. Her heart pounded like a sledgehammer against her chest wall. The man was tall, broad shouldered. He took a step forward.

"I hear you're looking for me." His voice was deep.

Olivia took a step back. "What?"

"You want to talk to me?" he asked.

Olivia was silent. She wanted to run but she knew he would catch her in two strides. She tried to calm herself, tried to think.

"I'm Kenny," the man said.

"I...I..." Olivia started. Her hands were shaking. She took another small step back.

"You've been asking questions about me." The man moved forward a step.

"I...my cousins...." Olivia didn't know what to say. She was afraid to incite him.

Kenny stared at her in the darkness.

"How did you get here?" Olivia babbled. She was thinking of swinging the bags of groceries at his head if he came at her. Then run for the car. *Where did I put the car keys? Did I lock the car?*

"You wanted to find me. I made it easy for you. Here I am."

"Do you want to go someplace we can talk?" Olivia asked. "To the bar in the center of town?"

Kenny snorted. "Yeah. Imagine how that would go. Look who's back. The murderer." He walked down the porch steps and stood in front of Olivia. "Let's go around back. I don't want anyone to see us."

Olivia's mind was racing. She tried to stall. "Um...I'd like to go in and put the groceries in the kitchen. Let the dog out." Her eyes darted around the yard trying to think of how to escape.

Kenny sighed. "Where's your cell phone?"

"In my purse," Olivia said.

"Take it out. Give it to me. I don't want you calling the cops."

Olivia placed the grocery bags on the ground. She started to reach into the purse, when Kenny said, "Give me the purse. I don't feel like being sprayed with pepper spray or something."

Olivia handed over the purse. She considered bolting down the driveway but knew he'd catch her before she got to the street, so she decided to continue to gauge the situation and wait for a better moment to get away. Kenny rummaged through the purse.

"Why do women have to carry so much stuff?" His hand came out with the phone and her keys which he placed in his pocket. He tossed the purse on the porch. "Come on, let's go in the back. I saw some chairs back there." They walked to the back of the house, around the sunroom under construction, and approached the deck.

"Let's sit," Overman said. Olivia climbed the steps and Overman followed. Olivia sat in the deck chair closest to the stairs.

"Why don't you take that chair," Overman said indicating the one in the middle of the deck. Olivia moved and Overman took the chair Olivia vacated.

"I'm going to talk," he said. "Then you can ask questions. Then I'm going to leave."

Olivia nodded. "Okay," she said softly. Her anxiety decreased a notch.

"I wouldn't mind if you kept my visit to yourself. But I can't force you."

Olivia didn't say anything.

"So I got word from a friend that you've been buzzing around. Asking questions."

Olivia nodded.

"You're like a horsefly. Buzzing around pestering people."

"I've been called things like that before," Olivia said.

"I'm not surprised." Overman rubbed his forehead and started talking. "I grew up here in Howland. Me and my old man lived on Wichita Road. Rented a ranch house over there. It was a dump. My mom took off on us before I was a year old. I went to the local schools. Hung out. Got in trouble. Dropped out of high school. It wasn't for me. I haven't been back here in almost forty-five years. It feels more like a hundred, like it was somebody else's life I'm talkin' about." He took a deep breath.

"I was good for nothing back then. Drank too much, took some drugs, screwed around with girls. I had no purpose." He paused and sat quiet for a minute. "There was one girl I dated for about two years. Emily Bradford. I had no business with her. I thought she cared for me but I finally figured out that the attraction was that dating me made her parents nuts. She was from a family with money. Her dad was a doctor. The mom was a socialite or some such thing ... thought she was too good for me ... her family was too good for me. She thought I was trash." He hesitated. "She was right." He stopped talking for a while. Olivia waited.

"I needed to do something with my life. I was going nowhere. I decided maybe it would be a good idea to join the Army. So on June 5, so many years ago, I decided to go to Boston to talk to a recruiter. I didn't get very far in my junk truck. It broke down on the road, a couple of miles from my house. I tried to get it going but it was dead. I walked home, got my motorbike, and took off again. When I got to the Boston recruitment office, there were posters in the windows...of soldiers, guns. I got a big fat lump in my throat, thinking what the heck am I doing. They're going to send me to 'Nam. How long will it be before I'm killed over there?"

He swallowed and tapped his hand on his knee absent-mindedly. "So I didn't go in. I got back on my bike, drove around some. Went over to Fenway. Parked. The Sox were playing but I didn't have any money for a ticket to the game, so I walked around. I had no idea that something happening back in Howland was about to change my life."

He continued, "I had a bunch of emotions jumping around inside me back then. If you asked me in those days what those feelings were, I wouldn't have been able to explain them. But now I understand better. That day in Boston, I was disappointed with myself for not going in and talking to the recruiter even though I knew the army wasn't for me. It felt like one more thing I failed at, one more thing that spelled 'loser'. I took the motorcycle and rode back to Howland. I went to my girlfriend's house to talk to her."

"What time did you get there?" Olivia asked.

"Oh, I don't know...maybe around 8pm."

"What did you do then? Did you stay at her house?"

"We sat in her car outside her house and talked for a while. Argued, actually. She was mad because I didn't go to New York City with her that day. We had talked about going, but I hated big cities. I didn't think we had made definite plans, but she went ahead and bought the bus tickets. That annoyed me, so I backed out. I had thought about the Army for quite a while and so I told her I wanted to go to the recruiter and not waste time in New York. She was furious. She said she would go by herself. When I got back to her house later that night and I told her I didn't talk to the recruiter after all, she mocked me...said I was useless, a pussy...stuff like that. She was mean about it...nasty. That was the way she was. She could turn on a dime...one minute all sweet and nice and the next minute, angry and mean. She was always telling me how lucky I was to be with her...how so many guys wanted her, came on to her. I knew she slept around with other guys but I stayed with her. I always made sure we used protection though. I didn't want to get roped into marriage. After a while, I started wondering why the heck I was with her. I didn't need her abuse. I tried to break it off with her a few times right before the Monahans were killed, but she kept at me and I kept going back to her."

He met Olivia's eyes. "Your name's Olivia, right?"

Olivia nodded.

"So anyway, the cops found my truck broken down on the road that Mrs. Monahan drove every day to get to her house near the center of town. The police figured she stopped to give me a ride, that we must have argued over something, and that I killed them. But I was in Boston when it happened. I've got no alibi though. Plenty of people saw me, but nobody knew me, so what are you gonna do? The police thought I did it. And so did plenty of people in town."

He paused. "What kind of cold blooded monster would do that to a little girl? They think it was *me. Me.*" He sighed. "Back then I thought 'What do people see in my face? What do they see when they look at me?' That's what I wondered. They think they see a monster? A monster, that could kill someone with a knife? And then after doing it once, go ahead and do it again? Like you've got no feelings. Like you're dead inside. People thought that was me? A monster who killed a little girl?"

Overman looked right at Olivia. "A little girl." He shook his head.

"I've got a daughter, you know," he continued. "She's all grown up. She's a teacher. Second grade. I've got a son too. In college. And, a wife. For thirty years, a wife who loves me." He looked down at his hands. "Every day, I thank God for her. Everything good in my life is because of that woman. I met her and she filled me up. All those hurt, lonely, no good loser places inside me. Those holes put there by a mother who left me and a mean drunk of a father who beat me, ignored me. In those days, I had a rock, a stone, a hard lump of granite stuck in my gut, in my heart... a heavy, hard stone of sadness stuck in me from all the loss and all the hate thrown at me." He held Olivia's eyes. "My wife filled the holes of my life and wore away at that old stone in my heart until it was just a speck of dust."

Overman coughed to clear his throat. "I know you don't understand what I'm saying. You're young. Have you ever been falsely accused, Olivia?" He didn't wait for an answer. "When I was accused, a switch flipped inside me. I figured somehow or another they'd pin it on me, and even though I was innocent, that I would spend the rest of my life in prison. Because, I was a loser. I promised myself that if I got out of it, I would make something of my life. I didn't want to be that loser who was such an easy mark. The loser that people looked down on. The loser that people expected nothing from but trouble. I didn't want to be that person anymore." He took a deep breath. "I left Howland as soon as the police said I could." He swallowed hard.

"You know something, Olivia? If that woman and her

daughter didn't get killed, I would have stayed here. I would have been just like my old man, a mean, empty drunk. I never would have changed. I would have let that stone of sadness sink me."

Overman rubbed his eyes. "On June 5, that woman and her daughter saved my life."

Olivia blinked at him.

Overman let out a long sigh. "Now you can ask me questions," he said.

Olivia didn't say anything for a minute. "I... You..." She coughed to clear the emotion that had tightened her throat. Then she asked, "Would you like some tea?"

Overman stared across the darkness at her. "Okay. Could you bring it out here?"

Olivia nodded and rose from her seat to go inside and make the tea. "I'm going to let the dog out."

"Okay," Overman said. He reached into his pocket. "Here's your phone. And, your keys."

25

Olivia returned with two mugs of tea. Lily bounded out of the door and sniffed the man in the deck chair. She wagged her tail at him and licked his hand before trotting down the stairs and heading to the far side of the expansive yard.

"Nice dog," Overman said, accepting a mug of tea from Olivia.

"She's good company," Olivia said returning to her seat. She had put on a sweater and pulled it around her against the nighttime chill.

"So," Olivia said. "This has taken me by surprise. Not just you showing up here, but what you've said to me. It's not what I expected."

Lily trotted up the stairs and sat next to Overman who reached over to scratch the dog behind the ears.

"Why did you come to see me?" Olivia asked. "Why not just let things be?"

"Because *you* weren't letting things be," Overman said. "It's been almost forty-five years. I thought my association with the crime was in the past. But I suppose that was naïve. I was worried. I was worried that your questions and your interest in the case would interfere with my life...drag my family into it. Create a circus." Overman leaned forward. "I'm innocent, Olivia. But I don't have any way to prove it."

"What about DNA tests? The police recovered samples from the crime scene. If they compared your DNA to those samples, wouldn't that clear you?"

Overman shrugged. "I don't know. Maybe the samples are lost. Why haven't the police tried to contact me about that sort of thing?"

"Maybe they have tried to contact you. Maybe they can't find you," Olivia said.

"I think the police could find me if they wanted to."

"Who is the friend of yours who told you I was asking questions?" Olivia asked.

Overman hesitated. "Father Mike. Over at St. Catherine's church."

"Father Mike?" Olivia sat up. "I talked to Father Mike. He didn't say anything about you."

"He said you didn't ask about *me*."

Olivia started to speak, but stopped. She played her

conversation with Father Mike in her mind. She only remembered asking about Father Anthony and Mary.

"Some detective I am," Olivia muttered.

Overman smiled. "After the murders, Father Mike came to see me when the police started to show interest in me. I wouldn't speak to him the first time he came by. But by the second time, I was shaking with fear. We talked and talked. He became a good friend to me. He treated me with respect. Gave me advice." Overman chuckled. "I think it is his great regret that he wasn't able to turn me to God. But I do believe he's proud of me."

"You keep in touch then? He knows how to contact you obviously."

"I changed my name a few years after leaving Howland. Father Mike knows my name and where I live. We're in contact."

"What did you do after leaving here?" Olivia asked. "Where did you go? You mustn't have had much money."

"I did odd jobs. Worked in restaurants, at garages. That first year, in the off season, I rented a small cottage in Hampton Beach. It was cheap. I did whatever work I could. I started going to AA to deal with my drinking problem. It took a good while but I haven't had a drop of alcohol in thirty-five years. I moved away from New England and went to a trade school. Father Mike helped me out with money so I could go full time. I did well. I built a business, expanded. The business is successful. I started a small foundation to help underprivileged kids. I have more money than I ever dreamed."

Olivia smiled. "Oh." She sat up. "That's how your father can live at the Manor. You support him."

Overman's brow furrowed. "My father?" He nearly spat out the words.

"Yeah."

"He's alive?"

Olivia stared at Overman. "You didn't know he was alive?"

"No." Overman looked pained. "Where is he?"

"In Worcester. At the Manor Senior Community."

"How?"

"I don't know. I thought you supported him."

"I don't," Overman said.

"Well, who does? It's a very expensive place." They were quiet. "Father Mike?"

Overman shook his head. "He couldn't afford that. Anyway, he lost track of the old man. I didn't care. I didn't want anything to do with him. I thought he was dead."

"Well, he's not," Olivia said.

Overman rubbed his eyes.

They sat in silence for several minutes.

Olivia broke the quiet. "Do you have any ideas about who killed my cousins?"

"I don't," Overman said. "I have no idea at all."

Olivia looked out over the dark lawn. "What the heck

happened? How did the killer get in the car with them? Why would Mary let some guy get in the car? She must have known him, don't you think?"

"Unless someone pushed his way in or threatened her. She supposedly stopped at a hardware store on her way home. The store was just over the line in the next town. Maybe someone approached her in the parking lot?" Overman said.

"But Father Mike said that Mary and her daughter stopped by the church hall after they had been in the hardware store. She dropped off gallons of paint."

"I didn't know that," Overman said. "What time was she there?"

"I'm not sure," Olivia said. "But the timeline was that Mary dropped off paint at the church recreation hall sometime after she was seen at the hardware store which was around 2:00pm or so."

"And the murders took place between 3:00-4:00 pm, so she had to run into the killer after she stopped at the church," Overman said.

"Yeah, and the church is only two miles from the crime scene," Olivia said. "So there wasn't much time or space where she could have run into the killer."

"Someone could have jumped in the car at the traffic light, I suppose. But that would have placed the killer on the main street of town. In broad daylight. You'd think someone would have seen a guy jump into her car," Overman said.

"It could have been quick though. Just open the back door of the car and jump in. And the town wasn't so populated back then so maybe there was a lull in the traffic so nobody was around to notice," Olivia said.

"Maybe the mom took her daughter to the state park after they were at the church. Maybe they were going down to see the lake or something and ran into the bastard?"

"But the husband told the police that Mary was always at home when he returned from work," Olivia said. "She was always getting dinner started. He never knew her to go to the park alone."

"What about the husband?" Overman asked. "I guess the cops looked pretty closely at where he was?"

"Yeah. The husband checked out," Olivia said. "His whereabouts were fully accounted and vouched for." She put her mug on the armrest of her chair. "Did you ever hear anything about that young priest at the church? Father Anthony was his name. Some women in town back then thought this Father Anthony had a thing for Mary."

"Never heard much." Overman shook his head. "Somebody mentioned it to me, but I didn't care, so I didn't pay any attention to it. I remember that the ladies all had crushes on the guy. I'd see him around town...didn't know what the fuss was about."

"I heard the same thing. The women at the church seemed to think he was pretty handsome and charming. I bring it up because someone in town wondered if he had something to do with the murders."

Overman's eyes widened. "The priest?"

Olivia nodded. "I know it's hard to believe. But the last place Mary was known to have been was at the church."

"Why would the priest kill them?"

"Speculation was that Father Anthony wanted a relationship with Mary and maybe he didn't like it when she refused him."

"The cops must have cleared him though."

"The cops cleared everyone," Olivia said. "So it seems."

"Do you know where this priest is now?" Overman asked.

"No."

"Maybe it would be worth finding him. See what he has to say."

"That was going to be my next step," Olivia said. "I don't expect *he'll* wind up on my doorstep."

"I'd bet not." Overman looked down at his watch. "I'd better get a move on. Anything else you want to ask me?"

"I don't think so."

They both stood and walked down the steps.

"I came through the woods. My car is parked off the road back there." Overman pointed past the backyard.

"I'm glad you came," Olivia told him. "I'm glad things worked out for you."

"Me, too. Take care, Olivia."

"You, too."

Overman started across the grass. When he was about forty feet away, Olivia called to him. Overman turned around.

"I believe you," she said.

He nodded, and raised his hand goodbye.

Olivia watched him walk through the darkness to the back of the property. Lily trotted along beside him until he disappeared into the trees. Olivia took a deep breath and turned her face up to the sky. *The stone of sadness.* It was in her heart, too, that stone, full of grief, heavy and hard.

She couldn't let it sink her.

26

Olivia decided to call the Catholic Archdiocese of Boston to try to find Father Anthony. It took several calls and suggestions of other offices to speak with, but eventually she received an address of the church where the priest was currently assigned. Turned out, he was in Connecticut, only an hour and half away from Howland. Father Anthony Foley was the pastor of Holy Rosary Church in Eastham, Connecticut. Olivia couldn't believe her good fortune.

Olivia arranged with Jackie to let Lily into the house when she was done working on the sunroom for the day. Because Olivia wasn't sure how long the trip to Connecticut would take, she left a bowl of dry dog food for Lily in the kitchen.

Olivia drove along the quiet country roads of residential Connecticut. The road wound past stately homes with wide expanses of lawn, wooded parcels, and through small villages with quaint stores and cafes. Olivia's GPS system indicated that the church would be coming up on her right in 4.4 miles. Father Anthony did not know that she was planning to pay him a visit. Olivia felt that surprise would benefit the conversation she hoped to have with the priest. She calculated that Father Anthony would probably be in his late-sixties now. She was interested in seeing the man that so many women back in Howland had been gaga over.

Olivia took the turn into the driveway that led up a slight hill past the church and into the parking lot near the rectory. She followed the crushed stone walkway to the front door of the Greek Revival home that was now used to house the priest and conduct church business. She rang the bell and after a few minutes, a grey-haired, stooped woman opened the door.

"Yes, ma'am?" she said brightly.

Olivia chuckled to herself. She couldn't remember ever being called "ma'am" before and wondered about the woman's eyesight. "I'd like to speak with Father Anthony if he's around. I don't have an appointment."

"Well, come in, dear. I believe he's doing paperwork. Let me pop into his office. I'm sure he can see you in just a minute or two." She indicated an upholstered chair along the foyer wall.

Olivia sat and wondered why so many older women seemed to be the receptionists for church rectories. She wondered if they felt they were doing God's work which might be beneficial when they went to meet their maker.

Olivia heard footsteps approaching. A tall, dark-haired man with gray showing at the temples offered his hand. Olivia stood and shook with him. The priest's eyes were deep blue. He had dimples in his cheeks. His smile was warm and welcoming. Olivia could see how he might have charmed a whole town of women when he was young.

"I'm Father Anthony," he said.

"I'm Olivia Miller. I was wondering if you might have some time to talk."

"Are you new to town?" The priest ushered her down the hall and into a den with wide windows looking out onto flower gardens. There was a large oak desk in front of the windows and a sitting area to the right next to a fireplace. He and Olivia sat in matching chairs placed on either side of the fireplace.

"No, I don't live in Connecticut. I was hoping to speak with you about a parish you spent some time at in Massachusetts."

The priest looked curious. "How can I help you?"

"I'm from Maine, but I attend school in Massachusetts. Right now, I'm house-sitting for my cousin while he is away on business. He lives in Howland."

The priest didn't say anything.

"I understand that you were assigned to St. Catherine's Church in Howland many years ago."

"I was. I spent just a few years there."

"You were there when my cousins were murdered. Mary Monahan and her daughter, Kimmy. They attended St. Catherine's."

Father Anthony's face lost its smile. "Yes. I was there then."

"I'm talking to people who lived in town at the time. Just gathering information. Trying to understand what happened."

"I see. What can I tell you?"

"You knew Mary?"

"Yes. She was active at the church."

"What was she like?"

"She was a wonderful person, kind, caring, a loving mother. She was devoted to her kids. She always had time to lend a hand at church. She had good friends."

"Did you consider yourselves friends?"

"Yes. We were friends. We had great conversations. She was well read. We talked about everything. She had a curious mind." He paused. Olivia could see tears in his eyes. "The murders hit me hard." He blinked and cleared his throat. "It still does."

"Was anyone at the church that day? Did you see anyone around in the afternoon?" Olivia asked.

"Just a girl from the youth group. She was out jogging, passed by the church. She didn't stay but a few minutes."

Olivia said, "Reports put Mary at the church between 2pm and 3pm on the day of the murders. Did you see her? Did you notice her car?"

"I was painting the recreation room of the church hall that day. Mary was supposed to come by with some gallons of paint. We miscalculated the amount we needed and she offered to pick some up at the hardware store. She was planning to stay for an hour or so and help me paint."

"So you *did* see her?"

"No. I had been painting for a couple of hours. It was a huge space and one coat didn't cover properly. It was a hot day. Humid. Maybe the space wasn't ventilated enough because I started to feel sick, light-headed from the fumes. I went back to the rectory to get a glass of water and then I went up to my room to change my shirt. It was drenched with sweat. I sat in my chair to finish my water. I just wanted to sit for a minute hoping I would feel better." He hesitated. "I fell asleep."

"So Mary stopped at the church hall to drop off the paint," Olivia said, thinking out loud. "She must have seen that you were in the process of painting. You must have left the paint and rollers and everything in place since you only intended to be in the rectory for a few minutes?"

The priest nodded.

"Mary probably waited a bit for you to come back?" Olivia leaned forward in her chair. "I'm just thinking out loud. Mary probably went to the rectory house and rang the bell to let you know she was there. Did the house-keeper see her?"

"The housekeeper was gone. She left at noon that day. Her husband wasn't feeling well."

"What about Father Mike? And the other priest that was there at the time, what was his name?"

"Father Paul Carlson," the priest said.

"Right," Olivia said. "Wouldn't one of them have answered the door?"

"Father Mike and Father Paul had gone to the hospital to visit with a parishioner who was in for surgery. Father Paul was new, so he went along to pay the visit, to get experience doing things like that. Father Mike was his mentor."

"So you were alone in the rectory?"

"Yes. I didn't hear the door bell. I don't know if it rang or not."

Olivia sat back. "Why wouldn't Mary have stayed and painted?"

"I don't know."

Olivia's eyes widened. "Maybe she did stay. Maybe someone interrupted her."

"I don't know. Possibly," Father Anthony said.

"How long did you sleep?" Olivia asked.

"I woke up when Mike and Paul returned to the house."

"Did you go back to the church hall after you woke up? Were the gallons of paint there that Mary was supposed to bring? Had she painted? Did you notice that more painting had been done?"

The priest looked at the floor. "I did go back. The paint was there, so Mary dropped it off. I don't recall if more of the walls were painted, so maybe not. She probably didn't do any painting."

"Okay," Olivia said. "So she dropped off the paint, probably waited for you to come back to the rec hall. When you didn't, Mary probably went to the rectory and rang the bell. No one answered. She decided to leave... maybe figuring you had been called away."

"I guess that sounds right," Father Anthony said.

"She must have run into the killer right after that," Olivia said. "According to the timeline."

The priest's face was creased with worry or sadness. Olivia couldn't read the expression. She remembered that the police often will remain quiet so that the person they are speaking with will start talking to fill the silence. Olivia sat quietly and waited. Father Anthony didn't speak. Olivia was afraid he would end their meeting and she was about to ask something else when he spoke.

"I've carried guilt about this since it happened." His

voice was practically a whisper. "If I had just stayed in the church hall, Mary would have stayed too. She wouldn't have run into the killer. If I hadn't fallen asleep..." His voice choked on the words.

Olivia knew feelings of guilt and pain. *If only I had done this...if only I knew that...I should have been able to prevent what happened. I should have been there for her. If I had just been there at the right moment I could have changed the course of what happened.* Regrets. If onlys. They were heavy and hard and pulled you down, down.

"It's not your fault," Olivia told him softly.

"I know that," Father Anthony said. "People remind me of that. But somehow, sometimes, it just doesn't help all that much."

"I know that feeling." Olivia nodded. "Did you transfer to the church in California because of the murders?"

"No. The transfer was in the works for some time. We just hadn't shared it with the congregation. Father Mike felt that the people should have a chance to get to know Father Paul better...have a chance to connect with him before we told them that I was being transferred."

"So was the transfer assigned to you or did you request it?"

"Oh, no. I didn't request it. I would have been happy staying in Howland my entire life. But we go where we're needed."

"I hate to bring this up, but I need to know," Olivia said. She met Father Anthony's eyes. "Please be honest with me."

"I know what you're going to ask. I know the gossip."

"Did you have a relationship with Mary?"

"No. And it was hurtful for people to talk like that. Mary was a good woman who loved her family. She never would have engaged in anything like that."

Olivia glanced away for a second. "What I've heard matches what you say. Mary would never have done that. Forgive me for bringing this up, but the talk I heard was that you wanted a relationship. That you were pressuring her to have a relationship with you."

Father Anthony's face reddened. He didn't answer right away. "I was attracted to her, Olivia. I'll admit that to you. I've never told anyone that before." He sighed. "I was young. She was a lovely woman in every way. Smart, kind, fun, pretty. I enjoyed being around her. Sometimes I imagined what life would be like if I had chosen a different path, a career outside of the priesthood, with a wife and children. Who doesn't think about other roads that might have been taken?" He leaned forward. "But I swear to you, I was careful to remain within the bounds of friendship with Mary."

"Thank you for being honest with me," Olivia said. "Thank you for answering my questions. I know it was a painful time." They stood up. "I do appreciate it."

Father Anthony walked Olivia to her Jeep.

"Mary's murder...her daughter...it shook the very foundation of my being," he said as they stepped outside. "My faith suffered. When something like that happens, your vision of the world is altered. One can become cynical, distrustful, hopeless. Ideas of safety, security, justice are destroyed. You ask yourself how horror can befall good people. My transfer to California turned into a blessing in disguise. It helped me to heal. I was assigned to a parish where the senior priest had served in World War II. The things he saw..." Father Anthony shook his head. "We had long, long talks. It took time, but I healed."

Olivia swallowed the lump in her throat. "So what's the secret? How did you restore your faith, your feelings about the world?"

"We can't know why things like this happen. Perhaps there is no reason. Or the reason is hidden from us. As hard as it is to imagine, maybe there is something good that can come from things like this, things far-reaching and long-lasting that we aren't privy to. There is good in the world, Olivia. I looked for it...and when I found it, I held onto it."

Olivia nodded. She looked off across the front lawn of the church grounds. It sounded so simple. And, so impossible.

27

Olivia was chopping vegetables for a vegetarian shepherd's pie and Lily was pressing against Olivia's leg hopefully watching for any food item that might slip off the chopping board and into her mouth. Drool was dripping from the corner of her lip. Jackie was staying for dinner after she finished working on the sunroom for the day.

The doorbell rang. Lily barked and checked Olivia's face to see if she should keep barking or not. "Let's see who it is, Lily." Olivia picked up a dish towel and wiped her hands on it as they walked down the hallway to the front door. The heavy oak door was open to let the breeze in through the locked screened door. Olivia could see Father Mike standing on the front porch leaning on his cane. He looked up when he heard their footsteps.

"Olivia!" Father Mike called. "I'm sorry to barge in on you." His voice had an edge to it.

Olivia unlocked the screen door and opened it wide. "Come in, Father Mike. Is everything okay?"

The priest stepped in. He had a death grip on the cane. His eyes were wide and red. He couldn't hold back and a torrent of tears cascaded down the valleys of his wrinkled face.

Olivia touched his arm. "What is it? Come sit." Her voice was thin with worry.

The priest tried to collect himself as he tottered into the living room, Olivia holding tight to his arm. Father Mike half fell onto the sofa. Lily sat down in front of him, her dark eyes searching the old man's face. He took out his handkerchief and wiped at his tears.

"What's wrong?" Olivia asked. "What's happened?"

Father Mike waved his hand and shook his head. "I'm practically sick." He pressed the back of his head against the sofa.

"Do you want something to drink? Some water?" Olivia asked.

"Olivia, did you know that Kenny, through his lawyer, contacted the police and offered to go in for a DNA test?"

Olivia's eyes went wide. "No, I didn't know. He did?"

"The lawyer just called me. The police have taken Kenny into custody for the murders of Mary and Kimmy." The words caught in a sob. "The preliminary testing showed that his DNA matched the DNA in the semen collected at the crime scene." He wheezed and clutched the top of his cane with both of his hands. "The complete test results won't be back for a few weeks but the police have probable cause to arrest."

"But." Olivia's head was spinning. "There has to be a mistake."

Father Mike's eyes held Olivia's.

"How can it be? It has to be a mistake," she said again. She stared at Father Mike.

"Why did he take the test?" Father Mike asked. "Why?"

"He told you we talked?" she asked. "He must have decided to clear his name once and for all." Olivia rubbed her forehead.

"How could it be a match?" Father Mike's words traveled on just a wisp of voice. His hands shook.

"It can't be a match. It can't be." Olivia looked at the priest's white face and trembling hands. His lips were parted slightly and his breathing seemed uneven. "Father Mike, let me get you something to drink. What if I make some tea? My boyfriend's mom says tea makes everything better." She smiled weakly. She watched his face. She wasn't sure if she might have to call an ambulance.

"He shouldn't have offered to take the test," Father Mike whispered. Tears streamed over his cheeks.

"Kenny is innocent," Olivia said.

"Is he? How can he be? If the DNA matches?" The priest's face crumpled.

Olivia took his hands. "Kenny is innocent. You've known that for forty-five years. Kenny needs you now. He needs help. We'll try to figure this out."

Father Mike swallowed hard. Lily rested her chin on the priest's knee.

"I'm going to make some tea," Olivia said. "Lily will stay here with you. I'll only be a minute. We'll take the tea out on the porch. We'll sit and talk. It's going to be alright."

Father Mike nodded.

Olivia walked down the hall to the kitchen to make the tea. She choked back her own tears. She couldn't show her worry and fear to Father Mike. *Oh, no. I shouldn't have talked to Kenny. I should have left it alone. I've ruined his life.*

Jackie came through the backdoor just as Olivia was filling the teapot with shaking hands. "Hey, I was thinking of ..." she stopped short. "What the hell is wrong with you?"

Olivia stood still with the teapot in one hand. She was afraid of saying anything for fear of bursting into tears.

"Olivia?" Jackie said. "What's wrong?"

"Father Mike is in the living room," she whispered. She told Jackie what was going on. She couldn't keep tears from falling.

"What a mess," Jackie said. She took the teapot from Olivia and put it on the burner. "This can't be. Maybe the evidence got contaminated. Maybe they made some kind of mistake handling the specimen. Maybe someone is trying to frame him."

Olivia wiped her eyes on the dishtowel. "I have to pull myself together. I thought Father Mike was going to have a heart attack. I have to be strong in front of him." She locked eyes with Jackie. "What a disaster."

"You'll figure it out, Olivia. You're smart."

Olivia rolled her eyes. "I'm stupid. I should have stayed out of it."

The kettle whistled and Jackie poured the water into the two mugs standing on the counter.

"You want me to sit and talk with you two?" Jackie asked. "Put our heads together?"

"I better talk to Father Mike alone first. He is still trying to process this. Will you come out to the porch in a few minutes? Help us think this through?" Olivia picked up the mugs and noticed the vegetables she had been chopping were still on the cutting board. "Oh, the shepherd's pie. Our dinner."

"Go," Jackie said. "I'll clean up. I'll put the veggies in the fridge. We can get takeout tonight. We'll have the shepherd's pie another time. I'll work on the sunroom for a bit. Then I'll come and join you on the porch. Call me if you need me sooner."

~

OLIVIA, Father Mike, and Jackie sat together and talked and they determined that there wasn't a whole lot they could do. They assumed the lawyer would have Kenny out on bail. Father Mike would gather news as a contact person with Kenny's lawyer and would share anything of importance with Olivia. Olivia would keep digging into the case with the hopes of finding something, anything, that the lawyer might be able to use to fight the accusation.

A question hung in the air between them but no one said it out loud. A wrinkle of doubt had edged into their minds. *Was it Kenny? Was he the killer?*

28

Olivia pulled her Jeep into a space in the lot next to Emily Bradford's accounting office. The business was on the first floor of a five story brick building situated on a tree lined street in Brookline.

Something Father Anthony Foley said to Olivia had been floating around in her head. He had mentioned that a jogger stopped by the church on the afternoon of the murders. Olivia had a question that she wanted to pose to Emily and she thought she might get a more truthful answer if she appeared at the office unannounced. She opened the heavy glass door that led to the lobby and saw the finely polished door that fronted the Bradford Accounting Firm. When she approached the reception desk, a thirty something dark haired woman glanced up and smiled at Olivia.

"May I help you?"

Olivia returned the smile. "I don't have an appointment. Would Emily have a few minutes to speak with me?"

"Ms. Bradford is out of the office at the moment. I'm not sure when she'll be returning. Can I make an appointment for you?"

"Oh, I see, no. It isn't business-related," Olivia told her. "I took a chance of catching her. I'll have to give her a call."

The receptionist looked over Olivia's shoulder. "You're in luck. Here she is now, actually."

Emily Bradford whooshed into the room dressed in a fitted tan business suit and beige heels carrying a caramel colored leather briefcase, tapping away at the phone in her hand. She briefly looked up as she headed to her office and when she saw Olivia she stopped in her tracks.

"Olivia," Emily said without emotion.

"Hi. I know you're busy. I stopped by to see if we could talk for a minute."

Olivia could see a negative response start to form on Emily's face. "I'd only take a few minutes of your time," Olivia said. "I just have a couple of questions that I hoped you could answer." She took a hopeful step toward Emily.

Emily sighed. "Come into my office." She turned and headed down a hallway that had office doors lining both sides of the corridor. Emily called over her shoulder to the receptionist. "If Mr. Martin comes in, just have him sit for a minute. I won't be long."

Olivia trailed after her.

Emily flung open the corridor's last door and dropped her briefcase on a cream colored leather sofa. She waved Olivia to one of the chairs in front of the massive walnut desk.

"What can I do for you?" Emily asked as she pressed some of the keys of her laptop without looking at Olivia.

Olivia was slightly taken aback by Emily's business-like manner.

"I was wondering what you were feeling about the arrest news," Olivia said. "I assume you must have heard."

Emily stared at Olivia. "You came to ask about my feelings?"

Olivia blinked. "It's big news. I wondered what you thought of it."

Emily seemed baffled by the question. "My focus is on my business. I've been straight-out."

"Surely you've heard the news that Kenny Overman was arrested?"

Emily nodded. "Yeah, I heard it."

Olivia was becoming exasperated. "You dated. You fought with your parents over him. He's been arrested for murdering two people."

Emily leaned back against her chair. "It's ancient history. I have no connection to him."

"But once you did. Aren't you curious? Do you have any thoughts on his arrest?"

Emily fiddled with the stapler on her desk. "My first reaction was what took them so long. After all these years they make an arrest. I wondered why they didn't arrest him years ago."

"They claim his DNA matched samples from the crime scene. They didn't have that technology years ago." Emily didn't say anything so Olivia continued, "Were you surprised that Kenny was arrested?"

"Surprised? I guess not."

"Because you think he was capable of such things?"

"Because you can never really know a person." Emily shrugged.

"Do you think he did it?"

"He must have. The DNA."

"What if he was set up?" Olivia asked.

"Set up how? I don't understand."

"I don't know. Contaminated samples. Someone who just wanted the case solved."

"That would be you wouldn't it?" Emily said. "The person who just wants the case solved?"

"I don't have access to the samples," Olivia said, a tinge of annoyance in her tone.

"Your idea seems off-base. How could someone contaminate samples? Kenny showed up at the police station. He said to test him. They did. His DNA matched."

"Exactly. Why would a guilty man show up decades later and asked to be tested?"

"Conscience?"

"Really? You think so?"

"I have no idea. I'm not a psychologist," Emily said.

"Would you like to see Kenny? Talk to him?"

Emily sat up straight. "Heck, no. For what? What on earth would we have to say to each other?"

"You were friends. You had a relationship. I thought you might have things to say."

Emily shook her head. "I'm afraid not. All we needed to say to each other we said forty-five years ago. It was a fling, Olivia. There was nothing deep. I liked how dating him drove my parents crazy. He was fun for a while. There was nothing long lasting about it. I knew it. He knew it."

"Aren't you concerned about the way things have turned out for him? About what's going to happen to him?"

"Really? No," Emily said. "We all make our own beds. We all make our choices. Then we have to deal with the consequences. I've worked hard for what I have. No one gave it to me. I made a choice to be a successful business-woman...to build my business...to make investments...to take care of myself."

"You had certain advantages that Kenny never had."

"True." Emily's eyes narrowed. "I also had some disadvantages that Kenny never had."

Olivia was about to speak when Emily said, "Listen. He'll have a trial. If he didn't do it, he'll get off. Case closed."

"I need to ask you a question about the day of the murders. I talked with Father Anthony Foley recently," Olivia said.

"Anthony?" Emily's voice was shrill. "He's in the area?"

"He's at a parish in a small town in Connecticut."

"How on earth did you find him?" Emily questioned.

"I called the diocese office and asked," Olivia said. "Were you at St. Catherine's on the afternoon of the murders? Were you out jogging?"

Emily's eyes clouded. Her lips were pressed tightly together. "Why would that possibly matter?"

"Did you see Mary that day? Did you see her at the church rec hall? In the church parking lot?"

"I went to New York that day."

Olivia studied Emily's face. "Why did you stay in the city for such a short time?"

"What?" Emily spit the word out.

"You were already home when your mother returned from Boston. If you *did* go to New York, you could only have been there for less than two hours."

Emily's eyes darkened. "I don't know what Father Anthony told you but I wouldn't believe everything that comes out of his mouth." She stood up. "I really need to get back to work."

Olivia hesitated then stood up and walked to the door.

She left the building and slumped in her parked car staring into space. Emily Bradford's reaction to Kenny's arrest stumped Olivia. She was surprised at how indifferent Emily was about the turn of events. But it was a long time ago and her relationship with Kenny was based solely on how it annoyed her parents. *What did Emily mean about not believing what Father Anthony said? Why would she say that? Was Emily at St. Catherine's that day? Or did she go to New York?*

Olivia sighed and started the engine.

29

In the afternoon, Olivia and Lily walked along the old raised rail trail. Dense thickets of oaks, maples and pines soared on either side of the path. A wide lake opened to their right. Lily's ears perked up and she turned her head to Olivia.

"Go ahead," Olivia said. She knew the dog was itching to leap into that water.

With permission given, Lily raced down the hill and ran along the edge of the lake, weaving between and under brush and bushes. Olivia kept walking. She knew Lily would find her on the trail when she was finished swimming and exploring the area near the water.

Olivia pulled her camera from her pocket. She knelt and shot some wild flowers growing next to a rocky cliff rising from the side of the trail. A path veered off to the left and Olivia thought she could hear water running.

She walked that way eager to find the source of the sound, hoping for a small waterfall. She knew Lily would locate her with her keen sense of smell.

When they went for their daily walks in the woods, Lily would often venture off sometimes for fifteen minutes and then, after she had had her adventure, would come bounding up behind Olivia at full speed and then jump around as if she were trying to convey to Olivia what she had seen or done.

Olivia crouched on one knee framing a shot with her camera when she heard rustling off to the side. Expecting Lily, Olivia turned. A Jack Russell terrier zoomed out of the woods straight at her. The dog ran past, turned on a dime, and shot past again. This went on several times, back and forth, back and forth. Olivia laughed, which caused the dog to slide to a stop. The terrier stared at her for a second, leaped into the air and began its running sequence again up and down past Olivia. Olivia sat, entertained by the crazy dog's antics. She heard feet crunching and turned to see Robin from the Sports Bar Restaurant trudging up the path. She was breathing hard, her face bright pink.

"Olivia! How are you?" The dog changed direction and tore down the path towards Robin. "How do you like this crazy dog?"

Olivia stood, brushing the dirt from her butt. "Hi,

Robin. I was enjoying the show." She laughed. "I was wondering how long he could keep it up."

"Oh, gee, for hours," Robin puffed. "Why didn't we just get a tiny lap dog?" The terrier took off down the trail and the women headed in that direction. "Walk slow," Robin requested. "This dog is killing me. I need to catch my breath."

Olivia looked behind them for Lily. She had been gone longer than usual.

"Lily went down to the pond for a swim," Olivia said. "She's been gone for a while."

"She's probably enjoying the water. You know how Labs are. So how are you? Enjoying your stay at John's house?"

"Yes, it's nice to be done with school and just relax a bit. Yesterday I worked some more on cleaning John's attic. I made good progress. Lily and I take a long walk every day or we go over to the recreation area by the lake and have a swim in the evening," Olivia said. "Thank you for setting up the meeting with Dan Waters. We had a long talk the other day. He's a nice man. Finding my cousins' bodies in that field took a heavy toll on him."

"I imagine so," Robin said. "Was talking with him helpful?"

"It was," Olivia said. "But I'm really no closer to understanding what happened."

"I suppose that's why there was never an arrest," Robin said.

The women walked and chatted as the Jack Russell continued careening through the woods.

"Is that dog on speed?" Olivia asked.

Robin laughed. "I wish I could bottle whatever it has inside it."

Olivia looked over her shoulder again. "Robin, I think I should go back. Lily never stays away this long."

"We'll walk with you. My car is in that direction."

When they passed the spot on the trail where they met, Olivia called for Lily. They reached the main trail and saw an elderly couple walking slowly along. They exchanged greetings.

"Have you seen a chocolate Lab?" Olivia asked.

They shook their heads.

"I'm getting worried, Robin. Where could she be?"

"She's just got involved in watching a rabbit or something. She'll be along."

Olivia called for her every few seconds.

"This is the place where she went down to the lake." Olivia pointed.

Robin's dog tore down the embankment to the water.

"Jasper!" Robin yelled. "Ugh, he'll be a muddy mess now. Jasper!"

The dog did not respond. He disappeared into the woods.

"Damn. He always listens. Even though he acts like a lunatic, he usually comes when I call him. I had to take him to doggy training classes. Otherwise I would have gone nuts with his behavior. What's got into him? Jasper!"

"He likes the water?" Olivia asked.

"Not usually. He would rather investigate and race along the edge in the mud. He can't stay relaxed long enough to actually swim," she joked. Robin checked her watch. "I need to get him and get back to the house. Jasper!" Robin waited. "I guess I better go down there," she moaned.

"I want to take the trail that weaves along the lake that way." Olivia pointed. "The trail is raised so I can look down on the water as I go. I'm worried about Lily. If you see her while getting Jasper would you call me?"

"Sure, thing. If you find Jasper, call me."

"I will."

They parted ways and headed to different trails. Olivia started jogging, calling Lily's name as she ran. Ten minutes of searching passed without Olivia locating Lily or Jasper. She stopped to catch her breath and turned, looking all around at the woods, listening. Nothing. *Where was she? She never goes off like this. What if she's hurt? Which direction should I go?* After a minute of weighing options, Olivia thought it might be best if she headed back to the point where Lily went down to the water. Her heart was pounding with worry. She took off running back to where she started. *Where could she be?* She called Lily's name over and over.

Olivia heard something behind her. Jasper was hurtling towards her like he had been shot from a cannon.

"Jasper!"

He overshot her position, slid in the dirt trying to stop, wheeled and turned back at full speed. He barked at Olivia and rushed past.

Olivia called Robin and reported Jasper's location.

"I can't get close enough to clip Lily's leash onto him. Maybe I'll head back to where we separated. Maybe he'll follow me and you can grab him."

Olivia jogged down the trail. Jasper raced by again, barking. He halted in front Olivia, and raced back in the other direction. *Nutty dog. He ought to be in some movie. He acts like he wants me to follow him.* Olivia skidded to a stop. She called Robin again.

"He acts like I should follow him. I'm going to run after him. Come this way, Robin. Stay on the phone and I'll tell you if this ends up being a wild goose chase."

Olivia was getting winded but Jasper was still running ahead. He stopped and waited for Olivia, and then took off again. He veered down the steep embankment that led to the water. Olivia heard him rushing through the dense growth. She eased down the hill after him. Her legs were getting tangled in the vines and the bushes scratched her arms as she stumbled after the dog. Her feet were wet from the marshy ground. Jasper was howling.

"Can you hear him?" Olivia wheezed into the phone.

"Has he lost his mind?" Robin answered. "I'm going to have a heart attack trying to get to you two." Olivia could hear Robin's labored breathing. Jasper was barking now. Olivia's heart was pounding in her chest.

"Lily!" Olivia called again. Only Jasper's voice responded.

Olivia's shoe came off in the muck. She bent to retrieve it from the sucking wet mess. Hopping on one leg, she pushed it back on her foot. *Ugh.*

The pond bent to the left and a sheer rocky cliff rose high above. Olivia had to walk in the water to continue. She climbed over a fallen oak. Jasper was howling again. He was close. Olivia stumbled forward around a thicket. Jasper stood beside the rocky wall. Next to him was a chocolate colored dog.

"Lily!" Olivia called.

The Lab barked and wagged her tail. One end of a length of yellow and orange cord was tied to Lily's collar, and the other end was wrapped several times around the base of a tree.

"Lily, Lily," Olivia said when she reached the dog. She stroked the Lab's head. "What happened? Someone tied you?"

Olivia could hear Robin's voice coming from the cell

phone she had stuffed in her shorts pocket. She grabbed it.

"Robin! I found her! Someone tied her up. Where are you? Are you close?"

"I'm coming." Robin was gasping. "I could hear Jasper but now he's quiet."

"He's here next to me. Call out as you get closer and I'll direct you," Olivia's voice shook. She tried to untie the rope that was attached to Lily's collar but she couldn't loosen it. She stroked Lily's head. Jasper licked Lily's face.

"Good dog, Jasper. Good dog," Olivia told him.

Robin stumbled around the cliff wall covered in mud. She sank next to Olivia and the dogs.

"Let me catch my breath." Her face was like a beet.

"Are you okay?" Olivia asked. "Look at this, Robin. Who would do this? Tie her to a tree? What if we didn't find her? Poor thing. Who'd do this?"

"Kids, probably. Punks," Robin wheezed. "Trouble makers."

Robin reached into the fanny pack she had around her waist and retrieved a Boy Scout knife. She pulled the blade out. Olivia's eyes widened.

"I'll cut the rope," Robin said.

Olivia held the cord and Robin cut most of it off. Only a stub of rope remained on Lily's collar. Lily woofed. She slurped Olivia's face with her tongue and trotted to the pond for a drink. Jasper dashed after her. Olivia and Robin sat on the wet ground, exhausted.

"She seems okay," Olivia said. "Thank you, Robin. What if I hadn't run into you and Jasper? How would I have found her?"

"You would have thought of something," Robin said, leaning back against the cliff wall, her eyes closed.

"Are you okay?" Olivia asked.

"I just need to sit a minute." She opened her eyes. She took a deep breath. "What bastard would do that? Tie up a dog and leave her? Too many creeps around." Robin put the knife into her fanny pack. "The knife used to be my brother's. I started carrying it around when I was in college a hundred years ago. Some jerk tried to jump me one night when I was walking back to my dorm. A guy saw the altercation and chased the loser away. I've carried a knife ever since. Probably not the best idea as someone could grab it and use it on me."

The dogs returned from the pond and lay down next to the women. Olivia checked Lily over to be sure she was alright.

"So since I've been getting older, fatter and slower, I also carry this," Robin said. She pulled out her keychain with a small canister attached to it. "Pepper spray. You should get some, Olivia."

"Maybe that's a good idea." Olivia sighed and pressed

her head against her knees. Tears escaped from her eyes and rolled down her cheeks.

Robin inched along on her butt to get closer to Olivia.

"It's okay. All's well that ends well, hon. The dog's as good as new."

She put an arm around Olivia's shoulders. "And look, Jasper's actually worn out."

Olivia raised her tear stained face and saw Jasper quietly lying next to Lily. Olivia smiled. "Jasper, you're a hero."

The light was waning when the four of them trudged off the trail and onto the gravel parking lot. Their two cars were the only ones left in the lot. The dogs and the women were caked with mud and grime. They were glad no one was around to see them come out of the woods like that.

"Call the police, Olivia, and report what happened. People should know to keep their dogs close while walking here."

Robin opened the hatch of her car and Jasper jumped in like his legs were made of springs. He woofed at Lily.

"Lily's going home," Robin told him. She closed the hatch and gave Olivia a hug. "Get some pepper spray."

Olivia nodded. "Thank you. I wish there was some way to repay you. And, Jasper."

"I'm sure Jasper would love to meet up with you and Lily for a walk some day. Maybe we can plan it. But no drama next time. My heart can't take it. I'll give you a buzz some afternoon when we're on our way over here."

They hugged again. Robin drove away and Olivia and Lily got in the Jeep and headed home. But first they had to make two stops, one at the vet and the other at the police department.

~

THE SUN WAS SETTING when Olivia turned the Jeep into John's driveway. Her stomach was growling and her muscles were heavy and sore. The vet pronounced Lily fit and unharmed after her ordeal in the woods and Olivia filed a report with the police who said they would post the incident on their website to alert those people who used the park to be aware. They assured Olivia that the perpetrator was probably just a bored, local kid looking for trouble. When she reminded the officer about the dead squirrels on her front porch, he shrugged and said it was probably only coincidence that she had the misfortune of two run-ins with trouble makers. Olivia wasn't so sure that the officer was correct about the incidents being coincidence. Worry picked at the back of her mind.

When she turned into the driveway, Lily put her head out of the half-opened back window and whined to be released from the car.

"I know, girl," Olivia said. "It's been a long afternoon. You'll get your dinner as soon as we go in the house."

Olivia parked in front of the garage, grabbed her purse off the front passenger seat, and opened the car's rear door to let Lily out. Lily was caked with mud from the trails so Olivia called her to the side of the garage where the faucet and hose were. Olivia turned on the hose and held Lily by the collar as she gently ran the water over her back, legs, and underbelly. The water was warm from being inside the hose in the sun all day. Olivia unbuckled Lily's collar and Lily ran around to the back-yard. She washed the mud from the collar, turned off the hose, and walked around to the deck where she put the collar to dry in the sun. A small piece of the rope that was used to tie Lily up was still attached and Olivia decided she would need the scissors to remove it. She knew there was a spare collar in the kitchen closet and she would put that one on Lily for now.

"Come on, Lily," Olivia called. "Let's go inside and have our dinner. Enough excitement for one day."

30

"The vet was open late luckily and he was able to take a look at Lily. He gave her a clean bill of health." Olivia was talking to Joe on the phone. "The police took the information and said they would post a news blurb in the local paper and on the town local access cable station to get the word out to people to be careful in the park."

"I don't like you walking there alone, Liv," Joe said.

"I'm not going to take Lily there anymore. Jackie told me that there are lots more people who walk the rail trail located about five miles from the house. The only trouble with that one is dogs have to be leashed and I like Lily to have a chance to run free."

"It's not worth taking a chance," Joe said. "Promise you won't go back to that trail alone."

"I won't. I would never put the dog at risk." Olivia

paused. "Joe, do you think someone's trying to warn me off from looking into the murders?"

"It's possible, I guess. But who would do it? That Overman guy has plenty on his plate without chasing dogs in the woods. Is he even out on bail?"

"I'm not sure."

"It could have been random. Or maybe someone who knows you've been researching the murders and decided to try to scare you."

"I guess so," Olivia said. "What was done to Lily was so cruel. It must have been premeditated. Why else would someone carry rope while walking in the woods?"

"I don't know," Joe said. "Maybe the dog just had the misfortune to run into a nut."

Olivia stood and paced around the kitchen. "It feels like a warning."

"Stay around people when you're walking," Joe suggested. "It's safer. And lock the doors when you're in the house."

"I will. Definitely."

"You could come home, you know. Bring the dog here until John comes back from his trip."

"John will be back soon. It seems silly to go running home," Olivia said.

"It wouldn't hurt to stop investigating."

"Jackie suggested the same thing."

"Smart woman," Joe said.

"My class is starting soon. Looking into the crime gives me something to do until then. You know how I am."

"Yes, I do," Joe sighed. "Do what you have to. You don't listen to me."

"Sometimes I do," Olivia offered.

"Please don't get into any trouble."

"How can I get into trouble in just a few days?" Olivia asked.

"You'll think of a way," Joe said. "I'm going to work now. Talk to me tomorrow."

"I will."

Olivia clicked off and just as she set the phone on the kitchen table, it rang.

She glanced at it but didn't recognize the number so she decided to ignore it. She went to the back door and checked that it was locked and then turned for the hall to go check the front door. The phone was still ringing as Olivia walked by the table. She changed her mind and decided to take the call.

"Hello?"

"Olivia." The man's voice cracked. "I need to talk to you."

It was Father Anthony.

31

Olivia and Father Anthony arranged to meet the next night at a diner on the Massachusetts and Connecticut border. He wouldn't say why he needed to talk but he was adamant about having to see her.

Jackie didn't like the sound of it and insisted on accompanying Olivia to the rendezvous. She said she didn't want Olivia going alone but would wait in the car while Olivia spoke to the priest so as not to spook him.

Jackie was going to spend the night with Olivia at John's house in one of the guest bedrooms. Her own house had the beginning of a carpenter ant problem so she arranged with a bug guy to spray inside the house. Olivia invited Jackie to stay with her in order to give the house a chance to air out.

They were traveling down the Massachusetts Turnpike in the dark with rain pelting the windshield. Jackie was giving directions using the GPS on her phone.

"I'm glad you wanted to come along," Olivia told Jackie. "And it works out well since you're staying at the house with me tonight anyway." Her head was tilted forward and she was squinting at the highway. "I can't see in the dark when it rains."

"Great," Jackie said. "That's good to know."

A gust of wind rattled the Jeep.

"I could drive, you know," Jackie said.

"Why would you want to do that?" Olivia teased.

"Maybe, because you can't see?" Jackie asked.

"You're worried?" Olivia deadpanned.

"Bah." Jackie looked out the passenger side window.

"I haven't been in an accident yet," Olivia told her.

"So what do you think Father Anthony needs to talk to you about?" Jackie asked. "He just saw you a few days ago."

"He wouldn't say. Didn't hint at anything either. He just said it was important."

"Obviously he must have held back something the last time you talked."

"Do you think maybe he saw something?" Olivia asked. "Did he see Mary at the church on the day of the murders? Maybe he was afraid to admit it for some reason."

"Maybe the reason is because he killed them?" Jackie

sighed. She pointed out the window. "Here's the exit. Turn off here."

The road was empty and dark. Olivia slowed the Jeep to take the narrow twists and turns.

"I don't like this," Jackie said. "I don't like that Emily Bradford said not to believe what he says. Maybe he can't be trusted. I'm glad you're meeting him in a public place." Jackie looked at her phone GPS. "I wonder if we should turn around?"

"Why?" Olivia asked her. "Are we going the wrong way?"

"No. I mean you should skip meeting him."

"We're almost there. We came all this way. I need to hear what he has to say."

"What if you've scared him?" Jackie asked. "What if he killed your cousins?"

Olivia swallowed. She gripped the steering wheel. "Then I need to know."

The country road got wider. There was a traffic light. They passed a town hall, a post office, a Dunkin' Donuts. More stores dotted the street.

"At least there's some civilization now," Jackie said.

"Here it is." Olivia saw the lights of the diner and pulled into the parking lot. The lot was crowded. Olivia maneuvered the Jeep into an open space.

"I need to use the rest room," Jackie said. "I'll go in first, use the bathroom, get a coffee. You come inside in a minute. We'll pretend we don't know each other. Give me the keys so I can come back and sit here in the car while you talk to Anthony. Call me if he makes you uncomfortable or you feel threatened."

"Come on, what can happen to me in a diner?"

"And don't you dare leave with him," Jackie warned. "I don't care what he says."

"Oh, for heaven's sakes. I wouldn't," Olivia reassured her.

"I'll go in. When I come back out to the car, I'll keep my eye on the door watching for you."

"Don't worry," Olivia said. "We're just going to talk."

Jackie got out and ran through the rain to the door of the diner. Olivia waited a minute and then followed. She stepped through the front door of the cozy diner and closed up her umbrella while she scanned the small room looking for Father Anthony. A waitress pointed to an empty booth and Olivia walked over and sat positioning herself to face the entrance so she could see the priest when he arrived. The waitress brought a menu and a glass of water. There was a corridor that led to an addition in the back and Olivia saw Jackie come out from the restroom and order a coffee at the counter. Olivia didn't acknowledge her. She pretended to glance at the menu.

Father Anthony came through the door just as Jackie finished paying at the register. They passed each other as she left and the priest stood looking around for Olivia.

His raincoat was drenched from the downpour and his hair was wet and slicked back. Olivia raised her hand to signal him. He spotted her, went to her booth and slid into the seat opposite. His face was drawn and serious.

"I was surprised that you called," Olivia said.

"Thank you for meeting me," Anthony said. "I saw the news about Kenneth Overman."

Olivia nodded.

The waitress came over and took theirs orders for coffee and tea.

"I need to tell you something," Father Anthony said. "It probably has no relevance to the case but I need to get it off my chest. You can decide what to do with it."

Olivia had no idea what to expect. "Okay," she said.

"When we talked that last time, I told you that I went into the rectory and fell asleep."

"You didn't?" Olivia asked.

"No. I did. But I left something out that happened before I went back to the rectory." He fiddled with the silverware on his placemat.

"What was it?" Olivia asked. She wanted him to spit it out, but she didn't want him to feel pressured and change his mind about telling her.

Father Anthony took a deep breath. "There was a girl who attended church. She had just finished her first year of college. She attended the young adult group activities that we put on...hiking trips, game nights, things like that.

She...I felt like she often tried to flirt with me. She made me uncomfortable. This went on for about a year. I was always careful around her. She was aggressive in her flirtation."

He met Olivia's eyes. "One night she was the last one in the rec hall. She was helping clean up after an activity. We were in the kitchen. She was standing close to me. She started telling me how attractive I was...how she felt compelled to be near me. She leaned in and kissed me. I took a step back, but she came forward. She said something like...'I know you think I'm pretty...I know you'd like to touch me.' And she was right...in that moment with her being so close to me, touching me...I *did* want to kiss her. She took my head in her hands and kissed me hard. For a second I kissed her back. Just for a second. Then I came to my senses and pushed her away. I was horrified at what I had done. I told her it was wrong. It was a mistake. I was a priest and that I would honor my vows. I told her she needed to find a young man who would love her."

"What did she say?"

"She laughed. I didn't know if she was mocking me or she was embarrassed for kissing me. She said something like 'you're the man I want.' She acted so cocky and superior and that laugh...she frightened me."

"Then what happened?"

Anthony was sweating. He went on. "She unbuttoned

the top few buttons of her blouse and pushed the fabric back. She licked her lips. She had a smile on her face. I felt like she was teasing me. Then she turned around and left. The whole thing was unnerving. There were several other times that she tried to kiss me. I didn't know what to do...how to handle it. I was afraid to tell Father Mike because I...I don't know, I felt like...could it be something I did to encourage the girl?" He cleared his throat. "I was afraid of her...I was afraid she might make accusations against me. So I put in for a transfer to another church."

"So you did request the transfer?" Olivia asked.

Anthony nodded.

"Do you think this has something to do with the case? Why bring it up now?"

"There's something else. The day I was painting. The day of the murders. I heard someone come in. I turned around expecting Mary to be arriving with the paint. When you and I met last time, I told you a girl from the youth group dropped by that day. Well, it was that girl again. She said, 'I came to help you paint.' There was no way I was going to be alone in the rec room with her. I told her that it was inappropriate for her to be with me by herself. She came over close to me. She said she loved me and that she knew I could love her too. I started to walk away. She tried to block me. She told me to just listen. I said that I was a priest and I couldn't be with her. She said things like... just give me a chance... I'll be good to you...I need you. She was pleading with me...kept saying she loved me. I raised my voice and told her to stop. I rushed around the table to get out of there but she blocked my way. She got angry, started to cry. She said 'Who were you expecting? Mary Monahan?' I told her that Mary was planning to help paint that afternoon. She started ranting, said 'Why is it alright to paint with Mary but not with me? I see how it is. I see how you look at her. You're having an affair with her'...things like that. She was saying crazy things. She lunged at me...tried to kiss me... she pulled at my shirt...pulled at my clerical collar and yanked it off me. I had to push her back. I hit her, I think. It was awful. She said, 'We can be together...I love you... you'll love me in time.'" Father Anthony wiped at his eyes. His face contorted trying to contain the emotion.

"What happened then?" Olivia asked.

"I pulled away from her. I ran to the rectory. I was physically sick. I felt like I was going to pass out. I felt guilty. I kept playing our encounters over and over in my head trying to figure out what I had done to lead her on. I was afraid she would accuse me of wrong doing. How could I defend myself against that? It would be her word against mine. I was just a young priest. She was from a prominent family. No one would believe me. I wasn't sure what to do, so I just went to my room. I thought it best to keep it to myself. I didn't want to embarrass her family. I lay down on my bed. I was exhausted. I ended up falling asleep." He took a sip of his water. "Now I wonder if she saw something. I wonder if she saw someone approach Mary in the church parking lot. I wonder if she saw Mary's killer."

"You didn't tell the police this?" Olivia asked.

"No. I was ashamed. At the time, I didn't see how it had anything to do with what happened to Mary. In retrospect, I should have told them."

"Who was the girl? Is she still in town?"

Father Anthony swallowed. "Yes. She's still in the area. Her name is Emily Bradford."

Olivia's eyes went wide.

"Kenny Overman's old girlfriend," Father Anthony added.

Olivia leaned against the back of her seat. Her mind was racing. "Emily Bradford. Her parents would have had heart attacks if they had known."

"You know her?"

"I've met her," Olivia said. "I've met her mother and sister, too. I talked to them about my cousins." Everything Olivia had heard over the past week flashed through her mind. "I met with Emily twice. I told her that you and I spoke. Emily told me not to believe what you say."

Anthony sat up straight. He blinked. "She assumed I would tell you about her interactions with me."

"I guess so." Olivia's mind was racing. "Emily says she was in New York City that day."

"Well, she wasn't," Anthony said.

"When did you last see Emily?"

"I don't think I saw her again after the Monahans died. She stopped attending church. Then I moved out to California. I haven't seen her since the murders happened."

"When you ran into the rectory to get away from Emily... she could still have been in the rec hall when Mary and Kimmy arrived there. If someone approached them as they were getting out of their car, Emily could have seen it. But if she saw anyone and she did report it to the police, nothing came of it, since they didn't make an arrest. Or she could have seen someone and never told the police about it?"

"Overman's DNA matched the DNA from the crime scene," Father Anthony said. "At least, that's what the news reported. The two of them were dating. Maybe Emily Bradford knows something. Maybe she saw Overman at the church. What if she knows what happened? Maybe she protected him."

"Why would Kenny be at the church?" Olivia asked.

"Maybe he had some idea that Emily had gone to the church? Maybe he knew she was interested in me? He could have gone to the church to stop her from talking to me."

"Kenny says he was in Boston that day."

"He must be lying," Father Anthony said.

Olivia shook her head slowly, thinking. "I don't think so. I don't get that impression."

"Olivia, the preliminary DNA test was positive," Father Anthony said. "Maybe he was in Boston for part of that day, but he obviously returned, since evidence puts him at the crime scene. The question is did Emily see something? Did Emily see Overman? Does she know who killed the Monahans?"

Olivia stared at Anthony. What she needed to make sense of all this was right there in her mind. All the pieces were swirling around but she couldn't grab them and make them align. She just couldn't make it gel.

"I'm missing something. The clues are in front me. I just can't form the puzzle." She looked at the priest. "Was Emily's car in the rec hall parking lot?"

"Her car?" He gazed into space. "I don't know. I don't remember. I don't even remember what she drove back then. Wait. She was in jogging clothes so she probably didn't have her car."

They both sat in silence, thinking.

"Can you think of anything else?" Olivia asked.

Father Anthony shook his head.

"I guess I should head back," Olivia said. "Thank you for telling me all of this." She got up from her seat.

"Should I tell the police what I told you?" Father Anthony asked.

"It can't hurt. Maybe you should," Olivia said. "Maybe you should tell Kenny's lawyer, too."

∼

OLIVIA LEFT the diner and headed for her Jeep. A passing car's headlights shined in through the windshield and she could see Jackie sitting in the driver's seat, so she opened the passenger side door and jumped in.

"You're okay?" Jackie asked.

Olivia nodded. "He had quite the story." Olivia repeated the entire thing to Jackie while they sat in the parking lot.

"So Kenny and Emily were at the church?"

"Anthony only saw Emily. He is speculating about Kenny being around. He wonders if Emily knows something or saw something and is protecting Kenny."

"But," Jackie said. "You don't think Kenny did it."

"No," Olivia said. "I don't."

"Maybe..." Jackie's voice was soft. "Maybe you're wrong about him."

Olivia raised her eyes to Jackie and then turned away and stared out of the rain streaked windshield.

"Am I?"

Questions and doubts swirled inside her head.

32

Jackie and Olivia were silent on the drive back to Howland, each one playing events and conversations over and over in their heads. The rain had nearly stopped and, now and then, the moon peeked through the clouds. Jackie was driving Olivia's Jeep.

Jackie glanced over to see if Olivia was sleeping, but Olivia was sitting straight in the passenger seat staring intently out the windshield. Her face muscles were tense as she worked at the puzzle of who had killed her cousins.

"Maybe give it a rest," Jackie said. "Sometimes the brain comes up with an answer when you give it a break."

"Yeah, I know," Olivia said. "It's just eating at me and I can't turn it off." She rubbed her eyes. "Am I wrong about Kenny?"

"I don't know." Jackie shook her head.

"I just don't think he did it but things keep pointing to him and it makes me wonder if I'm wrong."

"I don't know if you're wrong, but something's wrong with the car," Jackie said.

"Like what? What's the matter?"

"Feels like a flat tire."

"Ugh, no," Olivia said.

Jackie pulled to the side of the road. They got out and stared at the tire, soft and flat.

"Jeez," Olivia said. She turned to go to the rear of the Jeep to access the spare, the wrench to loosen the lug nuts, and the jack. "At least it isn't pouring rain," she groaned.

With Jackie's help, Olivia changed the tire with much effort and by the time she finished, they were both wet to the skin from the drizzle.

An hour later, Jackie pulled into the driveway of John's house and she pushed the button on the visor to raise the garage door. She drove the Jeep into the bay.

"I'm beat," Jackie said.

"Thanks for driving. I'm so distracted it was good that you drove back."

Olivia opened the door into the kitchen and went to the back door that led to the deck. Lily was waiting for them. She jumped up and down to greet them.

"Such a good dog," Olivia told her as she scratched her ears.

The women changed clothes and returned to the kitchen. Jackie put water in the tea kettle and set it on the burner.

"I still want tea even though it's so damn warm and humid," Jackie said.

"I set up John's AC units in the bedrooms so at least we can have a good night's sleep tonight," Olivia said. She glanced at the wall clock. It was already 11pm. "I'm starving. I'm going to make a fried egg. Want one?"

"Yeah, sounds good."

Olivia pulled out the big frying pan and got onions and tomatoes, eggs and cheese from the fridge. She put a little butter in the pan and when it was just starting to melt she added the onions to brown. She cracked eggs into a glass bowl, added some milk, and swirled it together with a fork. She set it aside, stirred the onions, and started to dice tomatoes.

"I thought you were just frying some eggs?" Jackie said.

"It turned into omelettes," Olivia chuckled. "I think better when I'm moving around."

"Well, it works in my favor," Jackie smiled. "Smells delicious."

Olivia added the egg mixture to the pan, let it set for a minute, and used the fork to move it around the frying pan. Lily sat close to the stove, ready in case something made its way from the pan to the floor.

Olivia topped the omelettes with chopped tomatoes and cheese, and then divided it into three equal portions. She scooped some onto two plates and bent to deposit the last third into Lily's dish. Olivia and Jackie dug into the meal while sitting down at the worn, oak, kitchen table.

"Yum," Jackie pronounced.

"Thanks." Olivia smiled. She put a forkful into her mouth and said, while chewing, "How am I going to figure this out?"

"Maybe you're not. The police haven't figured it out and they've been working at it off and on for forty-five years." Jackie sipped her tea. "It might be best to just let it go."

"I don't know. I feel close. And what about the squirrels left on the porch. Someone must be feeling squeezed. I must be on to something."

"Maybe..." Jackie gave her a look. "Maybe you don't want someone feeling squeezed. If it's the killer..."

"Then I'm on the right track," Olivia said.

"Then it might be dangerous was what I was going to say."

"Do you really think so? What would the person do?" Olivia asked.

"Kill again?" Jackie suggested.

"But that would be stupid. It was forty-five years ago. Why risk it?"

"Because he's thinking you're getting close, that's why. I think you need to be concerned about your safety."

"But the police haven't been able to solve the crime," Olivia said. "How could the killer really think I would be able to figure it out? Why would he risk leaving some evidence now that might tie him back to the murders? Wouldn't it be smarter to just lay low?"

"Who knows how he thinks? Suspects know where you're staying. Overman. Father Anthony. Other people you haven't even considered who could have committed the murders. They all know you're staying here."

"I have the dog."

Jackie made a face.

"Jackie, it was decades ago. No one would be dumb enough to chance the attention by hurting me."

Jackie sighed. "Let's talk more tomorrow. I'm really tired. I need to sleep. Construction people get up early, you know."

"I'm feeling sleepy, too."

They put the dishes in the dishwasher, shut the downstairs windows, and headed off to their rooms. Olivia was glad she had turned on the AC units before leaving for Connecticut. Lily followed Olivia into the bedroom and curled up on her blanket in the corner of the room. Olivia changed into shorts and a tank top, and

climbed into bed thankful for the air conditioned coolness of the bedroom. She was sound asleep in no time.

OLIVIA'S MIND fell into a dark dream of being drugged
last summer. In her sleep, she watched, helpless, as the
needle plunged into her arm. She snapped awake and sat
bolt upright. Her head was killing her. Her stomach was
queasy and she wanted to get to the bathroom but was
afraid that moving would cause her to vomit. She eased
herself down on the mattress, hoping the feeling would
pass. She turned her head to look at Lily on the floor and
when she did, a wave of dizziness flooded her. She closed
her eyes. She just wanted to fall asleep to escape how
horrible she felt. She tried to turn onto her side but her
muscles were heavy and sluggish, like she had been
drugged.

Panic pumped adrenaline like a tidal wave through
her veins. Her heart was thudding. She used all her
strength to sit up and swing her legs over the side of the
bed. The room was spinning. Olivia put her hands on the
mattress to try to steady herself. Her stomach lurched.
She slid to the floor, grabbed for the small trash can next
to her bed, and heaved into it. She leaned back against
the bed frame and broke out in a fine sheen of sweat.

The room wouldn't stop spinning. Olivia turned her head to the dog, wondering why she hadn't come over to investigate her distress. Lily was curled on her blanket. She hadn't moved.

Olivia's body trembled, her vision blurred.

"Lily," she croaked. Lily lay still.

Olivia crawled across the pine floorboards to the dog. "Lily." Olivia jostled the Lab with her hand. Lily didn't rouse. Olivia slid onto her side and lay on the floor next to the dog, her head spinning, her stomach roiling again. *What's wrong?* Her brain screamed. *What's wrong with us?*

"Lily." She pushed at the dog again. Lily opened her eyes for less than a second and then closed them.

What the hell? What the hell?

"Jackie!" she screamed. But the AC units were running and would keep Jackie from hearing Olivia's screams.

Olivia was sure she was going to pass out. *No. No.* She pushed onto all fours and crossed the room on her hands and knees inching across the floor. The edges of her vision were fading into black. Her hearing was muffled and her body felt like it was floating. She had to get to her phone on the side table next to the bed. *Keep going. Crawl. Stay awake.*

She reached the side table and pulled on it so it would topple. It crashed over but her phone slid out of reach across the wood floor. Olivia stared at it but her vision was twinkling. *Sleep.* She began to let her muscles relax.

A vision of Brad formed in Olivia's mind. *Brad. Joe.* She moaned and struggled to stay conscious. *Help me.*

The fog in Olivia's brain swirled and broke for a second and she knew. She knew what was causing her sickness. She turned and reached for the AC tube that vented out through the window. She yanked it free. She pulled herself up and pushed the window sash open as wide as she could. Her head spun and the room swirled around her. She fell backward onto the floor and her head cracked against the wood.

With the wind knocked out of her, she lay flat for a few seconds before pushing herself to a half sitting position. She scooted herself across the floorboards on her butt. Olivia grabbed the edge of Lily's blanket in her fist and dragged it across the room, inch by inch, with the dog on top of it. She had to get her closer to the open window.

Hot, humid, but fresh air streamed into the room. Olivia went to the side window and struggled to push it up. It opened and more fresh air flooded the room.

Olivia gulped the air and slumped back onto the floor. She turned and crawled across the room. She picked up her phone as she passed it. When she reached the wall, she put her hands against it and pressed hard to balance as she stood and opened her bedroom door.

"Jackie!" she called.

Olivia slid down onto the floor again. She took deep breaths before crawling into the hallway. She moved on all fours to the guest bedroom where Jackie was sleeping. She sat on the floor for a few moments trying to force away the feeling of heaving again. She pounded her palm on Jackie's door. "Jackie!"

Olivia stared at the phone in her hand. She was disoriented. Her mouth was so dry. *Push the buttons. Push them.* She turned the phone over in her hand. She lifted her heavy finger and aimed it at the button. "9" she pushed. Her finger hovered over the numbers again before falling. "1." *Once more. Lift the hand.* Somehow the finger hit it again. "1."

The call went through. "This is Howland Emergency. What is the nature of your call?"

Olivia had to get one word out. Just one word. *Say it.* Her lips parted. "Help," Olivia whispered into the phone. "Help."

Her hand dropped to her side and her fingers released the phone onto the floor.

The dispatcher spoke. "Ma'am? Ma'am? Can you talk to me?"

Olivia looked up at the doorknob. She lifted her heavy arm and clasped it. She turned it and leaned her back against the door to push it open. She crawled into the bedroom, to the window. Olivia repeated what she had done in her own room, yanking the AC venting hose from the window. She pulled herself up and slowly pushed the window, up, up. She turned her head and whispered, her voice hoarse, "Jackie."

Jackie lay still in the bed. Olivia put her hands under Jackie's armpits and pulled. Jackie's head flopped to the side. Olivia used the last of her energy to grip Jackie in a bear hug and drag her out of the bed to the chair beside the window. *Fresh air. Breathe, damn it. Breathe, Jackie.*

Olivia's vision twinkled to black and she slumped to the floor.

The siren howled as the emergency vehicle sped down the driveway to the Colonial home.

33

Emergency workers entered the house and removed Jackie and Olivia on stretchers to the waiting ambulances which rushed them to the emergency room of the nearby hospital. They were administered oxygen during the ride. Lily was given oxygen by the fire fighters who arrived on the scene and she was transported to the Howland Veterinary Clinic where the vet decided to keep her for a couple of days.

"It was carbon monoxide, wasn't it?" Olivia asked the doctor.

"It was, indeed," the doctor reported. "And if you didn't wake up when you did, you all would have died."

Olivia was to stay in the emergency room until morning so that she could continue to receive oxygen and the doctors could monitor her blood levels. Jackie was in worse shape but it was decided that she did not need to be moved to a hospital with a hyperbaric chamber as she was responding well to oxygen therapy. She was admitted to the hospital but the doctors were confident that she could go home in about twenty-four hours. The doctors told Olivia that they were both very lucky.

Olivia thought that they would have been luckier if it hadn't happened.

A police officer arrived to speak with Olivia. "We were able to get some technicians out to the house right away. The chimney flue appears to be blocked which caused the build up of carbon monoxide. The furnace runs even though its summer."

"I know," Olivia said. "John has a tankless hot water heater so the furnace runs now and then to keep the water hot."

The officer nodded. "That's right. All the windows were shut in the house which prevented some fresh air from minimizing the effect. In the morning, someone will be back to take a look at the chimney to find out why it's blocked. In the meantime, the windows have all been opened and there is an officer stationed at the house."

"Okay. Thank you."

"Also, Ms. Miller, the carbon monoxide detectors in the house have had their batteries removed."

Olivia looked quizzical. "John would never do that. He is very conscientious."

"Did they happen to beep recently? Did you remove

the batteries and forget to replace them?" the officer asked.

"I did not." Olivia was indignant. "I understand how important it is for carbon monoxide and fire detectors to be in good shape. I wouldn't forget to replace any batteries."

"Well, you should speak to your cousin about keeping up with the CO_2 detectors."

Olivia stayed quiet. She knew John would not remove batteries and forget to replace them. She wished she could get back to the house and inspect the detectors herself but the doctors insisted she remain in the emergency room for four more hours.

"What time will the technician be at the house to check the chimney? I'd like to be there."

"He is supposed to be there around 8am," the officer said.

34

At 7am, Olivia was discharged. She went up to the fourth floor to check on Jackie. They chatted for a few minutes and Olivia told her what the officer had relayed. She told Jackie she would come back and visit with her after she heard from the technician about what was blocking the chimney. She also told her about the carbon monoxide detectors missing their batteries.

"I don't think John would forget to put batteries in them," Olivia said.

"He must have though, since they're missing," Jackie said.

"I'm going to call John after I hear from the technician. I'll be back soon." Olivia gave Jackie a hug.

"Thank you," Jackie whispered. "If not for you..."

"If not for me, you wouldn't have been staying at the house," Olivia said.

She went down to the hospital lobby and out to the front circular driveway where taxis were parked. She approached one, got in, and was back at John's house in fifteen minutes.

A police officer was sitting on the front porch and Olivia greeted him just as a truck pulled into the driveway. A technician got out. Olivia and the officer walked to the truck.

"There's a ladder in back," Olivia told him. "We have construction work being done. You can use it to get up to the roof."

"Great. I'll leave mine on the truck then."

The three of them walked to the back of the house. The ladder was lying in the grass and the technician set it against the sunroom. He climbed up to the sunroom roof and, from there he swung up onto the main roof. He inched to the chimney.

He called down to Olivia and the officer. "Well, that was easy." He held up a large tool box. He eased back down to the sunroom roof, backed onto the ladder carrying the box, and stepped to the ground. "This was set across the chimney. It was completely blocked. One of the workers must have set it there and forgot to take it away when he finished."

Olivia stared up at the roof.

"Problem solved," the officer said.

"Why would a worker be up on the main roof?" Olivia asked. "The sunroom is the only thing being worked on."

"One of the workers had to be up there," the technician said. "The toolbox didn't fly up there itself."

"It doesn't make any sense," Olivia said.

"Talk to the workers. Ask why. Maybe one of them noticed a loose shingle."

"And tell them never to leave something blocking the chimney, for Pete's sake," the officer said. "We almost had two dead people here last night."

"That would have messed with the construction company's insurance rates," the technician said.

Olivia was scowling. She needed to talk to Jackie. But first she went into the house and looked at the carbon monoxide detector in the upstairs hall. She pulled it out of the electric outlet. *If it was plugged into an electrical outlet, why didn't it work? Batteries or no batteries. There wasn't a power outage.* Olivia opened it. The batteries were missing. She pushed the small panel aside next to where the batteries should have been inserted. Not only were the batteries missing, but so was everything else inside the thing. All the innards had been removed.

A chill ran down Olivia's spine.

She whirled, ran down the stairs, opened the door to the garage, got in her Jeep still holding the carbon monoxide detector, and roared out of the garage. She sped down the driveway and headed for the hospital.

~

OLIVIA SAT on Jackie's hospital bed. Jackie was holding the CO2 detector.

"Remember how I said you should be concerned for your safety, that you might be putting the squeeze on someone?" Jackie asked.

"No. Did you say that?" Olivia made a vain attempt to lighten the mood.

"Olivia." Jackie was stern.

"Why would someone do this? Why would they risk getting caught?" Olivia asked. "Could it be unrelated to the killings? Is it some nut?"

"It's a nut all right. One that has killed before."

"I don't know," Olivia said. "Check with your workers, Jackie. Could one of them have left the toolbox on the chimney?"

"They wouldn't. They're well-versed in safety rules."

"Ask them anyway if someone went up to the main roof. We have to eliminate them as the cause for the chimney being blocked." She thought for a moment. "But who disabled the CO2 detectors?"

"My guys didn't handle the CO_2 detectors," Jackie said. "That's for sure."

"Then I'd better start worrying because somebody besides us has been in the house."

~

OLIVIA WENT down to the hospital cafeteria to get two teas while Jackie called her employees. By the time Olivia returned to the room, Jackie had spoken with each of her guys.

"So?" Olivia asked.

"No one went up to the chimney."

Olivia removed the cover from the cup and sipped the hot tea. She looked at Jackie. "It's adding up to trouble."

"I'd say so." Jackie said.

"Someone went up to the chimney," Olivia said. "But it wasn't one of your guys."

"You need to tell the police."

"They won't do anything. What can they do? Assign a cop to tail me? Keep a cop at the house? They won't do any of that. They'll just say to call 911 if something is weird."

"Tell them anyway."

"I will, but I need to think. Someone feels squeezed. Enough to kill the person who's squeezing him." She pushed her hair back from her face. "It was clever, Jackie. Carbon monoxide. Makes it seem like an accident. Keeps the attention away from whoever did it."

"It certainly was clever. When did they do it, though? While we were in Connecticut?"

"It seems like it had to be done while we were in Connecticut. I was home most of the day. The workers were there too."

Jackie nodded.

"Somebody had to get up to the roof and get into the house to tamper with the CO_2 detectors," Olivia said. "It wouldn't take long to do those two things. I had left some of the windows open a crack while we were gone. That's why we didn't react to the carbon monoxide right away. I shut the windows after we ate the omelettes and right before we went to bed."

"But we might have kept the windows open," Jackie said. "Then the carbon monoxide wouldn't have affected us. The person who did this didn't know if we would shut the windows or not."

"The person figured I'd shut the windows sometime. The carbon monoxide would have done its job eventually," Olivia said. "Whoever did it knew that if it wasn't last night, it would be another night soon."

"It could have been Overman. He's out on bail. He could have been watching the house," Jackie said.

"But if Kenny killed my cousins why would he ask for

the DNA test?" Olivia asked. "Maybe someone is framing him."

"Who, though?" Jackie asked. "It would have to be someone important to frame him." Jackie sipped her tea. "Wait, maybe Overman knew the police were getting close to asking him for a DNA sample. Maybe his lawyer told him to go along with it to seem innocent. Maybe he has some made-up alibi. Maybe they planned to say someone had tampered with the evidence."

"My head is swimming," Olivia said. "I don't know what to think. What about Father Anthony?"

"But you were with him," Jackie said. "He couldn't have messed with the chimney."

"We stopped to change the tire on the way home. Anthony left the diner when we did. He could have made it back to the house before we did."

They thought for a few minutes.

"Did he arrange the meeting as a sort of alibi? No one would suspect he tampered with the house because he met me in a public place. People saw us. But he could have made it back here before we did," Olivia said.

"But he didn't know we would have to stop on the way back," Jackie said.

Olivia sat straight, her eyes wide. Her voice was excited. "Maybe Anthony caused the flat tire. To buy him time to block the chimney. You and I were in the diner before he showed up. He could have got to the tire before he came in to meet me."

Jackie looked stunned. "Does he know what kind of car you drive?"

"He walked me to my Jeep the day I went to his church to see him. Maybe he was in the parking lot of the diner waiting for us to arrive. I don't know what car he drives. I wouldn't have noticed him if he was sitting in his car waiting."

Jackie shuddered. "This is too dangerous. Olivia, you need to stay at my house. You shouldn't stay alone."

Olivia leveled her eyes at Jackie. "Then I'll put you at risk again."

"You cannot stay at John's house by yourself. I won't have it. We don't know what's going on. It could be someone we haven't even thought of."

"Jackie..."

"Wait. We can stay at my parent's house. Lily, too. For a few days. Until we get a handle on this."

Olivia looked out the window. She thought of last summer. Her stomach clenched. Anxiety and fear flooded her body. She closed her eyes. *I should have left this alone.*

"Olivia," Jackie's voice was firm. "I mean it."

"Okay," Olivia said. Her voice was small. She turned to Jackie. "You're right. It would be better to stay with your parents. More people around is better. More eyes watching things. Your parents won't mind?"

"They love excitement."

"Then they better meet me," Olivia said. "Excitement is my middle name." She didn't smile.

35

Jackie was discharged from the hospital the following day. Olivia picked Lily up from the vet and they all moved in with Jackie's parents. The parents were happy to have the houseguests. Everyone made dinner together and then they all sat around the table and played cards for a few hours. Lily watched.

Olivia had a long talk with John about what was going on. He was horrified and told her to stay at Jackie's with Lily until he came back home. Olivia also reported to Brad and Joe about what had happened. She tried to downplay the whole thing but Joe wanted to drive down to Howland immediately to pick her up. Brad agreed with Joe that she needed to come back to Ogunquit where it was safe.

"It wasn't safe there last summer," Olivia said.

Brad groaned. "It's safe here now. Please come home."

"I will. Soon."

"Liv..."

"Brad, the police know what's going on. I'm with Jackie's parents. I'm not alone. Everything will be okay." She was trying to convince herself too. "John will be back soon. Then I'll go to Cambridge to start my summer class. When the class is over, I'll come home."

"Please don't stay alone," Brad said softly. "Please, Liv. Stay there with Jackie's folks. Promise me."

"I promise."

THE NEXT MORNING, Olivia walked out of the Howland Pharmacy with a bottle of aspirin for herself and a prescription for Jackie. She was about to get into her Jeep when she saw Isabel Bradford sitting on a bench outside of the medical building attached to the pharmacy.

"Mrs. Bradford," Olivia said.

"Oh, Olivia. Hello."

"Is everything okay?"

"If you mean, am I, practically a cripple, alright sitting here, then the answer is no. This bench is killing me. That fool of an assistant of mine is late picking me up."

"Can I give you a lift?"

Mrs. Bradford's scowl softened. "Would you? How kind. I accept." She held out her elbow to Olivia, who gently helped Mrs. Bradford rise from the bench. She led her to the passenger side of the Jeep and opened the door for her.

"Would you like to use my phone to call your assistant?"

"I would not. Let her get here, whenever that may be, and wonder where I am."

Olivia backed out of the parking spot and swung out onto the main street.

"I appreciate the ride home," Mrs. Bradford told her.

"I'm glad to do it."

"You must be pleased with the recent news reports."

Olivia shot her a quick glance. "How do you mean?"

"Overman. He's been taken in for the murders," Mrs. Bradford said. "You must be pleased that there is closure on the case."

"Well, there still has to be a trial. He hasn't been convicted."

Mrs. Bradford snorted. "Formalities. The man is on his way to prison. The DNA evidence has put the nail in his coffin." The old woman watched the scenery pass by. "He is more resourceful than I suspected."

"Why do you say that?"

"How did he get back to Howland from Boston so quickly?" Mrs. Bradford asked.

"He says he was in Boston until evening."

"Well, he was there until afternoon at least."

"How do you know that?"

"I saw him."

Olivia slammed the brakes causing the car to slide to the right shoulder of the road and jerk to a stop.

"My god," Mrs. Bradford cried putting her hands out toward the dashboard.

"What did you say?" Olivia's voice was sharp.

"I said, 'my god.' What on earth kind of driving is that? Are you trying to kill us?"

"What did you say about Kenny?" Olivia demanded.

The old woman looked confused for a moment. "What?"

"You said you saw Kenny."

"Yes."

Where?"

"In Boston."

"When?"

"The day the Monahans were killed."

"You saw him in Boston that day? How?" Olivia asked.

"I saw him from the window of the hair salon we frequented. He was on his motorcycle, parked on the side of the street," Mrs. Bradford said.

"What was he doing?"

"Nothing. He was just sitting there."

"What time was it? Do you remember?"

"Of course, I remember. Even though my body has betrayed me, Olivia, I still have my faculties, you know."

"What time was it?"

"It was three o'clock."

"How can you possibly remember that? It was forty-five years ago."

"My friend and I met in Boston weekly. Every Tuesday. We had standing appointments at the salon. At three o'clock. We had our hair done, then we would go shopping, and after that, we would have dinner."

Olivia stared at her. She couldn't believe what she was hearing. "If you saw him at three o'clock, it would be impossible for him to have made it back to Howland in time to kill them."

"Not impossible."

"No? What did he do? Drive ninety miles an hour on that old motorbike of his?"

"How do I know?"

"Did you tell the police you saw him?"

"I did not."

Olivia's eyes went wide. "Why, not?"

Mrs. Bradford sniffed. "They didn't ask."

"This is ridiculous. You have information that confirms Kenny's whereabouts. You're withholding vital information."

"What if I was wrong?"

"You seemed pretty certain a moment ago. Why didn't you tell the police?" Olivia asked.

"How did I know if he was able to get back to Howland in time to kill them?" She batted at the air with her bony hands. "No one cared about him. He was inconsequential. If he didn't kill them, he would have committed some crime in the future. He was useless, ruined by that drunk of a father. If he was arrested and locked up, it would have been best for society."

"You mean it would have been best for your family," Olivia said.

"Don't accuse me of wrongdoing. I take care of my family. I wanted him out of our lives," she sneered.

"So, the hell with him? Let him rot in prison for a crime he didn't commit?" Olivia said. "You can't be judge and jury."

Mrs. Bradford collected herself. "None of this matters, my dear. The man's DNA was found at the crime scene. Somehow he found a way to get back to Howland in time."

Olivia was fuming. "Innocent until proven guilty."

"True," Mrs. Bradford said. "It is also true that it shouldn't take the prosecutors very long to put Overman away."

"You need to tell the police that you saw him."

"I will not."

"Then I'll tell them what you told me."

"Do what you must, Olivia, but I will deny it. Besides, what jury would believe the rantings of an old woman?" She smiled sweetly. "Now, may we continue our drive to my home?"

"Get out." Olivia spit the words out. "Get out of my car and walk home."

Mrs. Bradford turned to look at Olivia with wide eyes, incredulous that Olivia would leave an infirm elderly woman alone on the side of a country road, miles from her home.

"What do I care what happens to you?" Olivia said.

The old woman opened her mouth, horrified.

"Don't worry," Olivia said pushing on the gas pedal and edging back into the street. "Unlike *you*, I wouldn't abandon someone."

Neither one spoke for the remainder of the ride to the Bradford home. Olivia pulled into the long driveway and stopped at the front door of the mansion. She got out, her face like stone, and walked around to the passenger side of her car. She opened the door to assist Mrs. Bradford.

Angela burst through the front door of the home with Mrs. Bradford's assistant trailing at her heels.

"Mother, for Pete's sake." Angela stood next to Olivia and reached into the car to take her mother's arm.

Not waiting for a reply from her mother, Angela

turned to Olivia. "Thank you for bringing her home. Where did you find her?"

"I *am* able to speak, you know, Angela," Mrs. Bradford said. "You can ask me the question."

She pulled her arms away from Olivia and Angela, adjusted her cane and started to move slowly towards the front door. The women exchanged looks and Angela sighed.

Mrs. Bradford continued, "I was at the doctor's office."

"Lindsey got a call from the doctor's office saying you would not allow a blood test and that you had left the building. When Lindsey arrived, you were gone. You can imagine how upset she was when she couldn't find you," Angela scolded.

Mrs. Bradford gave Lindsey a wilting look. "No, I can't imagine how upset she was."

"I was leaving the pharmacy and saw your mother sitting on the bench there. I offered her a ride home," Olivia told her.

Angela touched Olivia's arm. "Thank you. I was becoming frantic."

"Oh, Angela, how dramatic," Mrs. Bradford scoffed. Lindsey was helping her up the front steps.

"Hold on. You need to return to the doctor's for that blood test," Angela said.

"I will not," Mrs. Bradford said.

"In fact you have to go right now," Angela told her. "Lindsey will take you back."

Mrs. Bradford glared at Angela.

"Your prescriptions have run out and they won't refill them without the blood test."

It was quiet for a minute while the Bradford women exchanged stern looks. Lindsey broke the silence.

"I'll help you to my car, Mrs. Bradford. We'll be back before you know it." Lindsey took the old woman's arm and steered her to the car. When Mrs. Bradford was ushered into the front passenger seat and the door was shut, Angela turned to Olivia.

"She will be the death of me. She becomes more belligerent every day."

Olivia didn't tell Angela just how belligerent Mrs. Bradford had been in the car when she refused to tell the police about Kenny Overman's whereabouts forty-five years ago.

"Won't you come in, Olivia? There's iced tea in the refrigerator."

Olivia started to protest but Angela cut her off. "Please. It would be nice to sit and chat with someone who isn't always so negative and pessimistic."

"Okay. Iced tea would be nice." They walked into the foyer of the mansion, down the hall, and into the kitchen.

"I shouldn't speak ill of mother," Angela said. "The effects of aging are quite a struggle for a woman who was once so active and involved." She removed two tall glasses from the cabinet, filled them with ice and poured the tea over the cubes. She handed a glass to Olivia.

"Let's sit outside on the terrace," Angela suggested.

When they were comfortably settled in the chairs overlooking the pool, Olivia spoke.

"Angela, on the drive over here with your mother she told me something that disturbed me."

"What on earth was it?" Angela asked, her face lined with tension.

Olivia put her glass on the side table. "Years ago, did your mother go into Boston every week with a friend?"

Angela's face relaxed. "Yes, she did. She and her friend, Pauline, would meet in town every week. They would get their hair done, then shop and have dinner. Mother would return around 8:30 or 9 at night. Woe to anyone who tried to interfere with that standing date." Angela chuckled and took a sip from her glass.

"Is Pauline still alive?" Olivia asked.

"No, she isn't. She passed away about ten years ago. Mother and Pauline continued to meet in the city each week until Pauline got sick. Why do you ask? Did mother mention Pauline?"

"Not by name. She mentioned a friend she met in Boston each week," Olivia answered.

"What did she say that disturbed you?"

Olivia didn't reply right away, weighing what she wanted to say.

"Your mother told me she was in Boston on the day my cousins were murdered."

"Did she? It must have been a Tuesday then. Tuesday was the day she met Pauline each week."

"Do you remember the day? What you were doing that day?" Olivia asked.

Angela looked surprised at the question.

"Yes, I remember some of the day. I was here in the afternoon. It was hot. My son and I came over to use the pool. He was only two at the time, but he loved the water." She smiled wistfully.

"Who else was here when you were swimming?" Olivia asked.

"No one. We had the house to ourselves. Mother had gone into Boston and dad was at work."

"Where was your sister?" Olivia asked.

"She wasn't here." Angela paused. "Oh, she went to New York City that day."

"Alone?"

Angela nodded. "Overman was supposed to go with her, but he backed out at the last minute."

"Do you know when Emily got home that day?"

"No, I don't. I wasn't here when Emily got home. I took my son back to our house for a nap." Angela's face clouded over. "But mother and Emily had that altercation that evening. You remember mother told you about the fireplace incident when you were here last?"

Olivia nodded.

"Pauline took ill that afternoon. Mother came home earlier than usual. Emily was here when mother arrived. I'm not sure what time it was. But it had to be before 8:30 at night."

"Could you make a guess about the time?"

"Mother said she hadn't had dinner with Pauline. She said that Pauline felt ill while they were shopping. Their dinner would often last about two hours. Driving home usually takes about thirty-five minutes but if Mother left before dinner she would have hit the commuter traffic, so it would have taken her longer to get home. I don't know. Maybe six or six-thirty that evening? Why don't you ask mother?"

"I will," Olivia said.

"Does the time matter?" Angela asked.

"I don't know what matters," Olivia said. "When your mother arrived home, Emily was here, standing at the fireplace?"

Angela nodded. "That's what she told me."

"It takes about four hours to get to New York by bus," Olivia said. "Emily would have had to leave the city before 2pm to have arrived home before your mother returned from Boston. Emily didn't spend much of the day in New York."

"I don't know. She left here early that day. I think the bus was at 8am or something. I remember because Emily had been complaining about having to get up so early to get the bus." Angela smiled and shook her head. "But that was nothing new. Emily was always complaining about something." She took another sip of her iced tea. "But what was it that mother said that disturbed you, Olivia?" Angela asked.

"Your mother said she saw Kenny Overman in Boston that day."

"Did she?"

Olivia nodded.

"I didn't know this," Angela said. "I never heard that mother saw Overman in the city."

"She didn't tell the police," Olivia said.

Angela's eyes widened.

"She won't tell them now either."

"Why, on earth, not?" Angela asked.

Olivia shrugged. "Back then, I guess, she thought it would be best for society if he was locked up."

Angela groaned and closed her eyes. When she opened them, she asked, "Why won't she tell the police now?"

"I suppose she feels the same way."

"Oh, no," Angela said. "I'll talk to her. She can't withhold information."

"You know that Kenny was taken into custody?" Olivia asked.

"I saw the news, yes," Angela answered. "Are you relieved, Olivia? That the killer has been caught?"

Olivia shifted her gaze out over the pool. "No. I'm not."

"But now the case will be solved. Isn't that what you wanted?" Angela spoke softly.

"Your mother said that she saw Overman in Boston around three."

Angela looked questioning.

"I don't believe he could have gotten back to Howland in time to kill my cousins."

Angela looked pensive. "But he must have returned to Howland in time since his DNA was found at the scene. The Monahans were killed between 3:00 and 4:00pm. He could have made it back. Or maybe mother was mistaken about seeing him in Boston."

"Kenny came to see me not long ago," Olivia said.

Angela leaned forward. "He did?"

"He told me his side of things." Olivia paused. "I don't believe he did it."

"But. But his DNA."

"I know. I know." Olivia passed her hand over her forehead. "I don't know, Angela." Olivia shook her head. "He didn't do it."

"He must have done it, Olivia."

Olivia met Angela's eyes and shook her head. "This is a big mess. It's my fault. I should have left it alone. Now an innocent man is going to go to jail." Olivia's eyes misted over.

"Olivia, Overman could be charming...persuasive. When he talked to you..."

"No. I believe him."

"I heard Overman is out on bail," Angela said.

Olivia nodded and slumped against the chair back. "I wish there was something I could do to help."

"Maybe you'll think of something." Angela tried to be encouraging.

They sat in silence for a minute.

"Did you ever ask your sister about the fight she had at the fireplace with your mother?" Olivia asked.

Angela looked down at her hands. "Mother called me that night...after the fight. She was beside herself. I drove over after our phone conversation. She wanted to talk. When I pulled up the driveway and approached the garages, my headlights caught Emily's car parked in front of one of the bays. The windows were steamed up." Angela cleared her throat. "Emily and Overman were in the car having sex. I was livid. First, Emily hits mother and then has the nerve to have sex with Overman right outside the front door of the house." Angela shook her head. "She was so disrespectful. I'm sure she hoped that mother or dad would find her out there with Overman."

She took a sip of her tea. "I parked my car on the far side of the parking pad away from Emily's car. I got out and when I reached the portico of the house, Overman slammed the back door of Emily's car, got on his motorcycle and rode away. I went inside and went to the kitchen looking for mother. I heard Emily come in the front door and go upstairs."

"Did you speak with your mother?"

"Eventually. She was in the shower. I was furious with Emily so I went up to her room. The door was closed. I knocked. I asked her to let me in. I didn't let on how angry I was. I was all sweet and gentle. Emily opened the door and let me in. I told her that mother called me and asked me to come over. I played dumb. I ignored the fact that I knew she and Overman were in the back seat of the car together. I asked what had happened with mother. Emily put on a show...yelling...blamed mother for the argument. She said mother hit her so she hit her back and mother fell and smacked her head. It was an accident that she fell. She didn't intend to push her that hard. She said the parents were smothering her, never trusted her, treated her like a child."

"I told Emily that she might want to just try and get along with mother and dad. That she would be able to get her own place after graduating college. Emily didn't like that suggestion. She started in on me...that I always took their side...never defended her."

Angela's face was lined with sadness. "I loved Emily. Loved her spunk. But her personality clashed terribly with my parents. They did smother her. They were very controlling. I hated the turmoil that went on. I always felt like I was taking sides. I didn't know how to mediate the mess between them. I was always worried about Emily. She drank, slept around. Maybe she did drugs. Her rebellious behavior was because of mother's iron fist. That night Emily had on a long kimono that father had brought each of us from a trip to Asia...it was like a bathrobe, it had wide droopy sleeves. Emily had it on over her sundress. I think she put it on to hide the fact that she had bruises on her wrist."

Olivia asked, "Bruises?"

"When Emily reached for something on her desk I saw cuts and bruises on her wrist. I asked her what happened. She told me that she fell. I didn't believe her. I asked if Overman had hurt her." Tears welled in Angela's eyes. "She pushed me. Told me to leave her the hell alone. Told me to mind my own business. Said to get out." Tears spilled over.

"You think Kenny had been rough with her?"

"I worried that he had hurt her. I knew she would try to protect him. She wouldn't tell me if he hurt her, but I think he did."

"Had you ever noticed bruises on her before?"

"No, but I didn't really ever have a chance to notice.

We didn't spend much time together." Angela's face was lined with sadness. "I didn't have the relationship with my sister that I always hoped for. I really don't think she ever liked me."

"I'm sorry, Angela," Olivia said, her voice soft. Her mind was racing. *Did Kenny hurt Emily? Why would he hurt her?*

36

Jackie and Olivia were riding in Jackie's red truck heading to the center of town for dinner.

"So I think Emily is holding back information," Olivia said. "When I was at her office and I told her I'd spoken with Father Anthony and then I asked her straight out, were you at the church on the day of the murders, she got a cold look on her face and told me not to believe what Father Anthony said."

"Strange," Jackie said. "Does she think the priest is telling lies?"

"I don't know. Does Emily believe that Father Anthony is hiding something?"

"Why doesn't she just tell you what she thinks he's lied about?" Jackie asked.

"I think she knows something," Olivia said. "Maybe she didn't go to New York like she claims. Maybe she was at the church. Did she see someone that day at St. Cather-ine's? Hear something? Is she protecting someone?" Her eyes widened and she turned to Jackie, her voice excited. "Remember I told you that Emily's sister saw cuts and bruises on Emily...that she suspected Kenny had hurt her? Could someone have threatened Emily into silence? Is that why she never wanted a family? Is she afraid someone would try to hurt them to keep her quiet? I need to talk to her again."

Jackie shot Olivia a glance. "I don't think she'll talk to you. Sounds like you got her angry last time."

"Do you think she's still at work?" Olivia checked the time on her cell phone. "People say she's a workaholic."

"It's kind of late, but maybe. Why? You want to go now?"

"Would you mind, Jackie? I thought if she was still in the office, I could just show up. She's probably alone there...everyone else would have left by now. Maybe I could get her to talk to me."

"I don't know. I don't think she will. We can drive over if you want to give it a try."

It's about twenty-five minutes away," Olivia said. "In Brookline. Afterwards, we could get a bite to eat."

"Okay. But I don't think she's going to talk." Jackie shook her head. "How do I get there?"

Olivia gave the directions and thirty minutes later they pulled into the accounting firm's parking lot. There were a few cars parked and some lights could be seen in the building's windows.

"Which floor is Emily's firm on?" Jackie asked.

"The first. She owns the building. She rents the other floors out to different businesses." Olivia craned her neck to look around at the parked cars. "I don't see Emily's car."

"What do you want to do?"

"Let's go see if anyone is in there."

Just as Olivia reached for the door handle, she spotted a woman leaving the building. The woman was carrying a stack of papers and folders in her arms. "That's someone from Emily's office. I'm going to go talk to her." Olivia jumped from the passenger seat and jogged over to the woman who was just about to open the back door of her car.

"Excuse me," Olivia called. The woman startled and wheeled towards Olivia who was coming up behind her. "Hi. I was here the other day to speak to Emily. I'm Olivia Miller."

"Oh." The woman's brow was furrowed. Her voice was tinged with annoyance.

"Sorry to bother you but I was...."

The woman fumbled with the door handle while balancing the load of papers.

"Here, let me help," Olivia said and opened the rear

door so the woman could plop the papers on the back seat. "Is Emily still in the office? Is she working late?"

The woman straightened. "Emily isn't, but I was."

"Oh." Olivia was disappointed. "What time does Emily usually come in to work in the morning?"

"She gets here early."

"Like 7am?"

"Earlier." The woman was searching in her purse. It was clear she wasn't interested in conversing with Olivia.

"Do you think it would be okay for me to come by early tomorrow morning?"

"I don't know." The woman opened the driver side door. "Why don't you just make an appointment?"

"I only wanted to see her for a quick minute."

"That's all you'd get from her anyway." The woman got into her car.

"I guess I need to make an appointment then?"

"Not with me," the woman said. "I just quit. I cannot stand that woman for one more day. She's a witch. I thought working for a woman would be great, but she may as well be a man. She puts everything on me. She's always leaving the office to go running or biking. Training for that stupid triathlon." She made a face. "I need to get going." The woman started the engine. "Call the receptionist and make an appointment." She backed out of the space leaving Olivia standing there.

Jackie walked over to Olivia who was watching the car drive away. "I take it Emily's not here."

"That was a weird exchange." Olivia told Jackie how the woman was hurried and unhelpful.

"Not good qualities for a receptionist," Jackie said.

"I think she was the office manager or something. She seems really annoyed with Emily. She called her a bitch and said, 'she's worse than a man.'"

Jackie shrugged. "Maybe Emily might not understand that it's possible to run a business and still be nice to people?"

"Yeah. Well, that was a waste of time," Olivia said.

"Let's go eat," Jackie said and they walked back to the car.

37

On Saturday, Olivia and Jackie made a picnic lunch of sandwiches, pickles, cut up veggies, water, chocolate chip cookies, and cherries and strawberries. They packed a snack for Lily and a bowl for water. The women changed into bathing suits and grabbed beach towels and a Frisbee. They loaded everything into Jackie's truck and opened the door to the truck's passenger cab so that Lily could sit back there. Jackie knew of a small, clear lake situated near Walden Pond in Concord that was unknown to most people in the area and where they would be able to swim with Lily.

The drive took about thirty-five minutes. Jackie parked well off the side of the road next to a trail that wound through the woods to the lake. The scent of pines filled the air. The dog ran a short distance ahead with her nose close to the ground, intrigued by the new smells along the pathway. They walked for about ten minutes to a smaller trail that led to the lake. A thin, sandy beach hugged the edge of the water. A large grassy field spread out behind the beach.

"What a great spot," Olivia said.

"My husband and I come here some weekends," Jackie told her.

An older couple sat in sand-chairs reading at the water's edge. A young couple sat whispering to each other on a blanket and another couple with two small children was digging in the sand making a castle. Jackie spread the blanket and Olivia placed the picnic basket next to it. They both agreed that this would be a hiatus from the events of the past few days and that there would be no talk of the Monahan murders or who could be responsible.

They swam in the lake with Lily, sunned themselves, dug into the lunch items, read books, and played Frisbee in the field with the energetic dog. They returned to the blanket and pulled cold drinks from the cooler.

"What was your aunt like?" Jackie asked.

Olivia's eyes widened at Jackie's unexpected question. She looked across the lake and her face muscles softened. The corners of her mouth turned up into a slight smile. "She was great. Aggie was fun and smart and kind. She loved the ocean...the Red Sox. She loved taking me into Boston and just wandering all around the city with me." Olivia hugged her knees. "Whenever I had a fever, she'd lay a cool cloth across my forehead and sit next to me until I felt better. She read to me all the time when I was little. We'd draw, plant flowers. She taught me to drive... how to sail...how to swim. She'd ask my opinion about things...even when I was just a kid."

"What did she do for work?" Jackie asked

"She was a lawyer, started out as a public defender and then worked as a law professor. Poverty, corporate greed...those things made her crazy. Social justice was important to her...she stood up for people who needed help."

Sounds a lot like you," Jackie smiled.

"Hmm...maybe, someday." Olivia sipped from her water bottle and watched Lily sniff along the water's edge, then she turned to Jackie and said, "You know, I'm lucky. Aggie gave me a great gift. Probably the best gift that one person can give to another."

"What was that?" Jackie asked.

"The gift of knowing that I was loved."

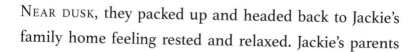

NEAR DUSK, they packed up and headed back to Jackie's family home feeling rested and relaxed. Jackie's parents had gone out for dinner, so the women made a frozen pizza and ate it in the den in front of the TV. Jackie lay down on the sofa while Olivia cleared the dishes and loaded them into the dishwasher.

Olivia returned to the den. "I'm going...," she started to speak but stopped when she saw that Jackie and Lily were asleep. She inched back out of the room.

Olivia wanted to go back to John's house because her cell phone was nearly dead and she had left her charger there. She also needed to pick up dog food from the house since Lily's food supply was running low.

Olivia opened a kitchen drawer and found a pen and small pad of paper. She left Jackie a note telling her that she was going to drive over to John's to pick up a few things and would be right back. Olivia grabbed her purse and keys and put her phone in her back pocket.

It was dark when she parked in front of John's garage. She got out, walked up the front porch steps and unlocked the door. The air in the house was stuffy and hot from being closed up. Olivia walked through the rooms checking that everything was in order. She climbed the stairs to the bedroom she used. The AC unit's hose was lying on the floor where she had thrown it after pulling it out of her window and the bedside table was overturned from her attempt to reach her phone the night of the CO_2 problem. She righted the table and sat on the bed. The police must have removed the trash can that she had heaved into because it was nowhere in the room. *Thankfully.*

The events of that night played in her mind. The dream that she had on the first night at John's house of the little blonde girl standing at the foot of the bed popped into her head. She glanced at the spot where the girl had stood in the dream.

Olivia sighed and left the bedroom.

She returned to the first floor and headed for the kitchen where she took a bag of Lily's food from the closet and set it on the floor by the table. She walked to the sunroom and flicked on a light to check the progress of the work. New floor to ceiling windows were now in place, the walls were being painted, and woodwork was in process. It looked beautiful and well constructed. While checking the new sliding glass door to the deck, Olivia spotted Jackie's sweater hanging over the railing. She unlocked the door and stepped out to retrieve it.

The air was warm. Stars were shining. Crickets and peepers were singing. Olivia sat down in one of the deck chairs and gazed across the dark back lawn. She clasped her hands together and laid them on her chest as she looked up at the stars.

Snippets of events and conversations she had had with townspeople over the past days played in her mind. The Bradford women. Kenny. Father Mike. Father

Anthony. The lawyer that Emily had dated. James Martin and his tragic swimming pool accident. The squirrels on the front porch. The psychic. Lily being tied up at the state park. Mary and Kimmy. *Why were they killed? Who did it?*

Olivia saw something on the deck. She leaned forward to better see what it was. Lily's collar. Olivia had forgotten to take it inside after washing the mud off of it from the state park incident. She stood and went over to pick it up. It still had a few inches of the rope attached to it. Lily's dog license and identification tag jingled in the darkness. Olivia fingered the piece of rope. *Who tied Lily up?* Anger and anxiety bubbled up inside her. She wanted that damn piece of rope off of Lily's collar so she turned to go back into the house to get the scissors.

She stopped short. She looked at the rope remnant. A thought formed. Olivia's heart beat sped up. She played her idea against what she had found out over the days of talking with people.

Thoughts aligned and, one by one, the puzzle pieces slipped into place. *Son of a bitch! Could it be?* Her hands trembled with excitement.

Just as Olivia was reaching around for her phone to call Brad to tell him what she suspected, it rang in her back pocket. She startled and dropped the dog collar on the deck. She pulled the cell phone out. *Angela Bradford.*

"Hello?" Olivia said. She listened for several seconds.

"Okay. Sure. I'll be there in ten minutes." Olivia clicked off.

She hurried back inside, got her phone charger and Lily's food, locked the house, and climbed into her Jeep. At the end of John's driveway, Olivia turned the wheel left towards Magnolia Hill and Isabel Bradford's mansion.

38

Olivia drove her vehicle down the long driveway, her headlights cutting through the inky night. She parked her Jeep along the edge of the circular driveway. As soon as she opened the Jeep's door, the front entrance to the Bradford mansion swung open and Olivia could see Angela's pale face visible under the lights of the front portico.

"Olivia, thank you so much for coming so late," Angela's voice quavered.

"It's okay, Angela. It's no problem at all," Olivia told her.

Angela's brow was furrowed and her lips were tense. She stepped back from the front door to make room for Olivia to enter.

"What's going on?" Olivia asked. The house was quiet and dark.

Angela twisted her hands and glanced down the hallway that branched off of the front foyer. "It's mother. She's been very angry the past few days. She hasn't been eating. She didn't get out of bed for two days. She's been complaining of feeling ill. I just got her up and out of bed this morning."

"Did you call the doctor?"

"Mother said she doesn't need a damn doctor. Her words." Angela sat down on the steps of the massive curved staircase. "Then she sent her personal assistant home early today...she said she wouldn't be needing her. I've been here all day. She's driving me crazy." She rubbed her eyes. "It all started when that lawyer came here to speak with her."

"What lawyer?"

"Overman's lawyer. He came to ask her questions." Angela looked up at Olivia. "She was not pleased."

"Were you there when the lawyer talked to her?"

"No. Mother wouldn't allow anyone to stay in the room with them."

"Did she tell you about their conversation?"

Angela shook her head. "I asked but she let me know in no uncertain terms that the conversation would remain confidential."

Olivia shifted her feet. "So why did you ask me to come over? I sure won't be able to get any information out of her."

"I called you...at mother's request."

"*She* asked me to come over? Why?"

Angela stood and shook her head wearily. "I have no idea. Come on. She's in the family room." She let out a heavy sigh. "This should be interesting."

The two women walked along the plush Persian runner that carpeted the hallway and emerged into the family room. The room was dark, lit only by one lamp on the side table next to the chair that held Mrs. Bradford's tiny frame. She was gazing out of the floor to ceiling glass walls towards the manicured lawns which were cloaked in darkness. She turned her head when she heard Angela and Olivia enter the room.

"Mother, Olivia is here."

"I can see that," Mrs. Bradford said, her voice curt and stern.

"Hello, Mrs. Bradford," Olivia said.

Mrs. Bradford's bony hand lifted from her lap and the long, skinny finger pointed at the sofa across from her. "Sit."

Olivia and Angela exchanged a quick glance and both moved across the room to the sofa where they took a seat.

"No, Angela," Mrs. Bradford said. "It's time for you to go home."

Angela's face was pained and she started to stammer, "But, I..."

"This is a private conversation between myself and

Olivia. It would make me very happy if you would head home now," Mrs. Bradford said.

Angela blinked at her mother unsure of what to do. Mrs. Bradford nodded her head. "Go ahead, Angela. You've been here all day. I'll be fine until Mrs. Adams arrives." Mrs. Adams was one of Mrs. Bradford's personal nurses hired to spend nights at the mansion.

"Mrs. Adams won't be here for some time," Angela protested. "You certainly won't be with Olivia until then."

"No, dear. But I will be happy to sit here quietly between the time Olivia and I finish and the time Mrs. Adams arrives to put me to bed." The kind tone Mrs. Bradford used threw Angela off. "Please, dear. Go home now. Do this for your mother."

Angela was shocked at the gentle words. She rose and went to her mother's side, where she bent and kissed her on the cheek. "Alright, Mother," she said, unsure. Angela looked at Olivia. "Is that okay with you, Olivia?"

Olivia nodded. "I'll be happy to stay until Mrs. Adams arrives."

"That won't be necessary," Mrs. Bradford replied. She patted Angela's hand and said, "You're a good daughter."

Angela's eyes misted over at the uncharacteristic kindness. She nodded at Olivia and hurried from the room. Mrs. Bradford trained her gaze out to the yard until she had given Angela adequate time to leave the house and walk to her car, then she turned her steely eyes to Olivia.

"So. Here we are," Mrs. Bradford said. She clasped her hands in her lap, the two index fingers touching and pointing towards the ceiling. Olivia remained quiet wondering where this conversation was going to go.

"Mr. Overman's lawyer came to see me recently," Mrs. Bradford said.

"I heard that," Olivia replied.

"He knew of our conversation regarding Overman being in Boston on the day of the murders."

Olivia nodded. "I told him. I wrote him a note. Father Mike delivered it."

"Of course, I denied everything. I said that you must have misunderstood my comments."

Olivia sighed. "I'm not surprised."

"You are a smart young woman, Olivia."

Olivia did not respond.

"But not smart enough to leave well enough alone," Mrs. Bradford said.

Olivia's blood started to boil. "Did you ask me here to discuss my IQ?"

Mrs. Bradford snorted. She flicked her eyes to the hallway entrance.

"I asked you here to discuss the case." She gave Olivia her full attention. "You have been persistent in your search for truth and justice. That might be considered admirable."

"But not by you," Olivia said.

"I would ask whose truth? What justice do you seek?"
Confusion furrowed Olivia's brow.

"What kind of justice would be appropriate in the case of your cousins? Some sort of deserved punishment for the murderer, say, a life for a life? Or, perhaps forgiveness for the murderer? An attempt to understand why the crime was committed? Or maybe, instead, an attempt at rehabilitation of the guilty party?" Mrs. Bradford asked, and looked towards the hallway.

"Maybe some of those things," Olivia said, her voice strained with annoyance.

Mrs. Bradford's eyes snapped back to Olivia. "Those things won't bring them back," she hissed. "Life is for the living."

"So?" Olivia asked. "What are you saying? We just forget about them? Let criminals get off? Crimes go unpunished?"

"You're young," Mrs. Bradford said. "You don't understand the depths of love."

Olivia's eyes went wide. Her mind was awash in confusion. She shook her head. "What are you talking about? Why did you ask me here? To have some sort of philosophical discussion about crime and punishment?" She heard footsteps approaching from the hallway. Emily Bradford entered the room. Olivia's pulse quickened.

Emily's head swiveled from her mother to Olivia.

"Hello, Emily," Mrs. Bradford said.

Emily again looked back and forth from Olivia to her mother. Her face was stern.

"Why did you call me?" she addressed her mother. "You said you were alone...and ill."

"Please sit down. I'll explain," Mrs. Bradford said and pointed to the empty chair positioned at the end of the coffee table between Mrs. Bradford's chair and the sofa Olivia sat on.

Emily exhaled loudly as she crossed to the chair. "How are *you* involved?" she asked Olivia.

Olivia's pulse quickened as she eyed Emily. "I have no idea. I only got here a few minutes ago. I didn't know you were invited as well." Olivia looked at Mrs. Bradford. "I thought you and Emily were estranged?"

Mrs. Bradford ignored Olivia. "Please try to be patient, Emily. Although I know that isn't one of your virtues."

Emily started to retort when Mrs. Bradford raised her hand. "I'm only asking for a bit of your time. We need to sort things out."

"Sort what out?" Emily asked. Her voice dripped with disgust.

Mrs. Bradford turned to Olivia. "So, Olivia, tell us what you have learned about the murders," Mrs. Bradford said.

The hair on Olivia's arms stood up. Intuition warned her to get out of the Bradford house. "I'm not sure what this powwow is about but maybe it would be better if just you and Emily continued the chat," Olivia said moving to stand up.

"Sit down," Mrs. Bradford commanded. "You will regret it if you leave now. You have questions that you want answered. Stay in your seat and you'll have them."

Olivia glanced at Emily and remained sitting.

"You have interviewed many people," Mrs. Bradford said. "I assume that you have an idea of who committed the crimes of murdering your cousins?"

Olivia said nothing. Her heart was thudding against her chest.

"Do you have a suspect in mind?" Mrs. Bradford asked.

"I might," Olivia replied. She looked to the hallway and then to the doors that led to the terrace, trying to judge which would be the best means for a quick exit.

"Have you told the police what you think?"

"No."

"Why, not?" Mrs. Bradford asked.

"I don't have any proof to offer them," Olivia said trying to modulate her voice.

"Do you think that you will be able to muster some evidence if you keep investigating?"

"I don't know."

"Do you think it was Overman?"

"No." Olivia's face was as hard as stone.

"But, his semen. The DNA test," Mrs. Bradford stated.

"His semen was there at the crime scene, yes." Olivia took a deep breath. "But *he* wasn't."

Emily shifted in her chair and her eyes shot daggers at her mother. "What is the point of this?" Her voice was shrill.

"If you are patient, Emily, you will see what the point is. So, Olivia, please tell me who the suspect is."

Olivia's head was buzzing. She rose from the sofa. "I'm done with this."

"No, you are not," Mrs. Bradford said icily. She pulled a small pistol from under the soft blanket that covered her knees and pointed it at Olivia. Olivia's mouth gaped.

"Mother!" Emily cried.

"Sit down," Mrs. Bradford said. Her voice was calm and even.

Olivia backed up, her eyes on the pistol, and sat.

"Now, you will both answer my questions. And don't think I won't pull this trigger. I am an old woman and I have nothing to lose." She pointed the gun at Emily and held it there for several seconds before turning it back on Olivia. "People can surprise you, can't they?" she asked both of them.

Olivia and Emily stared at the gun. Olivia's mind was racing. Her eyes swept the room searching for something she could use as a weapon.

"Who do suspect killed your cousins?" Mrs. Bradford demanded.

Blood was pounding in Olivia's ears. "I had two guess-es," Olivia seethed. "Father Anthony was one of them... initially," she said to Mrs. Bradford.

Mrs. Bradford threw her head back and cackled. "I wasn't expecting that. That's nonsense." She adjusted the blanket on her knees.

Olivia turned to Emily. "Do you own a gun?"

"What?" Emily spit the word out.

"Do you know how to shoot?" Olivia asked. Her voice was firm. "Squirrels?"

Before Emily could respond, Mrs. Bradford cleared her throat and demanded, "Olivia, who is suspect number two?"

Emily leaned forward clutching the sides of the chair.

Olivia leveled her eyes at Mrs. Bradford, and said, "Emily."

Emily almost jumped out of her seat.

"Don't you move," Mrs. Bradford said and brandished the gun at Emily. "Go ahead, Olivia. Tell me why you suspect her."

Olivia drew in a breath. "Emily dated Kenny to make you and your husband upset. She never had any inten-tion of staying with him. Emily was infatuated with Father Anthony at the church." Olivia stole a glance at Emily whose face was flushed. Her eyes looked black.

"Go on." Mrs. Bradford's voice was hoarse.

"Emily flirted with Father Anthony, made him

uncomfortable whenever she was around. Father Anthony and Mary were friends. People gossiped about them being more than friends. The idea that Father Anthony and Mary might be having an affair made Emily crazy."

"Shut up," Emily screamed. "You don't know me."

Mrs. Bradford shot Emily a warning look.

"Kenny spoiled Emily's plans to go to New York City for the day. Emily claimed she went, but she didn't. She couldn't have arrived home so quickly that day if she had taken the bus back and forth like she says she did. She would have only been in New York for two hours if she was home when you say you arrived back from Boston, Mrs. Bradford." Olivia paused to steady her voice. "Emily went to the church that afternoon to see Father Anthony. He rebuffed her. She was in a rage. Father Anthony went into the rectory to get away from her. Mary and her daughter arrived at the church hall with the paint, but only Emily was there."

Olivia faced Emily. "I don't know what happened next, but your fury and jealousy caused you to murder my cousins."

Emily's fingernails had pierced the fabric of the chair arms. Her eyes were wild and she was hyperventilating.

"Explain the semen." Mrs. Bradford's voice was tense.

Olivia wiped at her eyes and cleared her throat. She tried to speak but nothing came out.

"I would offer you a drink, Olivia, but this isn't a social occasion," Mrs. Bradford said. "Keep talking."

Olivia coughed. "Kenny came over that night...the night of the murders. You wouldn't let him in because of your earlier fight with Emily near the fireplace. So Kenny and Emily talked outside...in her parked car."

"Go on."

Olivia looked at Emily.

"Angela said she saw you and Kenny in the backseat of your car when she pulled into the driveway of your parents' house. You were having sex with Kenny in the car. I think you were high from the killings. You didn't care if your parents caught you screwing Kenny in their driveway. Your sister drove up to the house right when you and Kenny were finishing up. When she drove in, you or Kenny pulled off the condom and left it in your car. Later that night you got the idea to convince the police that the killer was a man. Maybe you planned to pin the murders on Kenny. So you got the used condom out of your car and took off through the woods behind your house to the field where the bodies were still undiscovered. You emptied the condom at the scene and ran home." Olivia kept her eyes fixed on Emily. "No one would ever suspect that a woman was the killer since someone left semen there, would they?"

"You bitch," Emily growled. "You have a vivid imagination." Emily made a move towards Olivia.

"Stay in that seat," Mrs. Bradford ordered.

Olivia's heart was pounding. Adrenaline coursed through her body. She wanted to put her hands around Emily's neck and choke her. "Angela said she went up to your room to talk to you about the fight you had with your mother that day. She said you had cuts on your arms, bruises. She thought Kenny had hurt you, but you must have gotten them when you ran through the woods in the dark. Or, maybe when my cousin was fighting for her life and the life of her daughter."

Emily's chest was heaving up and down.

Mrs. Bradford spoke to Emily. "After our fight at the fireplace that day, I decided to check the ashes after the fire burned out." She paused. "I found a piece of your blouse in the ashes. The blouse I bought you for your birthday. And the buckle of your belt...it was under the logs that hadn't fully burned." Her eyes searched Emily's. "You were burning the clothes you wore when you murdered them."

Emily choked on her words. "You can't prove it," she croaked. "You can't prove it."

"Why didn't you tell me?" Mrs. Bradford asked. Her voice was just above a whisper.

"You would have told the police," Emily said.

Mrs. Bradford shook her head, tears in her eyes. "I would have protected you."

"No, you wouldn't have." Emily's words dripped with

bitterness. "Your daughter, the murderer. That would have gone over well at the country club, Mother."

Mrs. Bradford blinked.

Emily stared at her mother, then looked off into space. "I went to the church to tell him."

"Tell who?" Mrs. Bradford asked.

"Anthony," Emily said.

Mrs. Bradford asked, her lips trembling, "To tell him what?"

Emily leaned forward in her chair, a wide, wild smile on her face. "To tell him I loved him." Her mouth contorted. "But he rejected me. He didn't want anything to do with me. He told me to get out." Her eyes clouded over and she glared at her mother. "I wasn't good enough. Never good enough. Not for you. Not for Anthony. Not for anyone. Even Kenny wanted to break it off with me." Emily stared across the room. "Anthony loved that bitch. That bitch, Mary Monahan." Her voice was like ice. Her head snapped towards her mother. "How would that have gone over with you, Mother? Isabel Bradford, the social queen bee of Howland. Your daughter arrested for murder. You would have been the talk of the town."

Emily's eyes darted around the room, looking at nothing. "Mary and her brat drove up just then. I was still in the rec hall. I wanted to kill him. I wanted to kill dear, saintly Father Anthony. There was a box cutter on the table. And, a knife. I picked them up." She sucked in a long breath. "They came in just then, carrying the paint. Mary. It was Mary he loved, not me."

Her hands gripped the arms of the chair. Emily's jaw was slack, she was breathing through her mouth. She shifted her eyes onto Olivia.

"I killed them," she hissed. Her face was triumphant.

Olivia clenched her hands into fists. She wanted to lunge at Emily and punch her in the face and it took all of her will power to remain in her seat.

"But that wasn't the end of it, was it?" Olivia asked.

Emily's eyes narrowed into slits. "What are you talking about?" she sneered.

"What about James, Emily?" Olivia could barely get the words out of her throat it was so constricted with rage.

"What?" Emily asked.

"James Martin."

Olivia and Emily stared each other down.

"No one can get in the way of what you want, can they?" Olivia asked.

Emily sucked in a breath.

"You killed him, too," Olivia said.

Emily's eyes were like saucers. Her facial muscles were tight and pulled her lips into a frightful grimace. She leaned forward. "Yes, bitch," she whispered. "I killed him, too."

Mrs. Bradford's face was wet with tears. She brushed them away with her bony hand. "James? Why?"

Emily turned to her mother. "He wouldn't help me. He wouldn't help me." Her breathing was fast. Her fists pounded the arms of the chair. "I told him. We were drinking that night. We were drunk. I told him what I did to the Monahans."

She swung her head back to Olivia and glared. "He was going to tell the police. I begged him not to. Oh, the way he looked at me." Emily paused, and then her voice was hard. "So I smashed him in the face with one of the loose bricks from the patio. He staggered back. He fell into the pool." Tears gathered in Emily's eyes. "I didn't want to kill him. But I had to." Her face was crumbling. "He held his hand out to me from the water. I let him drown. I watched him die."

Emily straightened in her chair and her eyes shot daggers at Olivia. "I let him drown because of your stupid cousin. It was Anthony's fault. He loved her. That bitch. That fucking bitch!"

Emily breathed in several quick breaths. Her wild eyes bore into Olivia. Her voice was so soft. "You should have died before tonight. Too bad you were with that fat cow on the rail trail when I tied up your dog. If you were alone that day you wouldn't be sitting here now."

An icy chill filled Olivia's body.

"And why didn't you die from the carbon monoxide?

You can't be a lucky bitch forever." Emily sprang out of her chair, her hands outstretched aiming for Olivia's throat. Olivia jumped up to meet her, lifting the palm of her hand forward where it connected with Emily's jaw. Emily's head snapped back.

A crack filled the air and a bullet hit the ceiling above the women. Both women spun to face Mrs. Bradford who held her pistol outstretched towards them.

"Emily!" Mrs. Bradford's eyes were blazing. "Sit! Both of you!" She moved the gun towards one, then the other, as warning.

They both sat. Olivia's mind was racing, thinking of how to get to Mrs. Bradford before she could fire the gun.

"Don't get out of those chairs," Mrs. Bradford said. "Or the bullet won't hit the ceiling the next time."

Emily turned to her mother, her eyes black with hate.

"I always suspected you killed the Monahans," Mrs. Bradford spoke. "But I couldn't explain the details." Her small voice was firm. "I had to know the truth. To be sure." She raised the pistol towards Emily. "Before I did this."

Emily's jaw dropped.

Mrs. Bradford shifted the gun away from Emily and pointed it at Olivia.

Olivia pressed back against the sofa.

"I won't let you destroy my daughter."

Just as Mrs. Bradford's finger was about to press the

trigger, Olivia hurled herself off the sofa onto the floor, Emily lurched from her chair to go after Olivia, and Angela Bradford and her husband ran through the entranceway into the family room.

"Mother!" Angela shouted.

Angela's sudden appearance caused the old woman's hand to jerk the barrel of the gun in Emily's direction, and the bullet hit her square in the shoulder. Emily stumbled backward onto the chair.

Screams from Emily and Mrs. Bradford rattled Olivia's brain as she leaped up, stepped onto the coffee table and was beside Mrs. Bradford in two strides. She grabbed for the gun and yanked it from the old woman's feeble hand before she could fire it again.

Angela and her husband were frozen in place in the doorway. Angela's face was white. Her arms hung at her sides. Her mouth was open in a large "O".

Emily was wailing and writhing.

"Take this," Olivia said holding the pistol out to Angela.

Angela stepped forward in a daze and took the gun from Olivia. She handed it off to her husband.

"Call 911," Olivia said.

Angela stared at Olivia.

"Angela! Call 911."

Angela hesitated like she was trying to process what

Olivia said to her, then she blinked and pulled out her cell phone to place the emergency call.

Emily was thrashing in the chair clutching her shoulder. Blood was soaking her blouse and dripping onto the white fabric of the chair. Mrs. Bradford was slumped in her seat. Olivia couldn't tell if she had passed out. Olivia grabbed the blanket off Mrs. Bradford's lap, balled it up and pressed it tightly to the wound in Emily's shoulder.

"This is your fault," Emily shrieked at Olivia. "This is all because of you!"

Olivia's face was lined with disgust. "Shut. Up."

~

It seemed to take an hour for the police and EMT's to arrive but it was really only fifteen minutes before their sirens could be heard wailing up the Bradford driveway.

When Jackie entered the mansion after receiving the call from the officers who arrived on the scene, Olivia was sitting on the sofa, shaking. Emily and Mrs. Bradford were already in the ambulances. Angela was crying, speaking with one of the detectives. Her husband was standing beside her chair, his hand on her shoulder.

Jackie glanced at the police, at Angela, the bloody chair where Emily had been sitting. She walked to the sofa and took a seat next to Olivia.

"I asked the police to call you," Olivia said.

"You're not hurt?" Jackie put her arm around Olivia's shoulders.

Olivia shook her head.

"What a mess," Jackie said.

Olivia nodded. "Yeah."

39

A fter dinner, Olivia and Jackie sat on the front porch in the white rocking chairs sipping drinks. With the sun lower in the sky, the air was cooling off. Earlier in the day, Olivia had spent a couple of hours at the Howland Police department answering more of their questions and speaking with Kenny Overman's attorney. All charges against Kenny were dropped. Emily Bradford confessed to the murders of Mary and Kimberly Monahan and James Martin, and was taken into custody. Isabel Bradford was in the hospital and would be charged with assault or some such thing but Olivia believed that whatever sentence was imposed on her probably would not be served.

"So when did you figure it out, Olivia?" Jackie asked as they rocked on the porch.

"When I went back to the house to pick up my phone

charger and the food for Lily, I went out on the deck. I saw you had left your sweater on the railing. I saw Lily's collar on the deck. I put it there to dry after I washed the mud off of it when we came back from the state park that day I couldn't find her. I picked up the collar. It still had a piece of the rope on it that Emily used to tie her up. I looked at that piece of rope and something in my brain made a connection. It looked the same as Emily's climbing rope that was in the box that dropped out of her hatch the day we went to the running event. Something clicked. So many things ran through my head. Remember what Emily's office manager said to me? 'Emily may as well be a man.' Little pieces of things started swirling around in my head. Angela told me that Emily and Kenny were having sex in the car in the driveway of the Bradford house on the night of the murders. Kenny told me that they always used protection. When Brad was here, we walked on the trails behind the Bradford house. Those trails lead right to the field where my cousins were killed. So many little things started to add up. James Martin's mother told me that James and Emily were having an argument the night he died in the pool. She thought she heard them talking about my cousins. All these things were swirling in my brain. Emily and James had been drinking. Turns out, Emily confessed to James that night about killing my cousins and he didn't take it well. He was going to tell the police, so she killed him too."

"How terrible," Jackie said.

"And climbing is one of Emily's hobbies. She wouldn't have been afraid to go up on the roof and put the toolbox across the chimney. It would have been easy for her. So many other things...little things...they were all pointing to her. I figured she was the one who put those squirrels on the front porch and, I bet the night she did it, she saw the construction here and got the idea to block the chimney."

"She knew you would figure it out," Jackie said. "You were getting too close."

Olivia continued. "When Emily walked into the family room at the Bradford house, I had all the pieces. Her presence in the room, something she was giving off, it was like my body was giving me signals to get out of there, that she was dangerous. It confirmed my suspicion that she was the one. I knew she was the killer. I could feel it." Olivia paused. "The day at the park when Lily was tied up. Emily knew I would search for Lily. Emily was going to kill me...in that isolated area of the park. Just like she did to my cousins." Olivia shuddered.

"Thank God you ran into Robin and her dog." Jackie closed her eyes for several seconds. "Emily was certainly clever... planting the semen at the crime scene. Making the killer seem like some pervert. No one would suspect the killer was a woman. Not with semen there. And, the carbon monoxide to kill you off. She is one smart monster."

"Yeah," Olivia said. "Emily was infatuated with Father Anthony. She wanted him and when he rebuffed her she was hysterical, it pushed her over the edge. In her head, she was sure it was Mary that he loved. Father Anthony said he ran into the rectory to get away from Emily. Emily was in the rec hall when Mary and Kimmy arrived with the paint." Olivia paused and swallowed. "Emily killed them in a fit of rage."

"And you believed Overman was innocent," Jackie said.

Olivia nodded. "After we talked, I just didn't believe he did it."

Jackie and Olivia heard the sound of a car approaching and turned to see who was coming down the driveway.

"It better not be another news reporter," Olivia said.

"We'll just go inside and tell them we'll call the cops," Jackie said.

A black Honda came around the trees.

"It's Father Mike," Olivia said leaning forward in her chair.

"Who's in the car with him?" Jackie asked.

"I can't see." Olivia stood up and walked down the front steps to meet the car.

"Olivia." Father Mike emerged with a wide smile. He took her hand and gave it a squeeze.

Father Anthony Foley got out of the driver's side.

Father Mike gestured at the other priest. "Anthony called me. He decided to come up when he heard the news."

Anthony walked around the front of the car. "You solved it, Olivia."

"Come sit. Have a drink with us," she said.

Olivia put her hand under Father Mike's arm and assisted him up the porch steps. The two men greeted Jackie and sat down in rockers. Olivia brought them drinks.

"Your interest and persistence has cleared an innocent man. Once and for all," Father Mike said to Olivia. "You found the person responsible for those terrible murders. May Mary and her daughter rest in peace."

"I think they were already at peace," Olivia said. She met Father Mike's eyes. "I think...maybe...justice is for the living."

Father Mike's kind eyes were bright. "Perhaps you're right, my dear."

Father Anthony spoke. "I wanted to come up and talk with Mike. And, with you, Olivia." He leaned forward, his face serious.

"I swear to you I did not know that Emily was the killer." He shook his head. "I am still coming to grips with it." He paused. "I never meant to lead her on. She accused me of having an affair with Mary. I didn't know what to do. If Emily made that claim publicly...would people have believed my denials, Mary's denials?"

"I don't know," Olivia said. "Some would have believed you."

"Emily was unbalanced. Angry. Desperate. I regret how I handled it. I should have confided in you," Anthony told Mike. "I was afraid you wouldn't believe me."

"I hope I would have," Father Mike said.

"If I had tried to calm her, if I didn't leave the rec hall..." Tears gathered in his eyes. "The Monahans would be alive."

"Don't," Olivia said softly. "You didn't know what would happen. It wasn't your fault. It wasn't." Olivia swallowed. "I think, when something happens, we blame ourselves. We wish we could have changed things, we wish we could have done something differently. But the truth is, things just don't work that way."

Anthony nodded.

They talked a little longer, and when the men finished their drinks, they stood to go. Olivia walked Father Mike to the car but before he got in, he turned to

Olivia. "Have you found what you were looking for, my dear?"

Olivia smiled. "I think so," she said. "I think I have."

Father Mike patted her hand. He reached into his pocket and retrieved an envelope. "Someone asked me to give this to you." Olivia took it and Father Mike hugged her.

"You take care, Olivia. Come back and visit us sometime."

"I will." She smiled at the priest. "Thank you."

Olivia took the envelope to the porch where she sat down and opened it. "It's from Kenny," she told Jackie.

DEAR OLIVIA,

Thank you for all you've done. Because of you, I can live without fear of the police coming to my door to arrest me. I'm safe now. My name is cleared. That is a gift for my family as well.

You'll be surprised to hear I went to see my father at the nursing facility. When I sat down next to him, his eyes got all watery and he gripped my hand and kept patting it. I was amazed, really, that he showed me affection.

You'll be even more surprised to hear that my father's benefactor for the nursing home is Emily Bradford. I nearly fell over when I found out. It seems that she set up a fund to pay for his care. It floored me. Maybe it's guilt for trying to frame me? I guess some things can't be explained.

Anyway, thanks for everything. You did good work. I'm happy.

Father Mike knows what happened to you and your aunt last summer. I was sorry to hear about it. Don't let a stone of sadness sink you. You're strong. Make yourself a happy life. That's what I wish for you.

Kenny

OLIVIA SMILED and handed the letter to Jackie so she could read it. When Jackie finished, she lifted her face and turned to Olivia.

"A happy life," Jackie said. "That's what I wish for you, too."

"I feel better, Jackie," Olivia said. "I'm not sure why but I feel lighter. I'm not afraid to go home now. Since Aggie was murdered I've had that stone of grief in my heart. I felt like it was sinking me, pulling me away from the people and place that I love. I guess I've been afraid to lose them too."

"Maybe," Jackie said. "Maybe you've been afraid to hold onto them for fear of losing them. To protect yourself from more hurt. So you pulled away."

"Father Anthony told me something when I first talked to him," Olivia said. "He told me that there's good in the world and when he finds it, he holds onto it. I want to hold onto the good in my life. I'm going to hold on tight." Olivia smiled. "I want to be with Brad and Joe. I want to go home."

40

Olivia made the drive from Howland to Ogunquit in just under an hour and twenty minutes. She pulled in and parked her car at the end of Joe's driveway. Joe's truck was parked in front of the garage bay. Olivia hadn't been home in almost a year. She sat in the Jeep drinking in the familiar lines of Joe's cape style home. She turned her head to her own brick ranch house on the lot next to Joe's, the house she shared with Aggie for so many years. An ache squeezed her heart.

The woman who was renting Olivia's house had planted flowers and greens in the window boxes and had placed a huge container spilling over with pink and white flowers on the front landing. The windows were open and Olivia could see the curtains fluttering in the light breeze. There was a pale blue bicycle leaning against the garage door. It was an old style bike with higher handle bars and a wicker basket attached between the bars. Olivia smiled. She had never met the woman who lived in her house. After Olivia returned to school, Joe had taken care of placing the ad, interviewing potential renters, getting the lease signed, and collecting the rental money.

Olivia stepped from the Jeep and walked up Joe's driveway to ring the doorbell. Just as she pushed the bell, she heard the slap of her own house's screen door closing and voices coming towards her. She stepped off the porch to see who was heading in her direction, and just as she did, Joe spotted her standing at his door as he was walking across the lawn from Olivia's house. A huge smile spread across his face and his step quickened.

"Liv!" He was carrying a bag of groceries and a petite blond woman was walking beside him holding a canvas bag. Olivia smiled at them.

Joe grabbed Olivia with his free arm and gave her a bear hug.

"What's this?" His voice was excited. "You didn't tell me you were coming home."

"I thought I'd surprise you," Olivia grinned. "Is the spare bedroom still available for me?"

"It's all yours, sweet pea. Any time."

Olivia turned to the woman who she guessed was in her late sixties. Her honey blonde hair was pulled up into a chignon. She had beautiful smooth skin and her brown eyes sparkled. She was dressed in tan Capri pants, a white linen blouse, and brown sandals.

"I'm Olivia." Olivia smiled and extended her hand.

The woman grasped Olivia's hand warmly. "I've heard so much about you. I'm Rose Williams. It's wonderful to finally meet you."

"Thank you for taking such good care of the house," Olivia said.

"Oh, it's my pleasure. This place is really heaven on earth. Thank you for renting it to me."

Rose handed Joe the canvas bag she had been holding. "I'll let you two catch up. I'll talk to you later, Joe." She turned to cross the lawn. "So nice to meet you, Olivia."

When Rose was nearly to her house, Olivia said, referring to the bags of groceries, "Were you two going to make dinner together? Don't change your plans on account of me."

"Oh, no. She was just helping me carry the bags," Joe answered hurriedly.

Olivia gave him a sly look as she took one of the bags and opened the front door for him. They entered the kitchen and started putting the groceries away.

"Do you mind that I came back early, Joe?"

"It's never early enough to have you back. You can live here all year round as far as I'm concerned," Joe told her.

"I'm going to walk up to town and surprise Brad at his store. I didn't tell him I was coming back."

"He'll be happy to see you. He's been straight-out busy." Joe leaned against the counter. "What about you, hon? Your summer class is starting next week?"

"Well, the classes start then," Olivia said. "But I'm not going to be there."

"Decide to take the summer off?"

"I've decided to take the whole year off, Joe. I put in for a leave of absence at school."

Joe's eyebrows went up and a smile played across his lips. "That, so?"

"Is it okay, do you think? For me to take a break? I thought I'd work in Aggie's shop for a good part of the year. Maybe do some other things."

Joe met her eyes and put his hands on her shoulders. "I think it's the best idea you could have come up with."

"Really? You think Aggie would approve?"

"Sweet pea, Aggie would want you to be happy."

Olivia hugged him. "I just need a break."

Joe patted her hair. "I understand," he told her.

Olivia stepped back and the two returned to emptying the bags.

"So what were you and Rose planning to make for dinner?"

"We were going to make..." Joe stopped, realizing

Olivia had tricked him into admitting he and Rose had dinner plans.

Olivia grinned. "She seems real nice, Joe. Classy."

"She is real nice." Joe's tanned cheeks showed a pink blush. "We're just friends," he blurted.

Olivia cocked her head. Joe turned and started bustling in the cabinet. Olivia stood still and stared at his back. When he turned around again, she was still staring.

"We're just friends," he said.

"Joe, I know you think I'll be upset. I know you think it's too soon after Aggie died. But I'm not and it isn't. It's okay. I saw the way you look at each other."

Joe swallowed hard and looked down at the floor. Olivia took his hand.

"I like her," he said. "I like being around her. She's good to me. She makes me happy."

Olivia's eyes brimmed with tears. The corners of her mouth turned up in a smile.

Joe looked up, sheepish. "Is it okay, Liv?"

"Yes. It's good." Olivia hugged him. "I want it for you. I love you, Joe."

Joe squeezed her tight.

"You deserve to be happy," Olivia said.

"We both deserve to be happy," Joe whispered.

Olivia smiled up at Joe. "Go get her and tell her to come back over. I'm going up to town to see Brad. I'll probably stay at his place tonight, so don't wait up for me." She grinned. "And don't worry that I might barge in on you and your lady friend."

"Liv," Joe growled, but he had the hint of a smile on his face as he turned to take a glass bowl from the cabinet.

41

Olivia walked up Shore Road to town. Golden light spilled from windows and streetlights and nudged at the darkness that was settling over the trees and buildings. She passed hotels and private homes, shops and restaurants. The closer she got to the center, the more people crowded the sidewalks. Olivia loved the bustle of the summer, the people, the flowers, the colorful clothing in store windows. As she passed the Front Porch restaurant she could hear the customers' jovial voices singing together as they shared a drink around the piano in the upstairs lounge. She waited on the corner of Beach Street to cross over to Brad's store. She was home.

Brad's store was full of patrons browsing books and magazines, and sitting at café tables in clusters of two or four sipping drinks from the coffee bar. Olivia spotted

Brad working as barista, filling glasses, mixing liquids in blenders, and swirling whipped cream on top of frothy chocolate drinks. She leaned against the wall and watched him, her heart swelling. Brad's brown hair flopped over his eyebrows. He needed a haircut.

As he reached for another mug, his eyes swept the crowded store, passed over Olivia, looked down at the milk jug in front of him, and then jerked his head back to look where Olivia was standing across the room. He stopped his activity and grinned at her, his blue eyes twinkling. Olivia smiled. He said something to the employee next to him, wiped his hands on a towel, and crossed the room in quick strides. He stopped in front of Olivia and locked his eyes on hers. Brad's eyes were like deep blue pools and Olivia was ready to fall into them.

"Are you in the market for a book?" he asked.

"I might be," Olivia said.

"Then you've come to the right place."

"Have I?" Olivia teased.

"Oh, yes. No doubt about it. You are definitely in the right place."

"I think I am." She reached for his hand and the touch of him warmed her to her core. He pulled her to him and hugged her, stroking the soft brown hair and inhaling her scent.

"Happy Birthday," she whispered.

"Best birthday gift ever," he said.

"I might have a better one for you later," she whispered.

Brad kissed her lips. "I'm glad you're home."

"Me, too."

"What happened in Howland?"

"John came back a few days early."

"I mean about your cousins. The case."

"It's solved," Olivia told him.

Brad's eyebrows went up. "It is?"

Olivia nodded. "It was Emily Bradford."

"Emily?"

"I got shot at."

"What?" Brad took a step back and his eyes scanned up and down Olivia's body looking for damage.

"She missed."

Brad pulled her to him.

"It's a long story. I'll tell you later tonight."

Brad led her to a vacated table and they sat. "How long are you staying?'

"A year."

Brad's eyes went wide.

"I took a leave of absence. I want to be home."

Brad opened his mouth but nothing came out. A smile spread over his face. He laughed. "I can't believe it."

"I shouldn't have gone to school this past year. I've been pulling away from everything I love. I'm still hurting, Brad...over Aggie's murder."

"I know," he said, squeezing her hand.

"I've had so much sadness in my heart. I thought I could bury myself in my schoolwork and it would go away. But it didn't. I need to be home. I need to be with you."

Brad's face was full of emotion. "I'll help you. We'll wear away at that sadness until it disappears. And we'll fill your heart with something else."

A tear spilled from Olivia's eye and traced down her cheek. Brad brushed it away. She reached for his hand.

Olivia swallowed. "I was thinking of fixing up the second floor over Aggie's shop. Make it into a studio apartment, like you have here over the store. The building's paid for. Joe can help me fix it up. I can live there almost for free. That way I can keep renting out the house."

"That's a great idea. We'll all work on it together."

"And I can keep the shop open all summer and into the fall."

Brad squeezed her hand. His eyes looked misty.

"Maybe we could go somewhere warm in the winter for a few weeks," he said. "After Christmas, when we close the shops for the off season."

"I'd like that," Olivia said.

Brad reached across the table and gently pushed a stray strand of her hair from her cheek. She leaned against his hand.

"How late is the store open tonight?" she asked.

"We close at ten. Want to get a late supper afterwards? Stay at my place? Tell me what the hell happened in Howland?"

Olivia nodded. She looked around the busy room. "Do you need me to stay here and help out?"

Brad held Olivia's eyes. "Always."

They stood and walked to the coffee bar, their arms wrapped around each other.

THANK YOU FOR READING!

To hear about new books and book sales, please sign up
for my mailing list at:
www.jawhitingbooks.com

Your email will never be sold, shared, or spammed.

If you enjoyed the book, please consider leaving a review.
A few words are all that's needed. It would be very much
appreciated.

ALSO BY J. A. WHITING

OLIVIA MILLER MYSTERY-THRILLERS

SWEET COVE COZY MYSTERIES

LIN COFFIN COZY MYSTERIES

CLAIRE ROLLINS COZY MYSTERY

PAXTON PARK COZY MYSTERIES

ABOUT THE AUTHOR

J.A. Whiting lives with her family in New England. Whiting loves reading and writing mystery, suspense and thriller stories.

Visit me at:
www.jawhitingbooks.com
www.facebook.com/jawhitingauthor
www.amazon.com/author/jawhiting

Made in the USA
Middletown, DE
27 September 2018